Erica downed the last of her Coke, then crossed her jeans-clad legs. Adjusting the ankle strap of her spike-heeled sandals, she suddenly looked thoughtful. "Thirty-five, maybe. I gotta admit, any older would be freaky."

"We'll make our meeting, then, an even twenty years from now," Della said, straightening as she always did with the brilliance of an idea or a piece of juicy gossip. "That means we'll be back here on this same day, at the same time—" she did the math, ticking off the years on her fingers, red nails flashing "—in the year 2005." Her gaze fell to her engagement ring, and she bit her lip. "Jeez, that sounds like something from a science fiction movie."

Mattie tugged Della's hand across the table, admiring the tiny diamond that adorned it. "At least one of us knows what's in her future."

Erica rolled her eyes, grabbed a bar napkin and tore it into four squares. She scribbled the future meeting date on every small scrap of paper, then slid the pieces of napkin across the table to the other three.

When each girl held a square, they looked up like reluctant knights of the round bar table, each making brief eye contact with the other. Shay looked relieved, hanging on to her scrap of napkin like a teddy bear. Della looked suddenly uncertain and Erica defiant, as usual. Mattie's gaze wavered under the scrutiny of her friends, then strayed to the stack of envelopes with a look of pure longing....

Kristen Robinette

Who says I even want to be married by thirty?

could never decide what she wanted to "be" when she grew up. She wanted to become an archaeologist, a firefighter, a psychiatrist, an equestrian, an artist, a police officer...all at the same time. After deciding that her affliction was actually the urge to *write* about such things, she set out to become a writer. Now a multipublished author with ever-changing fictional careers, she couldn't be happier!

Kristen lives in Alabama with her husband and three daughters. When not at the keyboard, she can be found horseback riding, boating and generally avoiding domestic chores.

Hell's Belles

✤ KRISTEN ROBINETTE ✤

To Josh and Christina

You're the only ending that fit.

Haddes, Georgia
May 11, 1985

The four girls crashed the Stop-N-Bowl a few hours before its official opening, as they had virtually every Friday night for the last two years. They were now perched at a long-legged bar table, sipping colas and wondering what they'd gotten themselves into. Four white envelopes lay piled in the center of the table, the name of each girl written in her own handwriting across the outside.

Erica Donovan reached for her envelope only to have her hand slapped away by her friend Della Murphy.

"Don't even think about it," Della warned.

Despite her blond starlet looks, Della was the undisputed matriarch of the group. Though the girls were all eighteen, she had a worldliness and maturity that made her the natural leader of the pack.

At last night's sleepover at Mattie Harold's house they'd

each agreed to participate in a self-improvement exercise found in a back issue of *Cosmopolitan*. "Make your own fantasy time capsule…" the article had dared. They'd since come off of their cheese-curl and pizza high and were now eyeing the envelopes with regret. Private thoughts took on a life of their own when pen met paper.

"This was so stupid." Erica tossed her straight black hair over her shoulder and pretended not to care.

Della shot her a look. "Then what did you do it for?"

The two girls were as opposite as opposites came but they had a bond that thrived in the gray area that separated their opinions. Della had managed to go from mood rings and Rod Stewart to an engagement ring and impending mortgage without flinching. Erica, on the other hand, thought Della had lost her mind and had every intention of sowing her friend's wild seeds *for* her.

"Search me. The only fantasy I have is to get the hell out of Haddes…"

"You've mentioned that." The comment belonged to Shay Chambers. Shay had long since grown weary of Erica's wanderlust. She pulled her long, shorts-clad legs up to sit yoga-style on the bar stool.

The pre-opening hustle and bustle as the waiters wiped down tables and stacked glasses was as close to the bar scene as the eighteen-year-olds had ever been. And it was as close as they were likely to come at the bowling alley, since Della's family owned the place. In fact, Jack Murphy, Della's older brother, would soon escort the underage girls out of the bar, ending their small taste of adulthood.

"I think it's good to write down our goals," Shay added. "It helps to know what we want in life. Right?"

"Um…" Mattie Harold pulled the napkin from beneath her glass and wiped up the ring of condensation that had bled through. "Were we supposed to be writing down our goals? I thought we were writing down…. Well—" she lowered her voice as Jack passed behind their table "—more like our fantasies."

Della scowled at her brother for the intrusion, oblivious to the way Mattie's eyes followed him as he disappeared behind the bar. What she hadn't missed was the way shy little Mattie had torn into her fantasy assignment like a groupie after Michael Jackson's white glove. She was clearly hot for something—or someone. Della eyed Mattie's envelope with a surge of curiosity. "Is there something you want to share a little early?"

Jack chose that moment to crank up the music. *"Like a virgin…."* Madonna's voice rang clear and excruciatingly loud as if in answer to Della's question. The foursome convulsed with laughter as Jack adjusted the volume.

"So now we need to agree on a date." Shay straightened, refocusing on the task at hand. Her gaze fell on Mattie. "What year are we going to open the envelopes, see if we made good on our goals? How about when we turn thirty?"

Mattie sniffed away her laughter. "What if we're not married by the time we're thirty...." She let her sentence trail, luminous blue eyes growing seriously horrified at the prospect. She stroked the bare skin of her arms below her tank top and shivered.

Erica shot Mattie a look. "Who said everybody's future fantasies included marriage?"

The other three stared her down, Erica's tough-as-leather exterior transparent to her friends. "Get real," Mattie said.

"If we're not married by thirty, we'll have to do *something*." Shay examined the ends of her long auburn curls for splits before nervously smoothing her hair into place.

Shay's life hadn't been as carefree as that of her friends. She'd lost her parents in a car accident at eight years old and had long ago stopped questioning fate. If not for the tragedy, she wouldn't have moved to Haddes to live with her aunt and uncle and would never have become part of this circle of friends. They were her family. But in three weeks they would graduate from high school and their adolescence would end. Who knew what lay ahead?

Mattie tugged Della's hand across the table, admiring the tiny diamond that adorned it. It winked in the dim light of the bar. "At least one of us knows what's in her future."

Della smiled, a lovesick expression on her face. "Donald," she whispered dreamily, then pressed the ring against her chin. "Wouldn't it be neat if we all got married and lived in the same apartment building—right here in Haddes?"

Erica groaned. "Spare me! Besides, who says I even *want* to be married by thirty?" She downed the last of her cola, then crossed her legs. Adjusting the ankle strap of her spike-heeled sandals, she suddenly looked thoughtful. "Thirty-five, maybe. I gotta admit, any older would be freaky."

"We'll make it an even twenty years from now," Della said, straightening as she always did at the brilliance of an idea or a piece of juicy gossip. "That means we'll meet back here on this same day, at the same time—" she did the math, ticking off the years on her fingers, red nails flashing "—in the year 2005." Her gaze fell to her engagement ring and she bit her lip, marring her perfect candy-apple gloss. "Jeez, that sounds like something from a science-fiction movie."

Erica rolled her eyes at the sudden change in mood, grabbed a bar napkin and tore it into four squares. She scribbled the future meeting date, down to the half-hour, on every piece, her large handwriting dominating the small scraps of paper. Then she slid the pieces of napkin across the table to each friend with a challenging smile.

When each girl held a square, they looked up like reluctant knights of the round bar table, each making brief eye contact with another. Shay looked relieved, hanging on to her scrap of napkin like a teddy bear. Della appeared suddenly uncertain, and Erica defiant as usual. Mattie's gaze wavered under the scrutiny of her friends, then strayed to the stack of envelopes with a look of pure longing.

CHAPTER I

May 11, 2005

Della spun the chair around with a *whoosh*, and Mattie found herself facing a familiar image in the salon mirror.

"Now then," Della announced. "You're presentable."

Presentable. Why did that word grate on her nerves? It was true, that was why. Presentable and totally boring, though she'd broken out the most alluring thing in her closet today. But from her mouse-brown hair to her white slacks and aqua twin-set, she was merely…presentable.

Mattie touched the freshly cropped ends of her hair, causing the bob to swing at chin level. "Do you think I should let it grow out a little?"

"Why would you?" Della asked, obviously confused. "It would just make it harder to care for. As it is, you can wash it and be presentable in ten minutes."

There was that word again. Normally Mattie didn't spend much time fretting over her appearance, but today was different. Or was it? She wondered if anyone else would remember the reunion date. She met Della's eyes in the mirror but couldn't detect anything out of the ordinary. Disappointment settled in her chest. Della had forgotten. It was foolish, but she'd carried the scrap of bar napkin in her billfold for twenty years. Lately, though, it seemed to serve more as a reminder of her failures than her fantasies.

"I guess you're right." Mattie responded to Della's comment and was rewarded with a satisfied smile. Della liked to be right.

The world could begin spinning again. Mattie Harold, spinster bookstore owner, wasn't going to let her hair grow out. Much less let it down. God forbid.

Mattie wrote out a check to Della and resisted the urge to dot her name with a smiley face as she'd done as a teenager. Her eyes stung. She was feeling ridiculously nostalgic today. Blinking away the tears, she glanced around the salon.

Della had hired a new stylist named Kimee. With jet-black hair cut in a geometric bob and more piercings than a pincushion, Kimee needed no introduction to Haddes's youth. She was the poster child for the generation gap, hired, as Della said, "to bring in the teens and their allowance." And bring in the kids she had. Teenage girls lined the waiting area, sitting two to a seat and giggling in nervous anticipation of their Kimee makeover. She was currently stroking fuchsia eyeshadow on a young girl of about fifteen. Her red hair had been cut frighteningly similar to Kimee's and now sported a streak of white down one side. The girl looked like she'd won the lottery. Her mother looked like she'd just swallowed one of Kimee's nose rings.

Just say no, Mom, Mattie thought. But obviously Mom was more interested in making her daughter happy than asserting her parental rights.

Several of the salon's patrons, all over sixty, were obviously waiting to see Della. Mattie sighed. It didn't look as if Della could get away even if Mattie reminded her.

Which she refused to do.

Mattie tugged off her cardigan as she left the air-conditioned salon and entered the Georgia heat. May had arrived with confidence, chasing away the cool air. Already the heat was pooling against the asphalt, swirling and rising against her ankles and sandaled feet.

She lifted her face to the sun, a little sad that her wrinkle-busting, age-defying youth-radiating foundation had an SPF of 30. She hadn't had an honest-to-God tan in a decade. Back in the good old days, they'd slathered themselves with baby oil mixed with iodine, plopped down on a quilt and fried like teenage eggs. No guilt involved. She forced herself to stop frowning and rubbed the furrow between her eyes. Maybe she should just ditch the wrinkle-defying foundation and zap any intruders with Botox. She'd been thinking a lot about Botox lately. She'd been thinking about a lot of things like Botox lately.

Mattie sighed. Too much thinking was bad for the soul, not to mention the complexion.

She tried to clear her mind as she began the three-block walk to her duplex but her thoughts circled back with a will of their own. It seemed like some cosmic joke that she was pushing forty and still single. In her mind she'd freeze-framed her age at about twenty-three. But lately she'd been catching reflections of herself in unexpected places—the window of the drive-thru lane at Hamburger Heaven, the mirrored tile behind the florist's counter. And the woman who looked back at her was definitely not twenty-three. More often than not, the woman in the reflection was scowling. Mattie touched her forehead again and massaged away the tension.

It suddenly occurred to her that she'd drifted through life like someone drifting through a supermarket, perusing aisle after aisle with an indefinable craving.

Despite the encroaching heat, which would soon rule Haddes during the summer months, it was a picture-perfect day. A few residential areas remained downtown, snuggling comfortably against the businesses as they had for decades. Not much had changed in the nearly four decades she'd lived here, but the few changes she'd seen were for the better. Old homes were being renovated by enterprising early-retirees, morphing into quaint tearooms and antiques shops.

The shops in the original part of the little city were old two-story brick buildings that shouldered one another along

Main Street, causing shoppers to wedge their SUVs in side alleys and narrow parking spaces. Mattie took it all in, both content and discontent to walk the same path she'd walked all her life.

But then she spotted the bookstore and the doubt melted away. Something in her chest swelled with recognition and pride. Looking at the bookshop was like looking in a mirror but actually liking the reflection. Or maybe it was more akin to looking at your child, an offshoot of yourself of which you could unabashedly be proud. She wasn't sure. But nothing and no one else belonged in that store.

She'd created it and it was hers alone.

Mattie had built the bookstore from nothing. In fact, the idea had come about eight years earlier when a stack of paperbacks on her nightstand careened over. When she went to pick them up, she realized they'd hit another stack of novels on the floor, knocking them over as well. She'd cleaned up, packing the books neatly in a plastic crate, but when she went to store them in her closet, there was no room—thanks, in great part, to her shoe collection. Mattie grinned at the memory. The left side of her walk-in closet had been stacked to the ceiling with crates of books, the right equally as jammed with shoe boxes. Since she refused to give up either prized collection, the idea for a used bookstore was born.

She took two weeks vacation from her clerical position at the bank and rented some space in an old building previously used as a saddle shop, signing for the run-down real estate on a month-to-month basis. The venture was little more than an organized yard sale at the time and she had every expectation of returning to her old job when her vacation time was up. But the day she opened for business a fierce spring storm blew through Haddes and the shop lost power. Mattie lit a half-dozen candles and opened the front door. The damp air lifted the dormant smell of leather and oil, mixing with the scent of the lemongrass candles and books. Mattie was in love.

Not only had the storm blown in that day, but customers had, as well. Somehow parting with her books had been not only easy but enjoyable when she watched them leave with a happy customer. When her own personal collection began to wane, Mattie went in search of more. Her clerical job was history. She began selling new rather than used books but also began acquiring books from estate sales. She lucked out on some rare editions and started educating herself on collectibles. Before long, she'd gained a reputation for handling antique and rare books as well as stocking popular fiction.

These days the bookstore was well known for hosting book signings and writers clubs. There was always hot tea and slices of lemon cake and good conversation. Mattie loved the shop like a friend, was proud of its success. So why did the accomplishment feel a bit abstract, as though the shop itself was responsible for the success rather than her?

She sighed. Possibly because, after nearly four decades in one place, she'd managed to misplace her self-esteem. Mattie ran her hand through her hair, surprised at the feel of the short strands. Della had been a little overzealous today. But then she thought of Kimee Scissorhands and shivered.

Though she'd hung the "Closed" sign on the door in honor of the big reunion—which suddenly seemed like a short road to depression—Mattie slipped through the door, locking it behind her. She breathed deep and smiled. It was home away from home. Like a favorite pair of faded Levi's, or slipping into fresh sheets at the end of a long day, the shop was an instant shot of pleasure endorphins, despite the work required to run the place. And it was hard work.

Three stacks of boxes sat next to her desk, their cardboard edges battered and suspiciously dirty. Mattie knew what was inside without checking. A large order of children's books had been missing in action for two weeks now, lost in the mysterious realm of overnight delivery. She dug her box opener from her desk and slit the wide tape from the top box. The first book in the shipment was a picture book. The artwork was delightful, sporting a neon-green cricket, the author's name boldly splashed across the front in blue. Mattie ran the pad of her thumb across the author's name, mentally substituting her own.

The goal of owning the bookshop had been consuming at first, and her need to see it become successful had fueled her for years. But two years ago the shop had settled into a sort of easy rhythm that worried her. Then that indefinable craving had returned.

Mattie thought of her writing and shook her head. She'd gotten the urge to see her own name in print, but the stories, the characters and erotic worlds she created under cover of night would never see print. That part of her would remain saved on a CD, safely tucked away in the closet where she did her late-night work. So she'd targeted the children's book market instead, a much better fit for Mattie. Or at least the Mattie the rest of the world knew.

With her usual determination, Mattie formed a local writers' group and had been working steadily toward publication ever since. But so far she'd only met with rejection. Some days she wondered if the goal to write was just another distraction, something no more achievable than marriage and children. After all, marriage required a man, and children required, well, something to which she didn't currently have access. *Especially* without a man.

The number of dates she'd had in the last ten years— or rather the lack of them—was scary. Some days, especially after a rerun of *Sex and the City*, when it seemed the whole world was having sex, she'd vow to join them and just do it. Like the Nike commercial. She was straight. She was still relatively young and attractive. But then she'd go out with the postman, or the nephew of her insurance agent, and somehow the urge was lacking. She really didn't want to sleep with the postman. In all honesty, she didn't want to sleep with someone she wasn't in love with. She'd only had sex with one person, her college boyfriend, Brad. A.k.a. a distant memory. Brad had been a disappointment. Or maybe she had. Who knew? But she'd sort of given in, then given up.

Now she considered herself a sort of pseudo-virgin, and she was actually kind of comfortable with that. She figured there was some sort of statute of limitations. If you hadn't had an orgasm in a certain number of years, you got to reclaim virginhood. It made sense to her.

She spent the next two hours unloading the boxes, making order out of chaos and managing to avoid smudging her white slacks with dust. Finally she shelved the last book, stacked the empty boxes for recycling and made her way to the ladies' room to freshen up before heading to the Stop-N-Bowl. *What's the point?* her inner crab complained. *Go home. Eat ice cream. Watch* Oprah. *Avoid more rejection.* No, she countered. She kept her promises. If she was the only one that showed, she'd at least have the satisfaction of being the only friend with enough honor to remember. She smoothed pale pink lipstick across her lips, powdered away the afternoon shine on her face and mentally braced herself. No one would remember the reunion date but her. Unlike her friends, the wheel of Mattie's life turned at a predictable pace. Manageable. Comfortable. Familiar. As easily shelved as one of her books.

She decided to walk to the Stop-N-Bowl rather than hoofing it back to her duplex to get her car. Besides, she wasn't too anxious for her friends, in the unlikely event that they showed, to see her recent purchase. The land barge, as she thought of her Crown Vic, had been retired from the local police force. And it was as ugly. Dirty white, with the outline of the police shield still visible from the side, it had turned out to be more embarrassing to drive than she'd expected. Mattie sighed, feeling a niggling of regret. Oh well, it was big and cheap, which was why she'd taken the plunge and bought it at auction. She could stack boxes of estate-sale books in the trunk and back seat and still have room for a pony.

When Mattie rounded the corner to the bowling alley, she was surprised to see several cars, none of which she recognized. Probably the cleaning crew, she reasoned. The Stop-N-Bowl shouldn't even be open this time of the afternoon. She paused when she reached the door, her hand icy despite the fact that she clutched the sun-warmed handle. In all likelihood, the door would be locked and she would spend the evening in a blue funk, watching someone eat bugs on reality television while she downed a pint of rocky road.

Mattie squeezed the latch and the door swung open easily, enveloping her in an air-conditioned cloud of familiarity. She took a deep breath. The Stop-N-Bowl was her own personal time machine. Her writers' group held its share of meetings there, taking advantage of the deli and private party rooms available in the back. But no matter how often she came, she always experienced the same sense that time had stood still.

As her eyes adjusted to the interior, she found that the lanes were darkened but the bar area was well lit. Only a few tables remained, the rest squeezed out by a new pool table. Pinball machines still lined the wall but were now frighteningly referred to as "vintage." Rows of neatly arranged liquor bottles topped a mahogany bar devoid of graffiti. Mr. Murphy, Della's father, had an imposing presence that kept the locals in line. His glare as he wiped down the glossy wood was usually the only warning necessary.

Della's brother Jack hadn't been behind the bar since his summers spent home from college. He'd moved to Atlanta fifteen years ago to start a career as a private investigator. Mattie could never seem to reconcile the quiet athlete she knew with her image of a PI, though Della assured her it was less gumshoe and more corporate inquiry than the books that filled the mystery section of the bookstore led one to believe. Still, the job sounded dark and mysterious and only fueled the fantasy.

As if her fantasies about Jack needed more fuel. They had been simmering since she was the ripe old age of thirteen. Though she knew he often made it home for the holidays, the Murphys were a tight clan and Mattie made certain not to intrude on their family time. She'd run into Jack a time or two, though, her knees turning to Jell-O and her brain becoming sixteen again.

Thirty-eight-year-old knees and a sixteen-year-old brain. A scary combination.

Muffled voices from the far end of the bowling alley caught her attention. Mattie froze. She could have sworn she was alone. She glanced around, still feeling like a trespasser. Mattie grabbed her purse and thumbed through it to distract herself from the acid burning in her gut. She found her envelope in the side pocket of her purse and tossed it on the table as if it contained flesh-eating bacteria.

She'd experienced absolutely nothing written inside. But the moment of truth was here.

She wasn't anxious to admit her failure. So why was she here, trespassing, wishing her friends had remembered their childish pact?

"Long time no see." Della's familiar voice rang out as she sidled up to the table and slung her ten-pound purse atop it.

Della was still beautiful, despite the fact that there was more of her to love these days. She'd styled her platinum-blond hair in an ultramodern cut picked up from a recent hair show in Birmingham. It barely brushed her shoulders, the ends moussed to messy perfection. Everything about Della's appearance spoke confidence. Tight, black capri pants said, "Love me as I am," and a spaghetti-strapped tank peeked from beneath a colorful mesh blouse, flashing glimpses of ample cleavage.

Mattie was so shocked that Della had showed up, that she was speechless. But Della didn't appear to notice. She lifted her well-padded hips onto the vinyl seat across from Mattie, sighing heavily.

"You little sneak. I thought you'd forgotten."

"Ditto." The knot in her stomach loosened considerably and she smiled. "I thought... You had so many clients waiting."

Della waved a dismissive hand, nails the identical shade of red they'd been twenty years ago. "I gave them to Kimee."

"You did not!" Mattie suddenly pictured hordes of Haddesians walking around with Goth haircuts like a scene from *The Night of the Living Dead*. "Oh my God, please tell me you didn't leave old Estelle Ashworth with Kimee."

Della grinned a grin so mischievous that Mattie had only seen it on one other face—that of Della's three-year-old son, Trevor. "I did." She giggled. "I can't wait to see what she does to her."

"You mean Kimee or Mrs. Ashworth?" Estelle Ashworth was no shrinking violet. She ran the local dry cleaners and had a reputation for being gruff. She kept a candy jar full of Dubble Bubble and handed pieces out to the children along with a fierce pinch and a smile. Half left crying and the other half knew to refuse the offer politely. "I don't know which one to be worried about."

"Good point. It should be worth showing up in the morning." Della laughed, then opened her purse and began sorting through the contents. "Estelle gripes every time I cut her hair. Maybe after Kimee gets through with her, she'll appreciate my talent. In fact, I'm going to consider it a crash course in Della appreciation."

Mattie nodded. That course should be mandatory for a few people she knew. Namely, Donald. But she kept that observation to herself.

"So have you heard from anyone else?"

Mattie knew the "anyone else" Della was referring to meant Shay and Erica. She shook her head.

"I have a feeling we'll be the only attendees at this little party." Removing a sandwich bag filled with what Mattie hoped were raisins and a Hot Wheels car, she continued fishing until she extracted her envelope, placing it atop Mattie's. "Last I heard Erica was out of the country and Shay was out of her mind."

Mattie chose to ignore the comment about Shay. It hurt that Shay had withdrawn from their lives, but her reasons were certainly valid. She'd left Haddes to free herself from an abusive marriage, and despite the fact that her life was totally unconventional—maybe even a little weird—Mattie understood. And what was worse—making every poor choice available, as her friend had, or taking no chances at all, as she'd done?

She lifted the corner of the sandwich bag and examined the contents. Was it possible for raisins to shrivel? She gave Della a questioning look and dropped the bag. "Last I heard, Erica was covering the war in Iraq."

Della ignored her silent commentary on the state of the raisins. "If a war breaks out without someone there to snap a picture, does it really break out?" Della slipped from her chair and sauntered to the bar, smiling at her humor.

Mattie considered the caustic comment. Okay, so maybe she wasn't the only one feeling a little ordinary. Besides, she knew Della well enough to realize that the comment was sheer bravado. Sarcasm was easier than worrying about Erica's safety.

"Do you have any red wine back there?" Mattie asked. She'd only recently learned to tolerate alcohol in the form of wine. Half of the articles in the medical magazines she stocked at the bookstore were now claiming that red wine was beneficial to your heart. But in all honesty, holding the stem of a graceful wineglass while she read in bed at night made her feel more like a literary connoisseur and less like a lonely spinster.

"No, no red wine," Della answered absentmindedly, ducking beneath the bar in search of something.

"Are you sure?" Mattie eyed the dozens of bottles on the shelf.

"No." Her friend's blond head popped up. "Besides, today I'm making margaritas." She shook a canister of salt for emphasis, cha-chaing her hips to the beat, then held up her hand when Mattie started to protest. "Don't be a wimp, Mattie."

She snapped her mouth shut. Tonight she was *not* a wimp. She was a successful small-business owner, single and still a size six. She bit her lip. Well, a size six most of the time. If she wasn't retaining water and if she held her breath. At any rate, she was going to drink a margarita without grimacing, dammit.

After sipping and perfecting, adding various potions and revving the mixer to a deafening RPM, Della returned to the table with the drinks, leaving a half-full blender on the bar.

Mattie took a sip and managed not to grimace. A muted burst of male laughter erupted from the direction of the conference rooms. Della waved her hand as she sipped.

"Chamber of Commerce meeting in the back."

Mattie was about to get the details when a soft rustle from the entrance caught her attention. Shay stepped out of the shadows, her tall form gliding gracefully toward their table.

"Shay!" Mattie jumped to her feet, scooping her friend into a hug as she neared. Della was next in line for a hug, though Mattie thought she detected a guilty expression, at least one that looked as close to guilty as Della ever came.

"We never dreamed you'd come." Della hesitated. "How are you?"

Shay took a seat and met their eyes, hesitating until she had their full attention. "I'm great," she answered, her voice breathy. Shay always gave the impression of being delicately out of breath, as if she'd just breezed in from somewhere important.

Mattie shook her head in amazement. Shay looked like some misplaced Celtic princess. The crushed silk sheath she wore came nearly to her ankles, the effect no less than stunning. Auburn curls wound to her waist, and her ivory complexion was ten years more youthful than it should have been. Cut crystals hung from her ears, matching the crystal pendant that swung between her breasts. The New Age garb was the only hint that Shay's life had taken a turn down the road less traveled. Mattie sipped her drink and suppressed a surge of jealousy. Did everyone else have to be so damn interesting?

"Cough up that envelope." Della got right to the point.

Shay opened a delicately crocheted handbag and removed her envelope. Mattie eyed her own pedestrian-looking purse, then Shay's. Heck, she'd probably grown the cotton—organically, of course—spun it and crocheted herself, all the while chanting good thoughts for the universe. Mattie sat her drink down with a *thud*. Was it the alcohol or was she just becoming a middle-aged bitch?

Shay added her envelope to the growing pile in the center of the table, her expression serene but not entirely natural. The envelopes themselves told part of the story. Della's was ringed with coffee stains, Shay's rumpled but clean, and

Mattie's pristine, having survived its twenty-year wait pressed between the pages of a dictionary.

Mattie thought about what her envelope contained. This was the one that had started them all, the first time one of her fantasies met paper. And for twenty years it had been her little secret. Proof that she could be naughty when she wanted to. But now she wasn't so sure. What had been deliciously wicked twenty years ago suddenly seemed a little, well, stupid.

There was a feeling Mattie got when she was about to do something colossally dumb. It was a creepy creeping sensation that started at the base of her spine and worked its way to her chest like a big hairy spider. It was crawling now. And once it got to her chest, she wouldn't be able to breathe. She flexed her shoulders as if she could dislodge it. It didn't work.

"Jack!" Della's voice shouted in Mattie's ear. "Come say hi."

What? *What?* She followed her friend's gaze to find the silhouette of two men frozen in the shadows of the entrance. One was thin and rather short. The other was obviously Jack. The shadows fell across his face but she'd know that perfect silhouette anywhere.

"He and his partner are moving back here from Atlanta."

Partner... Mattie's tequila-laced mind turned the word over, trying to make the puzzle piece fit.

Jack's posture spelled r-e-l-u-c-t-a-n-t as he crossed the distance to their table. Mattie's stomach clutched, then

froze in a spasm of denial as Jack stood before her. He was
wearing a charcoal-gray suit, a stunningly shy grin
and…bronzer? She squinted. Mother-of-pearl, he looked
like the local news anchorman after last season's disastrous
brush with self-tanner. And to make matters worse, his black
hair was spiked and so thick with gel that it could put out
an eye.

"Y'all remember Jack, of course."

Shay stood and embraced Jack without hesitation. Mattie watched her friend's ample breasts flatten against the la-
pel of Jack's suit, strained to make out her breathless greeting.
Unlike Shay, Mattie was frozen in place, cemented to her
seat. Something was off kilter, something—

"And this is Cal," Della said, as she motioned the second
man to the table. "Cal is Jack's partner."

The smaller man literally seemed to pulse with energy as
he approached. His head was shaved smooth, the shiny dome
interrupted only by a pair of goggle-like glasses perched atop
it. He wore a casual white shirt tucked inside eye-popping
striped pants. Mattie felt her eyes go round with realization.
No straight man she knew would wear tight white denim
with wide brown stripes. She cocked her head, thinking for
a moment that the vertical stripes had a great slimming effect. She blinked, forcing herself to focus as her gaze traveled
upward, finally resting on a diamond stud that winked in one
earlobe. Cal smiled in response to her scrutiny. He had blind-

ingly white teeth and one perfectly manicured hand resting possessively on Jack's shoulder.

Oh God.

"E-excuse me." Mattie stood.

"Mattie? Mattie Harold?" Jack held out his arms and her stomach lurched. "My God, you haven't changed—"

Neither have you. The normal response formed in her brain but ended as a strangled noise in the back of her throat. "I— I've got to…" She stammered, then reached for the obligatory hug. The sound of a million and one fantasies shattering was deafening. "Excuse me for a moment." Mattie swiped her drink from the table and dashed to the ladies' room.

As Mattie hightailed it, Della shook her head. Her gaze fell on her brother, sweeping him from head to toe before settling on his face. "What," she said slowly, "on God's green earth happened to you?"

Jack's jaw twitched and his eyes narrowed. "Kimee happened to me." He tried to flatten the spikes on top of his head but they only bent, instantly standing up again like a tinsel Christmas tree.

Della burst out laughing. "You look like Dennis Rodman and Peter Pan's love child."

"I can't believe you left me with her."

"You showed up out of the blue. I had no choice."

Jack's face was turning a threatening shade of red. "You

told Kimee I was on my way to get a photo made for the chamber of commerce."

"I did." Della pretended to swoon, pressing her hand to her chest. "Oh my God, I'm so sorry. What was I thinking?"

Jack raised an eyebrow, then pointed to her drink. "How many of those have you had?"

"Not enough. Now please explain to me how telling Kimee that you needed a haircut so that you could get your picture made has caused you to look like—" she wavered a little under Jack's glare "—like a tanning salon mutant."

"Because, dear sister, little Kimee was convinced that the photographer's lighting would…how did she put it?…fade me out." He rubbed at his face with his knuckle. "She put… What was it called, Cal?"

"Bronzer," Cal offered with a sly grin.

"Yeah. That's it. She put bronzer on me with a weird little sponge."

Della looked at Cal. "And you were…?"

"Reading *Cosmo*." He shrugged, a mischievous twinkle in his eye. "What can I say?"

"Yeah, about that," Jack interjected. "Try *Field and Stream* next time you're in public." He glanced at Cal's slacks. "I know subtle isn't your nature, but you might want to let people get to know you before you break out the tiara."

"Oh, please." Cal rolled his eyes. "This is Haddes, not Green Acres. I think they can handle one gay man."

Jack looked serious. "This is Haddes, not Atlanta." He shrugged Cal's hand off his shoulder. "And cut the touchy-feely stuff before you give everybody the wrong idea about us."

Della straightened. "A tractor and a head of cattle wouldn't hurt, either." She fell into a fit of laughter. Shay muffled a giggle.

Cal winked. "Cows. I'll get right on that." He looked at Shay, then gestured toward Della and Jack. "Can you believe these two?"

Shay smiled, laughter replaced by her usual Mona Lisa serenity. "Haddes is pretty good at taking folks in." She met Della's eyes for a moment. "Even people who are different."

"So." Della jumped back to her brother. "Why did you let Kimee do this to you?"

"I didn't *let* her."

"Then why are you, uh, tan?" Della leaned forward to get a closer look.

"Because when I said no thank you, she started to cry."

Della laughed. "Kimee does not cry."

"I can assure you that she does."

Della was horrified. "Why? Why would that make her cry?"

"You left the poor kid with a gazillion people waiting. When I got there Estelle Ashworth looked like she was going to a Pink concert."

"Uh-oh."

"Uh-oh is right. Kimee was in over her head. I thought putting up with this stuff—" Jack scrubbed his jawline with his knuckle again, but the uneven color appeared to have adhered permanently "—until I could get to the car and wipe it off would make her feel better. But now it's not coming off."

Della smirked. "Well…uh…it's kind of a stain."

Jack looked puzzled.

"Self-tanner. It's what we use in the salon. It's a semi-permanent application. It won't wash off, it has to wear off." Della flinched and jumped behind Shay when Jack straightened his six-foot-three frame to full height. "It may take a week."

CHAPTER 2

Mattie burst through the ladies' room door, stopped at the sink and stared at her own horrified expression. The tequila swirled in her stomach, threatening to swirl in the sink. Fighting fire with fire, she threw the rest of her margarita down her throat, sat the empty glass in the sink and headed for a bathroom stall, opting for a good pee instead of a good cry. What was the use, anyway? Jack wouldn't be any *less* gay if she burst into tears.

Jack is gay…. Jack is gay…. How could she not have known this?

Mattie zipped her pants and straightened with new resolve. She knew one thing: there was no friggin' way she was going to read that fantasy letter to her friends. The idea of sharing her thoughts on sex was like a bad joke. Nope. Unlike Jack, she was going to keep her secrets *in* the closet.

Only one time in her life had she considered herself sexually active. And even then, she'd probably been more inactive than active. Despite the fact that she'd been a virgin, she'd instinctively known that Brad, her college boyfriend, was a sexual underachiever. She squeezed her eyes shut, wincing at the memory of Brad pounding away while she sort of flopped about, her back pressed against the mattress, her expectations withering along with her passion. It hadn't been the kind of experience she'd dreamed of, definitely not the sort penned in eighteen-year-old handwriting and sealed in an envelope.

It hadn't been with Jack.

And all these years she'd been certain that, if it had been, it would have been perfect.

Not.

Mattie felt as if someone had just jarred her from a deep sleep. One that she'd been in for, say, about twenty years. She'd written down every passionate thought she'd ever had and had sealed it in that envelope. And there it had stayed, safe and sound, pure and unmarred. Looking back, she doubted that even Brad had gotten the benefit of that passion. How could he? It had been sealed away in an envelope and flattened in a dictionary.

The sense that she'd waited too long flowed over her, and her shoulders slumped. She looked at herself in the mirror. Defeat lined her eyes, softened her jawline. Mattie looked away.

Too late, too late, too late, the tequila taunted over and over in her brain.

She envisioned herself marching out of the bathroom and

to the table, snatching up the envelope and breaking the seal. And then what? What would she find? Would the glue crumble, would the pages be yellowed?

The sense that this was not all about Jack was pretty obvious, and yet... How could she not have known? Jack had never been too involved in small-town life, or small-town girls. She had always assumed he was destined for bigger things, had his sights set outside the city limits of Haddes. Of course, it had been easier to fabricate the perfect life for Jack rather than face her own. And in doing so, she'd somehow missed the obvious.

But now... Now she was beginning to feel entirely too sober. Mattie washed her hands, retrieved the margarita glass and gathered her courage. She willed the hinges to stay silent as she eased open the door to the ladies' room and peered out. Relief washed over her. Jack was gone. She marched straight to the bar, refilled her glass with the melting margarita mix and returned, none too coordinated, to her chair. She stared with hostility at the ominous pile of envelopes instead of making eye contact with Shay and Della. Surely fragments of shattered dreams were still clinging to her face.

"Jack said to tell you that he hopes to see you again now that he's back in town," Shay said.

Heaven forbid. "I didn't know that Jack was—" she hesitated, mentally rephrasing "—that Jack had a partner."

"I thought you did." Della shrugged. "Cal's great. They're opposites. Sort of yin and yang. A great fit."

Mattie flinched at the image Della's words conjured.

"I didn't tell you that they're moving back to Haddes because I just found out myself— Oh my God!" Della interrupted herself, her gaze glued to the entrance.

"Erica?" Mattie and Shay said in unison as they followed Della's gaze.

Erica's normally athletic gait was slow and as she neared, Mattie realized her friend's arm was in a cast. The three women hesitated, as if not quite sure what to do with the injured, solemn-faced woman in front of them.

Erica grinned then, her face transforming into a familiar expression of bravado. She shrugged. "Land mine."

The comment broke the ice and the next few minutes were filled with swapping comforting hugs and laughter.

Shay helped Erica into a chair with characteristic sympathy. "What really happened? Were you in an accident?"

Erica looked momentarily confused. "Land mine," she restated, her brows arching.

"You mean a real line mand? Land mine…" Mattie corrected, hoping no one else noticed the tequila-slip.

Erica nodded, her face serious. "It was activated by a humanitarian relief crew I was following in Afghanistan. They were killed instantly." Her gaze appeared distant before she straightened with a weak smile. "I'm okay, though. Just a few bumps and bruises." She held up her arm. "And one minor fracture. I'm taking a month or two off to recuperate."

"Here in Haddes?" Della asked.

"Um…maybe." She pulled a tiny black purse into her lap and unzipped it. The envelope she produced had been folded accordion-style, no doubt to fit.

Erica always did travel light, Mattie thought. Friendships and relationships included. Without fanfare she tossed the envelope into the pile.

Della brought a drink, but Erica declined, holding up her injured arm. "Better not mix it with the meds," she explained.

Mattie's gaze slid from Erica's arm to her face. She'd changed very little during the years that had separated them. Still strikingly beautiful, her dark hair spilled over strong tanned shoulders, and the calculated movements of her body fell somewhere between athletic and graceful. If you didn't look into her eyes, it would be easy to assume she spent her days on a tennis court. But there were new lines at the corners of Erica's eyes, and for reasons unclear to Mattie, she was certain that they'd been hard-earned.

Della slid the drink in front of Mattie instead and the next hour was spent filling in the gaps of information about their lives. It was awkward at times, a social dance that included accepting Shay's silence when the subject of men came up and the lack of detail surrounding the last few years of Erica's life. Della played hostess and gossip instigator like the pro that she was.

Conversation finally waned, and the four friends lapsed into companionable silence.

Mattie realized that their gazes had all inadvertently settled on the pile of envelopes. The creepy spider feeling began to walk up her spine again and her lips felt numb. The tequila? Maybe. The sight of the envelopes reminded her of an old black-and-white episode of *The Twilight Zone*, when the object of some paranormal event began to take on a life of its own—growing, heartbeat throbbing, spinning in the center of the camera lens...

"I just remembered..." She made a move toward the stack of envelopes.

"Oh no, you don't," Della said. She leaned her palms on the table, tenting the envelopes with her body.

Della looked like an angry rottweiler guarding its kibble. Was that a bit of drool at the corner of her mouth? Mattie stifled a hysterical laugh at the thought, then straightened, attempting to gain control of her ping-ponging thoughts.

"I'm sorry. I—I really can't say—stay..." she stammered. "I have a shipment of books from Ralph Barnes's estate that I need to go through."

"Ralph Barnes?" Erica shivered. "He gave me the heebie-jeebies. Always walking around in that silk smoking jacket like Hugh Hefner."

Della ignored her, focusing on Mattie. "You're not wiggling out of this one, Missy. I don't care if St. Peter died and left you the keys to heaven."

Erica fidgeted with a bar napkin, seemingly oblivious to Della's rising temper. "Isn't St. Peter technically already dead?"

"It's okay," Shay said, shooting Della and Erica disapproving looks. "We understand."

Erica shrugged but Della landed on her feet, pointing at Mattie. "No, we don't!"

Mattie cocked her head, studying the image of her friend. With her arm extended in perfect pointer position, she looked more rabid golden retriever than rottweiler.

"Mattie!" Della's voice cracked and Mattie jumped, suddenly alert. "I've waited twenty years to hear what's inside of that envelope of yours." Della's eyes widened, then narrowed. "What are you so afraid of, Mattie Harold?"

Oh crap. All sorts of things came to mind—bugs, the bottom of her garbage can when she lifted the bag out, the rejection of men dipped in self-tanner....

Mattie had never had an athletic moment in her life. She'd always assumed that whatever gene was responsible for hand-to-eye coordination was dormant in her body. She had a colorful history of sending tennis balls into outer space and gymnastic coaches to the ER. But for one shining moment, she was Olga Korbut and Chris Evert rolled into one. She was on her feet before anyone could blink. Her hand shot out, unchallenged, grasped her envelope and shoved it safely into her purse. She executed a perfect half-spin and was halfway across the room before Della knew what had happened.

"Gotta run!" she called cheerfully.

Then she tripped over the threshold on her way out the door.

Jack watched Mattie Harold weave her way hell-bent through the maze of bar tables and pinball machines toward the back door of the bowling alley. He'd suspected she was tipsy earlier. Her gaze had seemed a little out of focus and her face had been flushed. But when she stumbled over the threshold, arms flapping like she was an agitated flamingo in an effort to keep from falling, he realized she was more than tipsy. He grinned. Damn, she was cute. She'd always been the cute one in the bunch. She was Della's age, a few years younger than he was, but she still looked like the kid he remembered.

A kid who was about to walk into traffic drunk as a skunk.

He stepped out of the building and slipped behind Della's minivan, ready to intervene if necessary. But Mattie successfully made her way through the cars in the parking lot and to the sidewalk that lined Main Street. But she'd now stopped and was fiddling with a piece of paper. An envelope, maybe? What in the world was she up to? He thought he recalled seeing a stack of envelopes on the bar table, but hadn't paid much attention. The haze of his own embarrassment at his appearance had been pretty thick.

He watched as Mattie began tearing the paper into pieces. He couldn't help but grin. She appeared to be seriously pissed off at the envelope. Mattie then wadded the pieces of paper into a ball and tossed it into the roadside ditch.

Jack felt a rush of curiosity that he hadn't felt since he'd stopped taking on personal investigations. He slipped his shades on and repositioned himself by another car, making certain that Mattie wasn't headed toward a vehicle of her own. The last thing she needed to do in her condition was to get behind the wheel. Thankfully, she was leaving on foot, though her feet didn't look too steady, either.

He watched until Mattie disappeared from sight, then his gaze settled on the ditch. Whatever lay crumpled in that soggy ditch was none of his business.

But that wasn't going to stop him.

Mattie dipped the sponge into the soapy water and squeezed, her head pounding as she bent over the bucket. She straightened, pushing her sunglasses up the bridge of her nose with her free hand. She'd slept off the tequila last night—well, yesterday afternoon *and* last night—but woke this morning feeling like she'd been hit by an eighteen-wheeler. And had been dragged behind it for about a mile.

The midday sun was now glaring off the chrome bumper of her car like a laser, and the sunglasses were no match. And she was unnaturally hot, even in shorts and a tank top. Not to mention a little queasy. She wanted to go inside her duplex, pull the curtains and die. But she wasn't going to. Washing the land barge was her penance for drinking like a fish and buying the ridiculous vehicle in the first place. Besides, she wasn't exactly mentally sharp, and washing the car was one task that didn't require her to think. She'd managed to retrieve one load of books from Ralph Barnes's estate this morning, but by the time she'd hauled the heavy boxes into the store she'd felt bloodless and about as strong as a noodle. No more tequila, she vowed. Never, never, never.

She squatted next to the side of the car and scrubbed at the dingy silhouette of the police shield as if it would miraculously disappear. No such luck. Little flakes of faded white paint stuck to her sponge. Groovy.

Mattie stood and snatched up the hose. She shot a stream of water at the sudsy side and pretended the nozzle was an Uzi. More paint chips cascaded to the asphalt with the water and settled in a mocking little puddle around her bare feet. So much for improving the outside. Hauling the estate books this morning had left a trail of spiderwebs and grime in the back seat, so she traded the hose for her cordless vacuum, shoved her sunglasses on top of her head and crawled inside.

The car was like a vault. But it wasn't the size that unnerved her as much as the car's gender. Insane, she knew, but the car was a guy.

She'd always had a secret habit of assigning gender to inanimate objects. This car had male written all over it. Testosterone practically haunted the thing, left behind by the countless police officers that had driven it. It even smelled like a man. The scent of aftershave and the faint odor of cigarettes still lingered, forever embedded in the worn upholstery.

It was completely foreign to her.

Men in general were a mystery to Mattie. She was an only child and therefore had missed brother exposure. Her parents divorced when she was ten, wiping out any chance that she'd have a sibling and severely altering her view of her father, who'd gone from father extraordinaire to awkward director of every-other-weekend activities in the blink of an eye. Of her friends, Shay was an orphan and Erica's older brother had married and moved away by the time they'd become close. Della was the only friend with a brother still at home, and Mattie's feelings for Jack were hardly sisterly.

Mattie's gut took a one-two stomach-acid punch as an image of Jack, complete with bad self-tanner, formed in her head. She moaned, revved the vacuum and went to work on the upholstery. Her tenuous grip on mental and physical health just couldn't process the new Jack.

A mechanical scream suddenly came from the hand vac, ripping Mattie from her thoughts. She dropped the vacuum and listened with dread as a chopping sound replaced the screech, decreasing as the engine sputtered to a halt. She eyed the vac, which now lay on the floorboard like a dead animal.

Obviously something other than lint had been sucked into the lint trap. She sighed.

The day just got better and better.

She sat cross-legged on the back seat, pulled the vacuum into her lap and popped it open, exposing the disposable lint trap. Sure enough, a small hole had been ripped through the liner. She pulled the damaged lint trap out, holding the edge of the crud-encrusted thing with two fingers, then tossed it out the car door. But when she tilted the vac to examine the exposed motor, a ring fell out, landing on her bare thigh. She was shocked. She'd expected a small rock, maybe a penny, but not a ring. She picked it up. It was a thin gold band with a filigree setting, centered with what looked to be a ruby. The ring's band was marred with a few nasty scratches from the motor, but was otherwise intact.

She mentally backtracked, trying to judge where the nose of the vacuum had been when it sucked up the ring. Probably the seat's crevice, she reasoned. Mattie held the ring up to the sunlight, examining it. The setting was old-fashioned, either a reproduction or an antique—it was difficult to tell. She pushed it onto the ring finger of her left hand for safekeeping.

In all likelihood, the ring had been stored with the books she'd bought from Ralph Barnes's estate and had fallen out when she was transporting them. Since Ralph had no living relatives, she could only ask the Realtor handling his estate if she knew anything about it. If that didn't turn up anything, she could always ask around at the police precinct. But she doubted that would do any good, given that all Haddes's officers were male. Maybe she could keep it. A gift from the universe for having treated her so poopy lately. Mattie spread her hand, admiring the ring. It really was beautiful.

She retrieved a fresh lint trap from the duplex and reassembled the vacuum. To her relief, it revved back to life and she returned to work, keeping an eye out for foreign objects. She came across a quarter and a hairy cough drop but nothing else out of the ordinary.

Finally, exhausted, she treated herself to a cold cola and a break. She dragged a folding chair from her porch to the driveway and plopped into it. She wasn't wearing her age-defying makeup with an SPF of a gazillion and, frankly, she didn't give a damn. In fact, she spritzed her legs with a fine mist from the hose, hiked up her shorts a little, slid her shades down over her eyes and leaned back. Burn, baby, burn. She was still too hungover to do anything but succumb to the sunshine. And she didn't care who saw her. She wiggled her toes. Besides, her neighbors were all of the geriatric set. If you didn't steal the Sunday newspaper or play loud rap music, they generally didn't notice you.

"What say, Mattie Harold?" The voice was deep, a little raspy and a lot sleazy.

Mattie bolted upright and was rewarded with a pounding pain to her right temple and dancing spots before her eyes. She blinked up at the silhouette that was now blocking her sun, but she'd know the voice anywhere. She pressed her fingertips to her temple. The voice was about as welcome as a tornado siren. She adjusted her sunglasses as she stared up at Shay's ex-husband, Mac McKay.

"Mac." It was more of a statement than a greeting. Her voice was cold, lacking inflection. And that was just how Mattie intended it. "What are you doing here?"

He ignored the question. "Getting a little sun?"

"Yeah. Something like that." He shifted and the sun hit her full force, blinding her. If possible, she was even more annoyed. "What do you want?"

"I just saw the cruiser. And you." He hesitated and the comment suddenly seemed suggestive. "I thought I'd stop and see if it was still performing like it should be."

There was a certain emphasis on the word *performing*. What a creep. She thought of Shay and wondered if Mac had gotten wind that his ex-wife was back in town. She felt a surge of protectiveness and stood. He wouldn't learn of Shay's whereabouts from her, that was for sure. Mattie had been raised to forgive and forget, but she doubted that she would ever forget the sight of Shay's battered face.

At five foot four, Mattie was petite. Though Mac was average for a man, probably less than six feet tall, she hardly came to the center of his chest, especially in bare feet. But that didn't keep her from wanting to take a swing at him. Especially today.

"The car's running fine. Now, if you'll excuse me, I really need to finish what I started."

He shrugged. "Just thought I'd ask."

When he didn't make a move to leave, Mattie turned to find him staring at her with an odd expression. She suddenly felt vulnerable with her bare feet and legs, her thin tank top.

After a minute, Mattie accepted that he wasn't leaving without fulfilling some police quota of small talk. She sighed. "Any news on Christina Wilson?" Christina was a local teenager, just eighteen, who had been missing for almost a week now. Mattie was concerned, as were all the locals, and she figured the neutral topic was as comfortable a one as she'd get with Mac.

"Of course not." He shoved his hands into his pants pockets, made a kind of hissing noise and looked off into the distance as if the question perturbed him. "She's a runaway. Her daddy just needs to accept the obvious."

Whether Christina had run away or had been taken by force was a question being asked throughout Haddes. You couldn't go to the barbershop or the grocery store without someone engaging you in the debate. The way Mattie saw it, either scenario was heartbreaking, especially for Christina's father, Rand Wilson, who had been Jack Murphy's closest friend in school and as underfoot in the Murphy household as Mattie. She had a lot of respect for Rand and she wasn't the only one in town that felt that way. He'd unexpectedly become a father at nineteen and had raised his daughter alone when his young wife took off in search of a less demanding life. Rand had risen to the occasion and Christina had become the center of his world.

Mattie could only imagine what hell Rand was going through, and Mac McKay's callous dismissal of the girl was just another strike against him in her book. As if she needed another reason to dislike the man.

Mattie narrowed her eyes and picked up the hose, wishing for all the world that it really was an Uzi. She really didn't want to start a fresh debate with Mac, but she couldn't resist adding at least one last word. "Maybe," she said.

Mac threw his arms into the air, hissing again, like a punctured tire. "The girl left a note. How much clearer can you get? She's a runaway, plain and simple."

Mattie supposed he had a point. There had been a note left on her bed, a one-liner saying that she was leaving. But Rand thought she'd been forced to write the note, had pointed out the obvious changes to her handwriting, the cryptic wording. And the way Mattie looked at it, Rand knew Christina better than anyone else in the world. If he sensed something was wrong, it just might be.

"I don't suppose you've heard anything to the contrary?" He eyed her with suspicion, his gaze suddenly dark as it raked over her.

"No, of course not," she answered. As if she'd be calmly

washing her car if she had any useful information for the police. What an idiot.

She squeezed the nozzle's trigger and the hose jumped to life. Mattie sprayed the car, making certain that the overspray drifted in Mac's direction. When droplets began to cling to his dark uniform, he got the hint. Backing up, he lifted his hand. It was both a wave goodbye and a dismissal, as if he'd given up on the conversation. Good riddance, she thought as he turned and sauntered off in the direction of his shiny new patrol car.

Since the Crown Vic had gotten way more attention than it deserved and Mattie was ready to throw in the towel on the sorry excuse for a day, she emptied the mop bucket and gathered her sponge and wheel brush, then tossed them inside. She was coiling the garden hose over her shoulder when the *chirp* of an electronic car lock caught her attention. She looked up to see a man crossing the street toward her.

Good grief, no. Not now. Couldn't a girl wash her police cruiser in peace?

It was Jack Murphy. Six foot three, two hundred pounds of recently banished adolescent fantasy. And he was walking toward her with the same masculine stride he'd had at nineteen.

She wanted to run. Instead, she threw down the hose. Then instantly picked it up again. Mattie felt like a squirrel dashing about in the middle of the road, looking for the perfect place to hide, the best direction to avoid the wheels of the car. In the end, it was always the lack of a decision that got the squirrel. Taken out by a Michelin on the centerline stripe.

Her next thought as he neared was that he looked more like the old Jack than he had last night. It was strangely comforting. He was ruggedly handsome, like a smiling—and overly tanned—model from a Jeep ad. The tan was a little uneven, but what the heck. He wore faded jeans and a black T-shirt that only accented his dark hair. But gone, thankfully, was the spiky, over-gelled hair, replaced with a top-down, windblown look. Deceit like that should be illegal, she thought. It was false advertising in the cruelest sense.

"Hey, there," she said when he stopped before her. She heard the friendly lilt in her own voice, marveled at it. Talk about bogus.

"I was hoping to run into you today." Jack paused, a shy-looking grin lifting one corner of his mouth.

"Thanks. It's good to see you again." Liar, liar.

Jack put his hands on his hips and stared at her car rather than her, distracted, no doubt, by its sheer ugliness. He finally dragged his gaze to meet hers, picking up where he'd left off. "I know my appearance was a little weird last night. I hope Della filled you in."

Mattie bit her lip, not certain what to say. All the bizarre comments that popped into her head were far from politically correct. And she wanted desperately to be supportive. So she nodded and smiled. There was little you could do to offend someone when you nodded and smiled.

But now that he was within detail range, she could see that the self-tanner cut a jagged line along his jaw. More subtle today, true. But still there.

"Kimee should come with a warning label," Jack said.

Mattie realized, with a start, that the expression on his face was one of embarrassment. "You mean Kimee from the salon?"

"She ambushed me when Della had to leave early."

"Oh." She tried to process the information, but the conversation was moving faster than her recently damaged brain. "Uh, yeah. Kimee has half the mothers in Haddes stirred up. She's very, uh, innovative." Good, she congratulated herself. Nice benign comment.

"Innovative." He laughed and rubbed at his jaw. "That's a nice word for it. I can't get this crap off. I can't believe it. I've been away from Haddes for years and the first day after I move back, I'm walking around my hometown like a beauty queen. How's that for embarrassing?"

Mattie frowned. That comment was a little self-depreciating. Not to mention that he used the *Q* word. A niggling doubt crept in, but the questions that floated through her brain were sure to make her look like a hick, or worse, intolerant. Yet she wanted to blurt out, *Are you sure you're gay?*

'Cause I never thought so. Mattie bit her lip instead. She was surrounded by steaming piles of faux pas. And no matter what escape route she took, she'd be ankle deep.

So more nodding and smiling ensued.

"Listen, I was hoping maybe we could get together." Jack's eyes were concealed by the shades but his gaze flickered downward and, just for a moment, traveled over her body.

Mattie squirmed. She wanted to look down and see if she had a blob of mud from the hose on her tank top. That was probably it. Coming from any other man, she'd think he was checking her out. Flirting, even. Not that she got checked out much lately. But occasionally, when the moon and stars were aligned, it still happened. At least often enough that she still recognized it.

"Maybe we could have dinner. Catch up," he continued. "And I didn't get a chance to tell you how great you look. You still look eighteen." He lowered his voice. "Only better."

He was staring at her so intently that she couldn't think of a thing to say. It was like… Her brain felt like it was sloshing around in her head, still a little pickled by tequila and a lot off balance. It was like he was coming on to her. But why would he do that? To what end? She didn't get it. A glimmer of hope shone in the dark recesses of her brain. Maybe she'd misread the whole situation. It occurred to her that she could out-and-out ask Della, but then the jig would be up. Her feelings for Jack would be written all over her face.

She didn't get men. Never did. Probably never would. The old Jack was gone, that much was clear. But so what? He was always a great guy. And, no matter what, he was Della's big brother. Maybe the universe was offering him up to her as a sort of learning tool, a risk-free piece of her incomplete "man puzzle."

They could be buddies. Mattie fought the sinking feeling that followed that thought. At the very least she could learn from him, understand what it was—or wasn't—that made men tick. It would be like watching a football game from the safety of the press box rather than getting creamed on the playing field.

It was a consolation prize, but she'd take it. Mattie lived in a small town and that meant playing by small-town rules. Most of her friends were married, which meant they had little time left between soccer games and laundry for hanging out with her. And bonding with other women's husbands was a recipe for disaster. So for those situations where she mingled with couples her own age, she wore her bookstore spinster status like an access badge: Harmless— no threat to marriage. *Full clearance to barbecues and bar mitzvahs.*

In other words, she was boring.

But Jack could change that. Suddenly the image of him as her hip gay friend was appealing in an off-center sort of way. They could hang out. Maybe he would take her to Atlanta, introduce her to the club scene. She felt a sly grin tug at the corner of her mouth as her mind drifted to the boxes of unworn shoes that lined her closet. They were hers, bought and paid for, but off-limits in some self-imposed way. Yet in the back of her mind hadn't she'd always thought a day would come when she'd wear at least one pair? Up until now she just hadn't been able to imagine what day that would be....

"Mattie? You okay?"

She blinked, aware that she'd been drifting on her own thoughts. "Oh, I'm sorry." She looked up at Jack as if she were seeing him for the first time, the awkwardness suddenly gone. "Yes, I'd love that," she answered.

"Great." He seemed a little taken aback by her response, as if he'd expected her to say no.

"So..." Mattie took a deep breath and searched for something supportive to say. She could do this. "So have you and your partner found a house yet?"

"My partner has his condo on the market." Jack shifted uncomfortably, as though he wanted to say more but then decided against it. "As for me, I still need to look around, check out the local real estate."

Mattie managed to babble for a solid three minutes, offering advice as though Jack hadn't lived here for the first twenty years of his life. All the while her brain tried to process their new relationship, stalling while she fought for balance. Her old Jack fantasy was deteriorating somewhere in a ditch. That was okay: a new friendship was budding. She swallowed hard and forced herself to stop talking.

"Thanks." Jack nodded, an amused expression on his face. "I'll, uh, try and remember all that."

Humor the crazy babbling lady. She wanted to die.

"So what about dinner tomorrow night? Pick you up at seven?"

"Uh, sure."

"Good." He finally raised his head, looking over her shoulder. "I should go now." He frowned. "But before I do, I have something to ask you."

She frowned. "What's that?"

He grasped her shoulders and gently turned her to face the Crown Vic. "Is this your car?"

"Uh, yes." She met his eyes. "Why?"

He shook his head in mock distress. "Because I spent fifteen years of detective work developing a theory about vehicles and their drivers."

"And?"

"And you just blew it."

Mattie grinned, intrigued. "How's that?"

Jack traced his thumb over his jawline. "In my opinion, most people are basically uncomfortable in their own skin."

She felt her eyes go round with surprise. All this time Mattie had thought it was just her.

"That being the case, my theory is that people feel the

need to wrap themselves in a shell. And that shell is a vehicle. People therefore choose a vehicle based on who they feel they are inside."

Mattie looked at the Crown Vic. It was plain, ugly as sin, and its paint was crackling like the makeup of an old woman. Tears welled in her eyes.

But when she looked up at Jack, she found his gaze trailing over her bare legs. She watched in amazement as he paused at her breasts before meeting her eyes. She shivered.

"You, Mattie Harold—" he lowered his head to whisper in her ear "are not a beat-up Crown Vic." He sighed and little shivers danced across her bare shoulders. "You're a red Mustang. Convertible."

CHAPTER 3

Erica felt like an alien as she pushed the buggy through the supercenter. Thousands of products were crammed from floor to ceiling, and her head ached from trying to take it all in. After working in countries where a twist tie or a hair barrette caused fascination, the commercial explosion was overwhelming. The words jumped out at her, screaming "Buy me!" in English and Español, their brand names underscored with "New!", "Improved!" and, her favorite, "As seen on TV!" Well, guess what, oh wise advertising execs, she hadn't watched television in about a decade.

So take that demographic and process it.

And the people. God bless America, but she wanted to run screaming from the crowd. There were people from all walks of life, from senior citizens to pierced teenagers, but the majority appeared to be exhausted-looking women with a fistful of coupons and at least five kids in tow. Was it just her, or did every kid in the place have a runny nose, a bad attitude and the tendency to stare at her as she passed by? She'd like to think it was the sight of an adult with her arm in a cast, but Erica suspected there was more. They sensed she'd never been in a supercenter, smelled her fear.

And she *was* scared. Back-against-the-wall, shaking-in-her-boots, boogeyman scared.

Erica took a deep breath. She'd assessed the store's layout as she'd once assessed the danger of a guerilla-controlled village, finding the pattern, forming a safe plan of approach. If her instincts were right, she was getting close. She bypassed a little old lady who was reading the fine print on a roll of paper towels, then dodged a toddler who had stalled mid-aisle, her finger shoved up her nose. Jeez, where were all the cute kids when you needed one?

Her stomach did a little flip-flop when she spotted the feminine products at the end of an aisle. It was a bit of a contrast in needs, but she'd bet her combat boots that the pregnancy tests were stocked next to the maxi pads. She wheeled her buggy down the aisle, which was, not surprisingly, less crowded. Sure enough, boxes of douche were cozied up next to the personal lubricant, which shouldered the tampons and maxi pads. And, lo and behold, the pregnancy tests were hanging with the condoms. Well, someone clearly had a sense of humor.

She gripped the buggy handle even more tightly and fought the urge to make a U-turn. This wasn't Greene's Pharmacy back in Haddes. Here, no one knew who she was and couldn't care less that she was a single woman about to buy a pregnancy test. Even better, they didn't care that she was an almost-forty-year-old, single woman about to buy a pregnancy test.

Oh God. She was an almost-forty-year-old, single woman about to buy a pregnancy test. The air rushed from her lungs in sheer panic.

She'd driven ten miles out of the way to shop at the supercenter rather than Greene's. It wasn't as if the town of Haddes had formed a welcome committee to celebrate her return, but in Greene's she would be certain to run into a familiar face or two. The supercenter was much safer. The plan was to anonymously buy the pregnancy test under the cover of the hordes of other discount shoppers, then hightail it back home and take the test. A wave of light-headedness washed over her at the thought of actually peeing on the stick. How had she gone from taking photos out the open door of a helicopter in the mountains of Afghanistan to pushing a shopping cart in a rural Georgia supercenter? And why did that scare her more?

In truth, the test shouldn't scare her. She already knew the answer to the question. One thoroughly missed period and weeks of nausea were probably as confirming as the little plus sign on a plastic stick. But she had to know for certain. It was the responsible thing to do.

Of course, *responsible* should have come up six weeks ago.

Condoms didn't hold up well in hundred-degree heat. And she'd been in the desert. Do the science, Erica.

One thing she didn't "do" was regret. She was a pro at living in the present, and had two happy decades to prove it. Looking back served no purpose. Even if, in this case, it meant forgetting John Phillips. Erica's hand unwittingly went to her abdomen. John had been her friend and a fellow journalist for years before the two of them had given in to loneliness and desire, and become lovers. And now her friend was gone, lost in the seconds it took for the land mine to detonate. There was no bringing him back, and no amount of dwelling on the past would change either of their fates. Her arm suddenly throbbed as if reacting to the painful memory of the explosion.

"Excuse me, dear."

Erica whirled to face the elderly woman who had been so absorbed in reading the paper towel package. Her face must have flashed ten shades of red, because the woman's expression registered instant sympathy.

She pressed her soft hand against Erica's arm and patted her in a grandmotherly gesture. "I'm sorry. I didn't mean to startle you."

"Oh, not at all." Erica smiled, though uncharacteristic tears suddenly stung the backs of her eyes. The woman looked nothing like her own late grandmother, but there was something familiar about the comforting pat. It was a grandmother's touch. "I was just a million miles away." Literally.

"I hate to bother you," the woman continued as she fished the paper towels from her buggy. "But I left my reading glasses at home and can't make out the name of the manufacturing company." She waved her hand. "Such tiny print. Could you possibly read it for me?"

"Of course." Erica took the paper towels and turned the package to locate the print at the bottom. Jeez, no wonder, she thought. The print *was* tiny. She held it further away, as she struggled to focus, thinking how often she'd had to do that lately. "It says here—" she squinted "—Delcorda Paper."

"Oh dear," the woman exclaimed, a frown gathering the wrinkles on her face. "I was afraid of that."

"Oh?"

"My, yes." She took the paper towels and jammed them on a shelf next to a box of thong maxi pads.

Erica was temporarily distracted. There was such a thing as thong maxi pads? Wow. She'd been out of the States for too long.

"Delcorda Paper Company is a menace to the environment," the woman explained. "Their lack of reforesting is shameful. Sheer arrogance."

Erica wanted to laugh with relief. A kindred spirit. She'd been ready to dismiss the elderly woman, had judged her by her age and surroundings. But here, buried among the cat food and weight-loss pills was someone who realized there was a vast world outside their own city limits. And actually gave a damn.

"Oh." Delcorda... Erica pondered the name. She'd done a piece that exposed irresponsible harvesting. If memory served, that particular paper manufacturer was one of the companies named. She felt a barb of guilt that they continued to get away with it—and that she'd had no idea. She'd wrongly assumed that the coverage had resolved the situation, but that had been at least seven years ago.

"Well," the woman continued cheerfully, "back to the drawing board." She pointed her buggy in the opposite direction and smiled warmly over her shoulder, her gaze drifting toward the pregnancy tests before returning to Erica. "Best of luck, sweetheart."

A second round of tears threatened and Erica swallowed hard. The term of endearment made her feel young and, just for a split second, a sense of excitement had crept in. But she tamped it down without question. Her situation was what it was, and that was anything but exciting.

"Thank you," she responded, adding a small wave.

Erica pushed her buggy forward with new determination and, after glancing at the myriad boxes that all made similar claims of 99.999-percent accuracy, chose the most expensive pregnancy test. Today she was one of those uninformed consumers that she hated, the ones who blithely assumed cost equaled excellence. She thought of the elderly woman's determination to do the right thing and shrugged. So what? She knew when she was in over her head.

Erica looked down at the lone box sitting like a scream-ing conversation piece in the bottom of the buggy, and threw a box of maxi pads in with it. Then she leaned over and ad-justed the larger box so that it shielded the pregnancy test from view. The paper-towel woman was as close as she in-tended to come to a conversation about the pregnancy test. She glanced around for more camouflage and tossed in a box of vitamins.

She didn't waste any time leaving the Embarrassment Section of the store, and began winding her way back toward the checkout aisles as fast as her buggy's wobbly wheels would go. But a tangle of teenage girls was buzzing about a display of bathing suits, blocking her way, and Erica was forced to detour down the candy aisle. She instantly slowed, like Dor-othy in the field of poppies, smiling at the bags of candy. Only in the States, she thought. She'd missed a lot. There were new varieties she'd never before seen. What on earth were Nerds-On-A-Rope, anyway? But there were plenty of famil-iar faces, too. Jolly Ranchers, Lik-a-Stiks... Those had been staples at Mattie's sleepovers when they were teenagers. She threw a triple-pack of Lik-a-Stiks in her cart for old times' sake and picked up speed again. But just when she was about to make a clean exit, a buxom blonde came from out of no-where and their carts rammed with knuckle-rattling force.

"Erica?"

"Della?" She felt as if every pore on her body perspired at

once. "Jeez…" Her hand went to her chest, which felt like it was on fire. She wanted to look down at the contents of her buggy, make certain that the maxi pads and vitamins were still shielding the pregnancy test, but she didn't dare call attention to the buggy.

"Wow. I—I never imagined running into you here." Della looked every bit as flushed as Erica.

In fact, she looked not only flushed, but terrible. Erica forgot her own troubles as she took a closer look. Della's eyes were swollen and red-rimmed and she seemed at least ten pounds heavier than she had yesterday. She was dressed in a curious combination of a cleavage-baring aqua tank, sweatpants sheared just below the knee and a worn flannel shirt. A little eyeliner was smeared beneath the corner of her left eye and she wore no foundation.

Good God. Something was seriously wrong if Della wasn't wearing makeup.

Erica resisted the urge to grill her friend for answers. "I, uh, never imagined running into you, either." She hoped her voice sounded less alarmed than she felt. "You're a long way from home."

"Yeah. I just needed some stuff." Della's gaze darted to her buggy and Erica's followed.

Lying in the bottom of Della's buggy was a family-size bag of Caramellos, a pair of night-vision binoculars, a voice-ac- tivated cassette recorder, a camouflage blanket and a jar of ground white pepper. Erica frowned. "I see. Della, is everything okay?"

Della ran her hand over her hair and straightened with a challenging sniff. But rather than seeming imposing, as it had countless other times, the sniff seemed as though it belonged at the end of a long cry. "I'm fine. Everything's just fine." Della's gaze darted to Erica's buggy and her eyes went round.

Erica's heart stopped.

"Lik-a-Stiks!" Della exclaimed.

Her heart began beating again.

"Uh-huh. Isn't that something?" Erica pointed a trembling finger toward the shelf, which was liberally stocked with the candy. "They still make them. Right there," she directed.

Della whirled in the direction of the candy and Erica nearly collapsed with relief.

"I picked some up out of nostalgia," Erica continued, all the while maneuvering her buggy to one side, out of sight. She sent up a prayer of thanks that the pregnancy test had, apparently, gone unnoticed.

"Oh," Della crooned as she squatted down to retrieve four packs. "I think I'll get some, too." She straightened with effort, then forced the flannel shirt down over her hips. "The kids always expect a treat."

Erica didn't dare point out that each pack was a three-pack. Nor did she ask why Della was shopping like she was going on a covert military assignment while looking like a department store makeup artist on a drinking binge. She couldn't risk more conversation. She had to get herself and her pregnancy test out of the store and back home—a task that was beginning to loom like a matter of national security.

"I want us to get together again soon," Erica lied. It wasn't entirely a lie. She did want to see her old friends. Sort of. If things were different. Say, for instance, if it were 1984 again. And if Mattie hadn't turned into a drunken lunatic. Oh, and if she wasn't pregnant.

Della dragged her gaze up to meet Erica's, looking like the weight of the world was on her shoulders. "Yeah, me, too." She hesitated, then slumped in a defeated gesture. "You know where to reach me."

Erica nodded, her concern growing. "Listen, I'm staying out at Mom and Dad's place if you need me."

"You are?" Della sounded genuinely surprised. "It'll be nice to see some life back in your parents' place. It's been standing empty for too long."

"Yeah." Erica felt a familiar tightening in her chest at the mention of her parents. "You're right."

Della began to push her buggy slowly, hinting that she was anxious to make an exit. "So give me a ring at the shop or at home." Her voice drifted as she waved over her shoulder. "We'll get together...."

Erica watched her leave, reminding herself that whatever had caused Della to dress like a castaway was actually none of her business. She had her own set of problems.

The bubble-gum popping salesclerk didn't make eye contact and certainly didn't acknowledge the pregnancy test. Thank God. Erica felt like a bomb had been defused when she watched it finally drop into the plastic bag. She paid in cash, readied her keys and walked quickly through the parking lot to her waiting Jeep Cherokee. The black leather interior was like a sauna. She sighed and stale heat filled her lungs. Ugh. Georgia in June. She cranked the engine and turned on the air full blast, leaning her face toward the ineffective stream of air.

There was a certain empowerment about driving, Erica realized as she pulled out of the parking lot and onto the county highway that led back to Haddes. It was almost comical how little she'd driven her own vehicle. Though the Jeep was nearly five years old, the mileage registered less than twenty thousand. She was on assignment so much that she rarely used the vehicle or her efficiency condo in New York. Neither possession was really worth the effort, but the IRS refused to believe you were a real person unless you had an address, and her southern roots dictated that she own a set of wheels.

She rolled down the window and welcomed the rushing air. It actually felt good to be driving along a rural highway again. She breathed the scent of freshly cut hayfields and warm asphalt. The scents evoked childhood memories, as did the familiar landscape that whipped past: tall pines carpeted by honeysuckle vines, a winding shallow ditch banked with red clay. A surge of relief at being home welled and Erica almost ran off the road at the unwelcome emotion. "Oh, please," she muttered, thinking she would rather test her bumper against one of the tree trunks than wax sentimental about Haddes.

The one thing Della had been right about was that her parents' house had been standing empty for too long, she thought as she pulled into the drive thirty minutes later. She paid a local landscape service to mow the lawn twice a month, but the service obviously didn't cover removing fallen tree branches. Or doing anything other than mowing a sloppy circle around the house. A collection of chainsaw-worthy branches was piled around the perimeter of the lawn like a primitive attempt at a split-rail fence. Dandelions bloomed in the cracks of the concrete drive, and headless tulips peered out from tall grasses that had invaded the flower beds, looking like forgotten children.

The sight was more than depressing. A sense of shame rolled over her but was quickly replaced by a bout of fresh nausea. Erica laid her head against the dash and waited for it to pass. She should have sold her parents' place years ago. But every spring something came up, and she would vow to arrange it the next year. Eight years had come and gone and she still hadn't managed to accomplish the task. She moaned as a second wave of nausea washed over her. When she broke out in a sweat, she accepted the inevitable. Yanking open the car door, she puked on the invading dandelions.

The world ceased to exist in the span of time that she lost her lunch, but eventually came into focus again. She grabbed a pre-moistened wipe from her console and ran it over her face, wondering what idiot named it morning sickness when it lasted all day. Erica froze mid-swipe as movement at the neighboring house caught her eye.

As if going still would cause her to go unnoticed. She'd just burped at the top of her lungs.

On the upside, a liberal amount of property separated the two houses and a tangle of neglected shrubbery formed a natural screen. She didn't doubt that she'd been heard, but maybe she hadn't been seen. Muted cursing drifted her way, and Erica followed the sound to a dark-headed man who was dragging an obviously full garbage can from the curb back to the house. Strange. She angled her head to get a better view through the shrubs, her own misery beginning to fade. The man finished dragging the black plastic can to the house, then kicked it on its side, spilling the contents onto the drive. Erica flinched. The gesture was not only weird, it was downright hostile.

Funny, though she'd operated in the midst of war for years,

she'd found herself genuinely spooked on more than one occasion since coming home to Haddes. This was one of them. In a foreign country there was a sense of the abstract that made the danger surreal. Not so here. Of course, it hadn't helped that she'd been met by headlines of a local kidnapping, something she still couldn't imagine taking place in her sleepy hometown. Erica hadn't made it past the first few lines of the article before she'd folded the newspaper and slipped it into the trash. Maybe it was the possibility of life inside of her, the knowledge that she soon would be solely responsible for another human being, or simply post-traumatic stress, but she found she had to turn away from what she couldn't change.

Then, as if he felt her eyes on him, the man turned and looked her way. Erica ducked her head, her battered pride kicking in. Not to mention embarrassment at her voyeurism mixed with a healthy dose of fear. She grabbed her grocery sack, made a strategic jump from the Jeep and dashed to the house.

She entered the dark house, locked the door behind her, then flipped on an overhead light, illuminating her parents' living room. Its contents were in perfect order, just as they'd been when her parents passed away. They'd died within twenty-four hours of one another, her mother to lung cancer and her father from heart failure. At least that had been the official diagnosis. The truth was that her father had died from a broken heart.

Erica paid a local housekeeper, a longtime friend of her mother's, to drop by and maintain the interior of the house, so rather than smelling musty and abandoned, it welcomed her home with the scent of lemon furniture polish and floor wax. Just as it always had. It was easy to believe her mother would come through the front door with an armload of groceries, or that she could find her father in the backyard, planting tomatoes. The sense of them was so strong that she almost called their names. Her chest constricted with grief that begged to surface, but she forced it down.

She'd been out of the country, naturally, when her brother phoned, saying that her mother's condition had worsened. By the time he'd caught a flight from Maine and she'd caught a flight back to the States, both their parents were gone. There had been no goodbyes. No lingering chances to say things unsaid. Another assignment came on the heels of the double funeral and she'd jumped at the opportunity to leave her grief behind. And she'd been running ever since, staying one step ahead of the pain.

Only now she'd run home.

Erica sank against the door, surveying the house as if seeing it for the first time. On the walls were framed photos of her and her brother as children—pictures she'd seen so often that she hardly noticed them anymore. But there were other, more recent ones, snapshots she'd sent home as mementos. One of her on a camel, another of her taken in the

Amazon jungle... She had never dreamed the snapshots would be framed and hung in her parents' living room, had never realized they were so important to them.

Her work at the Associated Press had garnered awards, was routinely seen around the world. She was proud of what she'd accomplished and knew her parents had been, as well. It wouldn't have surprised her to see that her parents had framed her work, but evidence of her photojournalism was nowhere to be found. These were pictures of *her*. Tears threatened as she realized that it was her, not what she did for a living, that had mattered most to her parents. And that was the one thing she'd denied them.

She'd turned her back on Haddes with pleasure, but in the process, she'd abandoned her parents. And her friends, she realized. It was as if finding her place in the world and turning away from the people she loved had been a package deal. Regret shook her to the core. How could she have been so stupid?

Erica glanced at the stairwell that led to the second level of the house. The second story held the bedrooms. And the bathrooms. She clutched the plastic bag to her chest. Being able to take the test shouldn't be a problem, considering she needed to pee every five minutes, but working up the courage was another thing entirely. Rising to her feet, she climbed the stairs and entered the bathroom that she'd shared with her brother, pushing away the memories and panic that threatened her resolve.

She squirmed as she read the instructions. The mere sight of the toilet had her hopping on one foot these days. Finally, she uncapped the stick, dropped her shorts and held it *"for twenty seconds in the urine stream to ensure proper dampening of the tip."* No small feat when one arm was in a cast.

Erica straightened, juggling the zipper to her shorts, while keeping the stick in the upright position until she could prop it against the bathroom mirror. She watched the little window begin to dampen and turned her back. Three minutes. She had to kill at least three minutes before she allowed herself to look again.

Erica drifted out of the bathroom and into the bedroom that had been her childhood sanctuary. Her mother had turned it into a guest room when she'd left home, hanging lace curtains and replacing her old bedspread with a crisp white comforter. A Thomas Kinkade print now occupied the space that had once sported her John Travolta poster. But it was still her bedroom—from the scuffs on the walls to the tiny blob of neon-orange nail polish on the carpet that she'd tried to hide. She sat down on the bed, watching the sunlight dance through the lace curtains, and barely resisted the urge to curl into a ball on the familiar mattress and have a good cry.

A scraping noise permeated the quiet and Erica stood, crossing the bedroom to the window. She parted the curtains and looked down at the neighboring house, her vantage point giving her a perfect view of the driveway below. The man was now crouched on the concrete drive, his dark head bent over the scattered contents of the garbage can. She cocked her head, thinking there was something familiar about him, before deciding she must be mistaken. The older neighbors that once occupied the house had long since died, and they'd been childless. He was almost certainly a stranger, someone who'd simply bought the house after the Sims had passed away.

Still she watched, mesmerized by the man's strange behavior. He appeared to be dividing the garbage into three piles, his pace nearly frantic. He paused for a moment, shoving his hair from his eyes with what had to be a filthy hand. He didn't seem to notice, or to care, only resumed his bizarre task with the same intensity as before. He wore a pair of dark jeans and his arms were tanned and muscled beneath a white T-shirt. His sinewy build reminded her of John. Erica's heart gave a painful twist. She knew she should turn away from the window for a lot of different reasons, but couldn't. There was something desperate about the man that held her gaze.

A shot of yellow appeared from nowhere, and Erica watched as a golden retriever bounded to the man's side, sidestepping the neat piles of garbage. Instead of seeming irritated, he welcomed the dog with one outstretched arm. The dog leaned against the man, his tail thumping a slow cadence against his back. And rather than shooing the dog away, the man looped one arm over its side as if in a hug. They seemed to take some kind of solace in one another's presence.

Erica let the curtains fall back over the window, feeling as lost as the man looked. She turned to face the bathroom. She'd shut the door, as if by closing it she could contain all her fears. But the answer to her question waited on the other side and her watch said time was up.

She glanced over her shoulder at the window. The man and dog were still visible through the lace and a surge of jealousy shot through her.

She could use a hug herself.

CHAPTER 4

Mattie found the front door of Ralph Barnes's house ajar and gently pushed it open. She stuck her head inside and was met with a gust of hot air that jetted straight to her sinuses. She wrinkled her nose. The air conditioning had obviously been switched off after Ralph's death, and the temperature inside the old two-story house had reached at least ninety-five degrees. Worse, the interior smelled like cheese and damp sneakers.

Whoa.

She opened the door a little wider and welcomed the fresh air that rushed into the elegant old foyer. "Eve?" she called. "Eve, are you here?"

"Up here." A small voice came from the second story, echoing down the staircase. Footsteps followed, the unmistakable *tap-tap-tap* of Eve Dawson's designer pumps against the hardwood floors before her perfectly coiffured head appeared at the top of the stairs. Eve was the kind of woman that could simultaneously bake a cake, change the oil in her car and sweetly talk you into buying a house you couldn't afford without ever chipping a nail. Mattie admired her.

And hated her just a little.

"Mattie, hello." Eve waved. "Come on up. I was just thinking about you."

She noticed that Della had cut Eve's hair into a short choppy style that flattered her petite frame, and had darkened it to a rich coffee shade. Eve's cut was youthful, brave. It suited the real-estate dynamo.

Mattie tucked a lock of her own boring hair behind her ear and waved back at Eve. "Coming up."

She climbed the steep stairs, marveling that the temperature continued to rise with every step. She finally reached the top, breathless, sweat popping out on her neck.

Eve patted her arm. "How are you?"

Mattie stepped away from the stairwell, imagining herself tumbling down them in a dead faint. Then she looked at the perfect matte finish of Eve's T-zone and decided to buck up. "I'm great," she responded. "I just stopped by to ask you something."

"Sure, sure." Eve gestured toward the hallway. "But let's talk in the library. I have a window open in there."

Mattie followed Eve to the library, a ramshackle room that was charming despite the piles of debris that filled every nook and corner. Thin curtains billowed from two tall windows, filling the room with fresh air and sunshine. The bookcases stood empty, thanks, in part, to Mattie's purchase, their shelves sporting a pattern of thick dust.

Two cracked leather chairs remained, and Eve gestured toward them. "Let's have a seat." She kicked off her pumps and curled into the first chair, tucking her feet beneath her short skirt in a ladylike maneuver that only Eve could have managed.

"You've made progress," Mattie remarked as she sank into one of the chairs.

"Only you would say that. But then again, you saw it before I started." Eve shook her head. "Ralph was a true eccentric."

Mattie recalled Erica's remark about his smoking jacket. It was true. She never recalled seeing Ralph in normal clothing. And, come to think of it, she never *saw* him unless he'd stepped outside to retrieve the mail or daily newspaper. She glanced around at the stacks of yellowed, decaying newspapers. Seems he was particularly attached to the news.

Mattie suddenly remembered the reason she'd come and extended her hand toward Eve. "I found this ring in the back seat of my car." She tilted her hand and the pretty little ring winked in the sunlight. "I wonder if it could have gotten caught up in the boxes of books I bought from Ralph's estate."

Eve took Mattie's hand and examined the ring. "I don't know. It's certainly beautiful." She frowned. "It wasn't in one of the boxes?"

"No. Actually I found it in the crevice of the seat but I can't imagine any other way it could have gotten there."

Eve shrugged. "I don't have a clue, but if it was part of Ralph's things, you're welcome to it. I'm sure he would want you to have it. He was so fond of you, Mattie."

Mattie smiled, thinking back on the many curbside conversations she'd had with Ralph. He considered himself a man of the world, despite the fact that he never left the three-thousand-square-foot aging manor that he lived in. Ralph viewed Mattie as a kindred spirit and loved to engage her in talk about books. If he'd been fond of her, well, the feeling had been mutual. In a guarded sort of way. She was fine with the outdoor chit-chat but wouldn't have wanted to go inside without her cell phone fully charged. And maybe a Taser. A surge of guilt hit her. The misgivings she'd had about Ralph were probably all about the bizarre smoking jacket.

The distinct odor of stale cheese wafted her way, but when Mattie started to ask Eve about it, she found her friend openly staring.

"You look different today, Mattie. Radiant, actually."

She was instantly flattered, embarrassed and suspicious. Eve had a way of buttering you up right before she sold you something. But the truth was, Mattie, too, had noticed a difference in her appearance this morning. Her car-washing stint yesterday had left her slightly sunburned, and despite the fact that her shoulders were a little sore, she'd been pleasantly surprised by her reflection. She looked, well, different. Her eyes were brighter, her cheeks rosy. Even seeing the ring on her hand as she worked was a nice change. Different. God, she could use different.

"Thank you," she managed. She touched her cheeks. "I'm afraid I got a little too much sun yesterday. I'll probably peel."

Eve narrowed her eyes. "No, that's not it, though the sun looks good on you." She jumped to her feet as if suddenly overtaken by a thought. "I mentioned earlier that I was thinking of you." Eve drifted toward a box. "That's because I came across some more books, if you're interested."

"Of course." Mattie stood, then instantly froze.

A dog, if you could call it that, stood next to the box that Eve was approaching. He was huge, wide-shouldered and drooling, his upper lip drawn into a nasty expression. The dog's head was lowered and a shoulder muscle jumped beneath his tan fur as he fixed his stare on Eve.

"Oh my God, Eve…"

Her friend stopped and turned toward her. Mattie slowly raised her hand and pointed at the beast.

"Oh," Eve said with a smile, "I forgot to introduce you to Buddy!"

Mattie watched in frozen fascination as Eve marched over to the dog, grabbed him by the rolls of fat that flanked his crooked ears and gave him a mock kiss between the eyes. She kneaded the handfuls of loose skin for a moment before looking over her shoulder at Mattie. "Have you ever seen anything so precious in your life?"

Not since the movie *Cujo*.

"I—uh…" She breathed a sigh of relief when the dog left Eve's throat intact. "I didn't know Ralph had a dog." She wrinkled her nose, identifying the dog as the source of the cheese smell.

"Neither did I. What a nice surprise, though. Buddy is an absolute darling. I tell you, I have felt so safe with him here while I worked. Come and meet him."

Mattie took a step and the dog widened his stance, lowering his head with a throaty growl. She stopped and looked at Eve.

"There, there, Buddy. Mattie's our friend." Cujo had a band of fur like a lion's that covered his dense neck, and Eve primly plucked at it as if she were applying mousse. She made eye contact with Mattie. "He's protective. Isn't that a wonderful quality in a dog?"

"Uh…yes." She felt herself blanch, feeling like a ninny, while Eve was completely at ease styling the dog for the Mr. Rabies contest. "I suppose it is."

Eve's hand flew to her throat, a huge grin splitting her face. "Oh, Mattie, I have the most wonderful idea. You should take him. Buddy needs a home and he'd make the most wonderful companion. Oh, do say yes!"

No. No, no, no, no, no.

"Oh." She blinked. "Oh, I'm afraid I couldn't."

Eve's face dropped like that of a rejected puppy, then she went in for the kill. She hiked up the skin that hung slack around the dog's neck, wadding it around his ears until his eyes completely disappeared. "Just look at this face...."

Exactly.

Eve pursed her lips, then stared at Mattie as if awaiting an explanation.

"I—I just stay so busy." That was a nice, fat lie. "I'm constantly on the run with the bookstore." Another lie, but immensely more polite than saying how she really felt about the drooling. And snarling. Not to mention the cheese. "I just couldn't give him the attention that I'm sure he, um, deserves."

"I see." Eve abruptly released the dog and stood, brushing a few stray hairs from her hands and skirt. She sighed, eyeing Buddy as if he were a real estate deal that had just fallen through. "Let me know if you change your mind."

Buddy gave Mattie the evil eye, yawned as if she weren't worth eating, then plopped down on the floor, suddenly looking as discarded as one of the boxes of old newspapers.

Mattie felt a tug of sympathy that was, thankfully, interrupted by a strange vibration at her hip, followed by the *Pink Panther* melody. Her cell phone. It never rang, which was why she hadn't bothered to figure out how to turn it off vibrate;

not to mention disconnect the *Pink Panther*. She opened her purse and began digging, eventually retrieving the unit.

She punched the answer button. "Hello?"

"Mattie, it's Shay." Her friend sounded more breathless than usual. "We have a problem."

For a moment she just stared at the phone in confusion. How did Shay even have her cell number? And *we* have a problem? Did she mean the singular "we" as in *we* could certainly use a drink right now?

She found her voice. "What? I don't understand. What do you mean?"

The cell phone crackled, and Mattie could hear an angry female voice in the background.

"It's Della." Shay almost shouted, then seemed to catch herself, lowering her voice. "She's…" Ranting and raving escalated in the background. "Mattie, I need your help. Can you come over to Della's house?"

"Sure. Just give me a few minutes to—"

"Mattie," Shay interrupted, "come now."

Shay watched from a safe distance as Della paced the small bedroom. She'd tried following her at first, but had given up about ten minutes ago, flattening herself into a corner behind an ironing board instead.

"Unbelievable!" Della shouted.

In fact, Della had been shouting the word *unbelievable* at

regular intervals for about forty-five minutes, followed by intense bursts of laundry folding, suitcase packing and toiletry throwing.

"Twenty years." Della looked up, making rather manic eye contact with Shay. Her eyes were red-rimmed and she bit her lower lip when it began to tremble.

Shay could see a dark bruise beneath her lip where she'd undoubtedly bit it before, and ached to pull her friend into a hug. Just as she made a move to do so, Della shouted "Un-damn-believable!" and turned back to the laundry-strewn bed to begin digging though a stack of men's underwear.

"Della," she ventured. "Please, let's sit down and—"

A frayed pair of briefs flew through the air, hit the wall near her head and slid to the floor. Shay retreated back into the corner.

The room resembled the inside of an upturned laundry hamper, but an odd sense of order was beginning to emerge from the chaos as Della continued to rage. Hanging on the door facing were four of Donald's dress shirts, now perfectly ironed. A large brown suitcase centered the unmade bed and, though it was surrounded by mounds of unfolded clothes and an empty laundry basket, inside was a neat row of Donald's black socks, flanked by a second row of folded undershirts.

"Della, I just don't think you're being rational. You can't be certain that Donald is having an affair, and until you are, you can't—"

"Can't?" Della paused mid-fold and looked up at the ceiling as if she needed divine intervention. "That's all I ever hear, you know?" She dropped her arms to her sides. "'You can't, Della,' she mocked. 'You *can't* trade the minivan for the two-seater, Della. You've got three kids.' 'You *can't* wear that knit skirt, Della. You've put on too much weight.' 'You *can't* go on this business trip with me, Della. Who would run the shop while you're gone? Who would take care of the kids?' And all the while he's screwing his secretary. *Unbelievable!*"

"Della?" Mattie appeared in the doorway, her car keys still in her hand.

Shay felt a rush of relief. Backup had arrived. She took a deep breath, unaware that she'd been holding it. Lord, she'd never been so relieved to see Mattie in her life. She'd called Erica first but had gotten her voice mail. Mattie, dependable as ever, had answered her cell. Thank goodness.

"What's going on?" A dark frown marred Mattie's face, and a telltale lock of blond hair curled at her ear.

Shay felt a stab of nostalgia. Mattie had a childhood habit of twisting her hair as she worried.

And, from her vantage point behind the ironing board, they had every right to be worried.

"What's wrong?" Mattie met Shay's eyes in silent communication.

"It's Donald," Shay offered. "Della thinks he's—"

"No." Della glanced frantically between the two friends.

"Della *knows* that he's screwing his secretary." She began pacing again, seemingly fueled by Mattie's question. "And *Nita* of all people. I sent her a fruit basket on her birthday. I do her *hair* for God's sake."

"No way." Mattie shook her head as she dropped her keys into her purse and inched toward Shay's corner. "Not Nita and Donald. No way."

Shay held out her hand and Mattie grasped it as she neared. She tugged Mattie safely into the corner. They cast one another worried glances as Della dropped to her knees and began to calmly lay a neat row of Donald's briefs on the edge of the bed.

"He can have her for all I care," Della muttered, digging beneath the bed skirt. "But he won't enjoy her."

"Della?" Shay whispered, stepping forward. "What do you mean?"

Della pulled a small metal canister from beneath the bed, opened the fold to a pair of Donald's briefs, and began filling them with the contents of the canister. She completed the task a second time before holding up the can for inspection. A mad-scientist grin split her tear-streaked face.

"White pepper," Mattie read.

"White pepper!" Shay shook her head. "Oh, Della. You're not planning… No!" She scooted from behind the ironing board. "You're not going to pack those! Think this through. You love Donald. Draw that love around you and—"

"Mattie!" Della screeched. She pointed at Shay. "Make her stop. I can't hear that New Age mumbo jumbo right now. Somebody's likely to get hurt."

Too late. Shay felt the barb and it did hurt, though she'd been pricked by that same thorn enough times to have grown immune by now. She'd spent a lifetime trying to figure out the universe, and had ended up with more questions than answers. Still, she made no apologies for the road she'd chosen. Most days it brought more ridicule than respect, but sometimes she tapped into something that was bigger than all of them. And just that minuscule glimpse of the big picture made the injustices seem bearable.

Shay straightened her shoulders. "I don't pretend to know everything, Della. But if there's one thing I know for certain, it's that you get back what you put out into the world. All of us do. If you seek revenge, it will find you again. And when it does, it will be uglier than before."

"She's right, Della," Mattie said from behind the ironing board.

"No, she's *not* right." Della grabbed another pair of briefs, twisting them as though she were strangling Donald. Or maybe Donald's crotch. "I didn't ask for this. Donald brought it on himself. You don't understand. It's been twenty years. Twenty wasted years. I deserve a little revenge." A sob tore from her throat and she dropped the underwear, her shoulders sagging in defeat.

Shay's hand went to her own throat as the current of

Della's pain vibrated through her. She closed her eyes, welcoming the emotion for what it was.

It was both affirming and unsettling, this connection she shared with Della, Mattie and Erica. Even after nearly two decades of separation, she felt Della's pain, as raw and real as her own.

"But I do understand," she whispered.

"No, you don't." Della laughed. "No one does. I was the one who got stuck here, remember?" She gestured toward Mattie. "Mattie is free to go wherever, whenever she pleases. Erica left to go gallivanting around the globe. And you—"

"Ran away," Shay supplied. She forced the memories back into the same dark corner of her brain they'd been in for the past eighteen years, then met Della's gaze with determination. "I had a good reason, remember?"

Della unexpectedly burst into tears, cradling her face in her hands. "What happened to you was my fault, you know." She hiccuped on a sob. "You married Mac because you wanted what I had. What—what Donald and I had." She hiccuped again. "What I thought we had."

Shay felt herself being tugged backward, pulled into a world that she'd barely escaped. She shook her head, trying to find the words to tell Della to stop. If there was one thing she'd learned, it was to not look over your shoulder when you were running. That was when the monster attacked, when the root leaped from the ground and tripped you.

Della wiped her eyes and turned to stare out the bedroom window. "I made out like my marriage was perfect. But it wasn't. Not even then." She looked at Shay. "And that wasn't fair to you. I made you want some stupid fairy tale—and look what it cost you."

Shay felt Della's gaze fall on the small white scar beneath her left eye that Mac had left, a constant reminder of why she'd left Haddes in the first place. But it wasn't the scar that ached. A deep pain tightened in her womb, and she felt the emptiness. She gripped the ironing board until the tips of her fingers stung.

"Why did you come here this morning?" Della whispered.

"I just did." Shay's hand went to the crystal around her neck, praying Della wouldn't scoff. "I just felt that you needed me."

Instead of ridiculing her, Della wiped her eyes with the back of her hand and smiled. "Just like the old days."

Shay felt a rush of relief. It had always been this way between them, among all of them. Some thread connected the four women—permanently, it seemed. For better or worse. It was as if they were all connected and she was the conductor, the psychic lightning rod. This circle of friends was special. And they accepted that she was different, kind of shrugged away the psychic intuition that had isolated her from others.

"Just like the old days," Shay agreed. And in that moment, the years began to melt and the world felt like home again.

"Sometimes I have the worst thoughts." Della's voice rang out, unexpectedly dark. "I picture myself dead. Getting run over by an eighteen-wheeler or something."

Shay stared, open-mouthed, then looked over her shoulder at Mattie, finding her own horror mirrored in her friend's face. Della was talking about suicide? She prayed for the right words as the silence stretched between them.

When she didn't see any help on the horizon, Shay reluctantly plunged in. "You—you're a mother, Della." She kneeled down next to Della and placed her hand on her shoulder. "Try to imagine how you'd feel if one of your children said something like that."

Della looked at her like she'd lost her mind.

She took a deep breath and tried again. "I—I mean, how do you think your Creator feels when you talk about killing yourself?"

"I think he'd be pretty pissed off." Erica's voice rang from the doorway.

Shay released a pent-up breath and sent up another prayer of thanks.

Erica crossed her arms over her chest and leaned against the door frame. "After all, you've been pretty high maintenance all these years."

Della glanced at Erica as though she wasn't at all surprised to see her. Erica walked into the room, let her purse drop to the floor and leveled a stare at Mattie.

"Why are you hiding behind the ironing board?" She looked down at Della. "And why are you talking like a fool?"

"That's not what I meant. Jeez. I didn't mean it literally. I don't want to kill myself. I don't want to be *dead*." She narrowed her eyes. "What are you doing here, anyway?"

A look passed between Erica and Shay that spoke volumes. "Obviously, I'm coming in on the middle of a really weird conversation. Want to catch me up?"

Della sighed. "I don't want to kill myself, for Pete's sake. I'd just like to be good and gone for a little while. Then what would Donald do?" It was her favorite secret fantasy and it felt kind of good to say it out loud. "Honestly, he doesn't know his ass from a hole in the ground when it comes to his own family."

She never bad-mouthed Donald, not even when the other women in the salon were on a man-bashing tangent. In her mind he'd been close to perfect. But now that she'd learned he was boinking his secretary—God, how cliché—his faults seemed to scream out for public exposure.

"I'd like to see him do a load of laundry. Just one." Something tight in her chest loosened, so Della decided to try another zinger. "Or pack a lunchbox." An image of Donald searching for a Twinkie in the predawn hours made her smile and she allowed the fantasy to grow. "He doesn't even know the kids' teachers' names." She sat up a little straighter. "Hell, he couldn't find the orthodontist's office if he had a guide dog."

For fun, she pictured Donald *as* the dog. Then, as an en-
core, she envisioned him chasing his tail. The sadness lifted
marginally. She wiped her eyes with a pair of his yet-to-be-
peppered briefs. When that felt wickedly good, she blew her
nose on them.

Della looked up at her friends. They looked confused but
attentive. Then she remembered that none of them had ever
conducted a predawn Twinkie search, either, but that was beside the point. She decided to take advantage of the captive
audience.

"Oh, and I'd like to see him handle Teacher Appreciation
Day." She narrowed her eyes. "Which, by the way, some idiot decided should be the same week as Mother's Day." She
blew a stray stand of hair from her eyes. "Ha! *Appreciation*
isn't in his vocabulary." She narrowed her eyes. "Do you
know that last year on Teacher Appreciation Day I managed
to get three kids, three lunchboxes, three backpacks and
three *glass* bud vases with roses filled with *real* water to school
without getting a tardy slip or cutting an artery?" She paused
for breath. "Well, we did break one bud vase because the dog
was in the car. He had to go to the vet because he had ear
mites. He wagged his tail when he saw Andy's best friend
Josh, who does safety patrol, and he knocked the bud vase
out of Elizabeth's hand." She waved a hand. "Anyway, it
didn't matter because I had stuck an extra bud vase in the
glove compartment just in case and…"

Della glanced up to find her friends looking more perplexed than ever. They didn't get it. But they seemed ready to agree with her, which was something.

Erica risked a smile. "*Real* water, huh?"

Mattie began inching her way from behind the ironing board. She gestured with her hand, as if signaling for permission to speak. "I agree. Kind of. At least, well, I think Donald doesn't appreciate you like he should."

"Damn straight." Della looked at Mattie, calm enough now to really see her for the first time. "Why *were* you behind the ironing board?"

"Well, you've got to admit…" Mattie grinned, looking relieved. "You were a little scary there for a while."

"I was just, uh, venting," Della replied.

"Della, you booby-trapped your husband's underwear with white pepper," Shay added.

"She what?" Erica's face registered disbelief before she burst out laughing. "Good one."

But it wasn't. Not really. Despite the humor in Erica's eyes, Della suddenly felt like a child pulling some stupid summer-camp prank. In truth, she was an aging, sagging naive woman who, up until two days ago, believed in soul mates and forever. And her best response to her husband's life-shattering betrayal had been to pepper his Fruit-of-the-Looms. God, she was pathetic.

Her marriage wasn't perfect, but whose was? Sure, she and

Donald sometimes spent an entire evening without talking to each other. But she was usually helping the kids with homework and he was busy paying bills or mowing the lawn. She didn't think it was unusual. They didn't make love as often as they used to, but they always fell asleep holding hands. She closed her eyes, imagining Donald's warm calloused hand in hers, curled beneath her familiar pillowcase—and the pain that followed caused her head to swim.

Now the rest of her life loomed like an empty tunnel with nothing waiting on the other side but more dirty laundry. And dishes. And book reports and hamster cages, dirty soccer uniforms and car pool.

The tedious tasks were the glue that held it all together, and the knowledge of that usually made it all worthwhile. But now there was no "together." It had fallen apart while she'd been busy scrubbing the toilet. And now, the next time she tackled those tasks, it would be alone. She couldn't quite wrap her brain around that. And every time she tried, she couldn't breathe.

Della tugged the hem of her plus-size sweatshirt over her knees as she sat on her bedroom floor. It was late spring, yet she hadn't been able to get warm since she'd found the plane tickets tucked in Donald's nightstand drawer two days ago. The *two* tickets.

She'd gone to Donald's office that day, looking for reassurance. But what she'd gotten was a good view of Donald and Nita embracing through the cracked door of his office. She'd gone numb all over.

Now her emotions were a swirling mix of betrayal, blinding anger and something that felt curiously like freedom. She envisioned herself standing in the vortex of it all, trying to capture the tempting bits of freedom as they flew by, but they were so foreign and small that she couldn't seem to grasp them. Maybe because, from most angles, they looked a lot like abandonment.

Della had a brilliant thought and practically dove beneath the bed. She extended her arm as far as it would reach, risking dust bunnies and god-knows-what-else until she grasped the gallon-size Zip-loc bag. She dragged it out, blew away the dust and held it up like a prize fighter holding up a championship belt.

"Lik-a-Stiks!" she declared.

Mattie, Shay and Erica filed over like eager thirteen-year-olds and sat cross-legged on the floor, joining Della to form a circle. Their knees bumped one another's as Della handed out packets of candy.

They each tore into the treats in silence, eventually dipping the candy sticks into the tart powder. They dipped and licked, dipped and licked. One by one they made eye contact, punctuated by more dipping and licking and a few moans of pleasure. Despite the sadness weighing heavily on her soul, Della felt a strange contentment that she hadn't felt in years.

"I'm glad y'all are here," she said. And meant it.

The moment was so familiar and perfect that she felt an overwhelming urge to go back in time. And to stay there. The thought brought instant guilt. She envisioned the faces of her children, the only good thing about adulthood that she could claim at the moment, and reminded herself that she couldn't run. Not back in time. And not anywhere else.

Andy was twelve, and was currently going through a bizarre phase of drinking coffee and dressing like a cross between Andy Warhol and Ozzy Osbourne. A kind of Goth poet. She grinned. He insisted on being called Andrew these days and was starting to sprout hairs in interesting places. At least the places that she could see.

Elizabeth was eight going on forty-five. She had more brains than the rest of them put together and wasn't afraid to use them. She memorized facts, her favorites coming from the underside of Snapple lids. Just this morning she'd asked if Della knew the gestational period for a zebra. The answer was twelve months, not that Della knew—she'd been trying to figure out how an eight-year-old knew the meaning of *gestational*.

And Trevor. Lord help her, but if Trevor the Terror had been born first, he'd be an only child. At four, he zipped around from one thing to the next, leaving a trail of happy destruction in his wake. And all the while he never said a word. At least not until bedtime, and then the entire day would come spilling out of him, told in excruciating detail.

It was as if no one else was worthy of experiencing his day but his mother. Della loved him so much that her heart hurt to try to contain it.

And yet to be thirteen, when nothing mattered more than the telephone and the boy next door... Except that that boy had been Donald.

Beside her, Erica shifted. "What will you do?" she asked.

Della licked a blob of Lik-a-Stik powder from the corner of her mouth, then looked at her watch. It was 2:15. She met Erica's gaze and shrugged. "Car pool," she answered.

CHAPTER 5

Jack stared at the crumpled notebook paper for about the millionth time. It had been torn to pieces, and was soggy and almost illegible when he fished it from the ditch. But after the paper dried, he'd smoothed the wrinkles and taped the jagged pieces back together.

And had gotten the shock of his life.

The ink had run in numerous places, but Mattie's name had been spared. Otherwise, he would not have believed it.

It was also dated twenty years ago—to the day—from the day he'd found it. But the amazing part wasn't the date or the author. It was the content. It was darn near erotica, and he'd cursed the ink smudges more than once when an arousing part had been obliterated. He'd salivated over the parts that were legible. In fact, the details had been permanently seared into his brain.

As had a brand-new image of Mattie Harold.

He'd always thought she was a pretty girl, kind of the poster child for the girl next door, with her slender frame, a perky haircut and a few requisite freckles scattered across her nose. And she'd grown into a classic beauty that exuded a kind of woman-you'd-want-to-marry innocence.

Except that she wasn't. Innocent, that is. At least not on paper.

He'd bet his last dollar that she wasn't picking up one-night stands in seedy biker bars on the weekends. But he was pretty sure it had crossed her mind. Or at least maybe it had twenty years ago. And the things she'd been willing to try with the lucky man she'd been writing about would make a sailor blush. He'd searched the papers for a name, a clue that would reveal the identity of the man, but came up empty-handed.

And like the good detective that he was, the absence of a name had driven him nuts. And like any red-blooded American man, he'd done nothing since but think about it.

Mattie had looked the part of the seductress yesterday when he'd caught her washing her car. Her cheeks had been flushed with sun and, despite her petite size, her legs seemed to go on forever. Her small breasts had been pressing against the fabric of her tank top and the image had wreaked havoc on his body and put his mind straight in the gutter.

He needed to be concentrating on other things. He and Cal needed to secure office space and begin the process of transferring their office equipment and files. They'd intentionally kept their client list light for the sake of the move, but there were still case details to wrap up. When all was said and done, he didn't have time to pursue a relationship right now. And Mattie wasn't the kind of woman he was willing to have a one-time encounter with. Though, the thought kept tapping him on the shoulder every time he tried to focus on anything else.

She'd agreed to have dinner with him, which was a small miracle given his overcooked appearance. Della had given him something called exfoliant, which she'd explained was a kelp-based concoction laced with ground walnut shells. It was about as pleasant as scrubbing his face with muddy gravel. But it was slightly less painful than sandpaper, which he had threatened to use. Anything to look less like a rotting carrot.

But the real challenge was going to be keeping his hands off Mattie Harold. He'd thought of canceling the date, saving himself the potential entanglement, but he frankly just didn't want to. He was fascinated by her. Knowing what he knew now, he couldn't wait to study her during casual conversation. His PI practice had made him an expert at judging people, at seeing through the facades people loved to erect. But he hadn't seen that one until it had hit him square between the eyes.

And Mattie had seemed quite neutral about the prospect of going out with him. She hadn't exactly balked at the idea, but she hadn't seemed anxious to go, either.

He chewed on that thought for a minute. He'd blatantly

flirted with her a time or two and had gotten no reaction. Maybe she thought of him as strictly friend material, Della's big brother. That would be good, he told himself. It would make things a lot less tempting.

Yes, he told himself. He was going to keep his date with Mattie, catch up on old times, maybe even figure out what made her tick. But he was going to keep his hands to himself.

For now, anyway.

"I thought maybe I'd gone and slung a rock into it." Elmo Garrett pointed toward his riding lawn mower, then back to the broken window on the side of Mattie's duplex. "But when I took a good look, I saw that the window wasn't locked down. That's when I told Ruth to ring you up, down at the bookstore."

Mattie crossed her arms over her chest, rubbing at the chill-bumps that seemed to have taken up permanent residence on her skin. "I really appreciate it, Mr. Garrett. I never dreamed…"

"Oh, I knew straight away that someone had broken in. I was sure you always locked down your windows. You always lock down your windows, don't you?" He took off his straw hat and waved at a bee. "It's just not safe if you don't lock down your windows."

Mattie ground her teeth, summoning patience for her elderly neighbor. "Oh, yes, sir. I do." That wasn't entirely true. She loved to sleep with her windows up on warm evenings, letting the gentle breeze and moonlight fill the room. Sometimes, on those nights, she even slept in the buff. It had always seemed entirely safe.

Until today.

She shivered. The broken window belonged to her bedroom.

"Well, that's good. Some folks don't. But a woman like you, living alone..." He made a soft clucking sound. "Folks know when there ain't a man around. That's when trouble starts."

Her mind went instantly to Della and Shay. Sometimes the trouble started precisely when a man was around. But she wasn't about to argue that point with Elmo Garrett.

"Ain't no place safe," he muttered.

She couldn't agree more at the moment.

"Mattie!"

Mattie looked up to see Gerald Randolph waving at her from the porch of her duplex. Gerald was a longtime Haddes police officer and friend of her mother's. He had also been a very welcome sight when he'd pulled up to the curb earlier, lights flashing. But now, with all the neighbors plastered to their windows and curious drivers slowing as they passed, she'd give her eyeteeth not to have to join him.

She waved to Gerald, thanked Elmo again, then began

trudging her way back to the front of the duplex. Her feet felt like lead. She blinked back tears, dreading the moment that Gerald would complete his report and leave. She'd never been as frightened as in the moment she'd opened her front door and found that the place had been ransacked. And now the thought of being alone in her own home made her blood run cold.

Truth be known, she'd considered Elmo's suspicions nothing more than the work of his overprotective nature and had resented having to close the bookstore to investigate. Never had she imagined that she'd actually been burglarized. Mattie rubbed the ache that had settled between her eyes and reminded herself that the Botox industry wasn't worth billions for nothing.

The sight had been like something out of a television drama. Drawers had been yanked from her dresser and thrown upside down, their contents scattered. Her mattress had been pushed from the bed frame, her antique nightstand kicked over. Even her bathroom linen closet had been emptied, towels scattered about. She'd only made it as far as the bathroom before she'd bolted. Lord only knows what the rest of the place looked like.

Mattie climbed the front stairs like she was headed for the guillotine. When she stood next to Officer Randolph, he clasped her shoulder and looked into her eyes with fatherly concern. "Are you okay?" he asked.

She blinked back tears. Sympathy was always her undoing. She was as stoic as they came until someone offered her a shoulder. She nodded, not trusting herself to speak.

Gerald lifted his clipboard and studied it. "It's a mess in there," he commented. "You already know that. But what bothers me…"

Mattie felt a new jolt of alarm and straightened. "What is it?"

"Well, maybe nothing," he commented, still studying his notes. "Obviously I don't know if anything was taken, but some key items, items that logically should have been taken, were ignored."

Mattie frowned, trying to recall what detail she could from her few minutes in the house. "My laptop?" she asked, the image of it springing to mind. "I left it sitting on my dining table, didn't I?"

"In plain view." Gerald nodded. "As were a lot of other things. I noticed a camera, a DVD player. Other small items." He tapped his clipboard. "I'm puzzled that they weren't taken. Maybe the perp was just frightened away. Elmo had begun mowing just beneath your bedroom window."

"But?"

"Let's step inside." He opened the front door and gestured for her to follow.

Mattie held her breath as she stepped over the threshold, concentrating on Officer Randolph's capable form beside her. He stopped just inside the doorway, making a calculated sweep of the place with his practiced cop's eyes. Mattie imitated him, trying to see things as he did.

"It seems to me like someone was looking *for* something rather than looking to *take* something," he commented.

The thought made her want to bolt. Still, there was no logic in the theory. What could someone possibly be looking for? Yet Mattie could see her laptop from where she stood, just as she remembered. She took a few steps into the interior of the house and glanced around. Her microwave still sat on the kitchen counter, and her digital camera was fairly noticeable on top of the refrigerator.

What if the person who'd broken in had simply been looking for *her*? Mattie thought of Christina Wilson and shivered. The world—including Haddes—suddenly seemed like an impossibly scary place.

"Most of the damage seems to be in the bedroom and bathroom," Gerald said behind her.

She started at the sound of his voice and began flipping light switches, as if more light would chase the fear away. It certainly couldn't hurt, she decided. She marched into the kitchen and turned on the oven light. As an afterthought, she grabbed her emergency flashlight from under the sink and switched it on, too.

Gerald gave her a curious look and headed down the hall toward her bedroom. Mattie, brandishing the flashlight like a weapon, followed him, flipping light switches as she passed them. This type of fear was new to her. She'd known insecurity as a child when her parents divorced, and had experienced the occasional bump-in-the-night fear, as had most adults. But this was different. This was a violation of her home. One that she wouldn't be able to put out of her mind when the sun set tonight. Or maybe ever.

Her stomach tightened when she and Gerald rounded the corner to her bedroom. Unlike when she'd first seen it, this time the details jumped out at her. A romance novel from her nightstand lay facedown on the carpet, surrounded by a littering of bottom-of-the-drawer junk—a pack of gum, pennies, two mismatched barrettes. She gripped the flashlight even tighter when a bout of nausea hit.

"You can clean up anytime you're ready. I've already taken what photos I felt might be useful."

Mattie whirled to face him, surprised. "You took pictures? Like on *CSI?*"

"The photos are just a precaution." He shrugged. "I don't mean to alarm you, but this feels a little personal to me. Are you having any trouble with anyone? Maybe someone you're dating?"

"No. I'm not seeing anyone…." She shook her head, almost laughing when she remembered her date with Jack. Then she tried to fathom who in her life could be considered an enemy. The idea was absurd. "No, not at all."

Officer Randolph studied her for a moment, then smiled. "That's a shame, Mattie. You're a beautiful girl. You should be dating. In fact, you're the spitting image of your mother at the same age."

Mattie didn't know whether to be flattered or to scream. She had bigger problems than her social calendar at the moment. But would a little breaking-and-entering keep people from commenting on the fact that she was still single? Apparently not—

"Mattie?" Officer Randolph's voice penetrated the irritation. "Are you okay?"

She nodded, then froze as Gerald began to drift toward her closet. *Oh God. Not the closet...* She'd forgotten about the closet.

Gerald casually opened the closet door, then stepped aside. "They hit the closet, as well." He shook his head. "But again, the most obvious item—your computer—wasn't taken."

Mattie didn't budge, not wanting to see what had become of her precious walk-in closet. It was her own private corner of the world. A sob caught in her throat. It was supposed to be off-limits to all eyes but her own.

She'd lovingly painted the walls two different colors, free in the knowledge that no one would see it but her. Mattie had chosen gold for the far wall and had painted the other three a deep violet. She'd centered her small computer desk against the golden wall and had hung a gothic-looking wrought-iron candleholder beside it. A beaded Indian-print scarf with deep sensual hues of red and gold covered her office chair. The candle she'd chosen for the votive smelled of ripe pears and earthy, exotic spices. She loved the small space, loved losing herself in the cocoon of comfort as she wrote her stories. In that tiny room she was safe to be herself. No one would tell her the colors didn't match, or comment that she'd gone too far.

But someone *had* seen it. And it was here that she *had* gone too far. At least with her stories. More than once. The closet was her private sanctuary, but her stories were her real secret. While to the rest of the world she was a budding children's book writer, in her closet she gave words to the fantasies that filled her mind.

Her heart pounded in her chest. Had she hidden the latest CD? She only saved her writing on CD, fearing that her hard drive might one day need to be serviced. No way was Peter Causey down at Haddes Business Machines going to have the opportunity to read her stories. She'd found that the only way she could free her mind to write was to indulge her admittedly crazy compulsion to hide her work. So each day she saved her stories to CD, slipped them out of her computer and hid them in the front pocket of her suitcase.

But had she remembered to hide the CD last night?

She closed her eyes and envisioned the way she'd left her

closet this morning. It had been pristine in its usual harem-brothel kind of way, a collision between her well-ordered life and her sensual alter ego. All seventy-plus of her carefully labeled shoe boxes had lined the side walls. Mattie always chose two pair of shoes when she was writing, one to wear and one to be displayed for inspiration. Last night she'd worn supple black leather boots that hugged her calves and clung just above the knee. For inspiration she'd liberated a pair of snakeskin pumps from their box. She cringed. She'd even placed one pump on top of her computer monitor as she'd written. Mattie never imagined that anyone would see what she'd done.

But someone had.

She took a hesitant step forward and felt the bottom drop out of her stomach as she got a good look at the closet. Shoes were everywhere. Mattie shuffled halfway into the closet and found herself knee-deep in shoe boxes and shoes. Her desk chair was overturned and Mattie felt her face heat with anger as she spotted her Indian-print fabric caught in the greasy wheels of the chair. She tried to inch in a little farther to rescue the fabric but was jabbed by a red stiletto. She cursed beneath her breath, then froze in embarrassment, realizing how bizarre it all must look to Gerald Randolph.

A computer in a closet was weird enough, but the sheer number of shoes was downright bizarre, she knew. Yet for those that knew her, and Gerald had known her since she was a child, her taste in shoes was probably the most shocking. They were, well, rather sensual choices. Which was exactly why she mail-ordered them. She'd die before she ever wore them outside of her closet, but inside her closet they were inspiring.

When Gerald didn't comment, she found herself more embarrassed than ever. Out of all the damage done, this was the most personal. Mattie resisted the urge to drop to her knees, tunnel her way to the suitcase and search for her CDs.

"I'm afraid you have your work cut out for you," Gerald commented.

Very diplomatic. Mattie turned and shuffled her way back out of the chaos.

"Let's take a quick look at the rest of the place. Then I'll head to the station and file the report."

Mattie followed Officer Randolph as he made his way toward the bathroom. When he came to a stop at the doorway, she saw the carnage. Her arsenal of grooming tools was now scattered about the small tile floor. A can of hairspray had rolled against the baseboard and a glass jar of face cream had cracked against the tile and was now oozing out in a giant overpriced blob. Tampons and vitamins littered the room. She heard the crunch of a tampon beneath her shoe as she took a step backward, and her face flamed in embarrassment.

Whoever had broken in had seen these most personal of items, as well. Mattie covered her mouth to hold in a sob, then turned and ran. She made her way to the front porch, collapsing into a wicker chair just before the tears started. A few seconds later she felt Gerald's familiar touch against her shoulder. A car door slammed nearby as she struggled to gain control of her emotions. Mattie looked up to see Eve Dawson hurrying in her direction. She didn't know whether to be grateful or cry harder.

"You have every right to be upset, Mattie," Gerald said. "But everything will work out. You'll see."

Eve came to a breathless stop in front of her. "What's wrong?" she asked.

Mattie blinked up at her, aware that her eyes were probably swollen into little slits. Eve glanced at Gerald, then squatted down to look her in the eye. "I was driving by and saw the squad car. Someone tell me what's going on." It was less a request than a demand.

When tears threatened again Mattie shook her head. Gerald filled in the blanks.

"Her duplex was broken into," he said. "Mattie's not hurt, Eve, just a little shaken up."

"Oh, Mattie!" Eve's voice was dripping with sympathy and Mattie felt her resolve begin to fray again. "Do you need a place to stay? You know you're welcome to stay with me. Or at Ralph's place if you need something long-term."

The image of neglect and the odor of rotting cheese leaped to mind and she shivered. "No, no thanks."

"I'm afraid she's going to need someone to stay with her," Gerald commented to Eve as though Mattie wasn't sitting right beside him. "Do you think her mother or father might be available…"

The rest of Gerald's sentence was lost in a haze of anger. Mattie was a grown woman, perfectly capable of taking care of herself. Yes, she was scared half to death, but it wasn't every day that someone broke into your home and played pick-up-sticks with your tampons. But, no, her mother wasn't going to stay with her. Neither was her father. The image of her and her father struggling to make conversation on a daily basis was more frightening than the break-in.

Normally she'd turn to Della, but Della had her own crisis to deal with right now. She thought of Shay and Erica and cringed. The last thing she wanted was to appear weak in front of her friends after so much time apart. She thought of Erica's war coverage and Shay's infinite spiritual tranquillity. Yeah, the last thing she wanted to do was look like a spineless wimp in front of her friends.

Mattie wiped her eyes, glaring at Gerald and Eve until they noticed and, wisely, stopped talking. "I'm going to be fine," she announced. She straightened with resolve and looked Eve in the eye. "But I think I do want that dog after all."

"I don't know why she's not answering." Shay looked at the cell phone as if something must be wrong with the unit.

A few seconds later, when she lifted it to try Mattie's number, Erica forced her hand down. "We can handle this," she whispered. "Besides, you're going to call attention to us."

Shay had thought to gather the friends for lunch to discuss how to best help Della. Erica had agreed, though rather reluctantly. When Mattie hadn't answered her cell phone and couldn't be reached at the bookstore, the plan had taken a serious blow. And now, from all indications, it was too late to help Della form a rational plan.

"I'm surprised she hasn't noticed us yet." Shay allowed her hair to fall across her eyes, then peeked around the cascade of auburn curls.

Shay and Erica were at a patio table at Pasco's Pizzeria. Della was seated just a few yards away, unaware that they were watching. Donald sat opposite Della, and immediately to his left was Nita, the adulterous secretary. The table was small. *Very* small.

"Oh God, she's picking up a knife," Erica whispered, scooting her chair back to stand.

"Wait." Shay urged her to sit. "She wouldn't…" She shook her head. "Oh, good, that's just a steak knife."

"Uh, yeah. Which makes it sharp and pointy and gives it the ability to cut through flesh. Are you following me?"

"Della wouldn't resort to violence."

"You're kidding me, right? This is the woman who was going to marinate her husband's testicles in white pepper. Ring a bell?"

Shay snatched up the cell phone and dialed Mattie again. This time she left a whispered message.

Erica and Shay had the misfortune, or fortune as it turned out, of being seated next to the kitchen door. Their clever waiter had tilted the table's umbrella at an angle, apologizing for the midday sun. In truth, he'd thought to shield them from the noisy comings and goings of the wait staff. But in the process, he'd provided them a perfect view of a buxom blonde with ramrod-straight posture and an unhappy expression. Della wore a dressy black pantsuit, and dark, Jackie O. style sunglasses that masked her intentions. She looked as if she was on her way to a funeral, which didn't seem like the best of signs. Her body language was stiff, unreadable, and her two lunch guests looked nervous.

Rightfully so.

And so Shay and Erica watched. And waited. Nibbled cold pizza and wondered what the hell to do while the little drama unfolded before them.

Della toyed with the knife for a moment, then leaned across the table and grasped Nita's hand. Her ample breasts were flattened against Pascoe's little wooden table, no doubt giving Nita a full-cleavage view as she stroked the other woman's hand. Erica and Shay exchanged glances.

"You don't think she's proposing a *ménage à trois?*" Erica asked.

Shay leaned to get a better view around the umbrella. "At

this point, I'd believe anything. But Donald looks angry, don't you think?"

Donald had shoved his chair back from the table and was watching the two women intently, his face an unnatural shade of red. He looked over his shoulder as if choosing the quickest exit route through the maze of tables.

"Maybe they're cutting him out of whatever deal they've got going."

"Oh, Erica, honestly… Oh!" Shay ducked down behind the umbrella. "He's getting up."

Erica, better shielded behind the umbrella, watched as Donald threw some money on the table, then turned to leave. His chair fell over in the process, the heavy iron frame thudding against the concrete. He ignored it, his face twisted in anger as he stormed from the restaurant.

Pasco's other customers fell silent and turned to stare. Della adjusted her sunglasses more tightly against her face and gazed after Donald. Her face was so pale and stricken that she was hardly recognizable. Nita scurried to right the chair, then returned to sit next to Della, wringing her hands.

"Is it just me," Erica asked, "or does it seem like Della is the one who should be mad?"

"Right. Unless…" Shay pressed her hand to her chest. "Unless he didn't do it." She met Erica's gaze. "Oh my God, he didn't do it."

CHAPTER 6

Della stared after Donald as he stormed from the restaurant.

Liar, she thought.

The thought no sooner formed in her head than it was replaced by another: *You fool. You've accused an innocent man.*

She gripped the edge of the table until her fingers ached, her thoughts warring. Didn't all men deny what they'd done when they'd been caught in an affair? *Don't believe him*, a voice whispered. *He's lying…*

A surprise vacation getaway. No way. The embrace nothing more than a thank-you to Nita for making the arrangements. Ha! It was all just an elaborate lie. The ticket hadn't been meant for her, it had been meant for Nita. Just as she'd suspected.

And yet she'd believed Nita as the other woman had explained the so-called misunderstanding. Donald's secretary had looked genuinely horrified when she'd calmly accused them. But Donald was another story. He'd just stared at her in stony silence. He hadn't even added his denial to Nita's.

So why was her heart twisting inside her chest? Why was every instinct she possessed screaming at her to go after her husband, to beg his forgiveness?

"Some days I think I'm in love with Donald."

Nita's voice sliced through her heart like a knife. Della slowly met the other woman's eyes. Nita was like a sparrow, with delicate features and luminous gray eyes devoid of makeup. At least ten years Della's junior, she was petite and quiet, her clothing understated. They were opposites. Nita was everything that Della wasn't.

And at that moment Della learned what it meant to honestly hate another person.

A tear spilled down Nita's cheek and she wiped it away with a quick stroke of her fingers. Della noticed that her nails were short clipped and without polish. Had those innocent-looking hands touched her husband?

"What I mean is…" Nita looked around her, as though she were about to impart a terrible secret. "There have been days when I wished that he and I could be together."

Della shook her head, not understanding. Her throat tightened and her ears rang. She ached. Lord, she ached all over.

"He's so handsome and so sweet. A good person through and through." Another tear trailed down Nita's cheek. "There were days when he would lean near me to read a document and—and I wanted him to kiss me. I thought about it. Forgive me, Della, but I thought about it."

Della opened her mouth to speak, but no words came out. What was Nita trying to say? She couldn't decide if she was trying to explain something—badly—or get herself killed.

"I don't understand." Della's voice sounded like it belonged to someone else. Someone ancient and in pain. "You just told me that you and Donald never..." She gripped the vacation pamphlet, and the photo of the cruise ship crumpled beneath her fingers.

"Oh my God, no." Nita shook her head. "We never. I would never. I just—"

"Wanted to?" Della offered.

Nita nodded.

"Did he..." She straightened, bracing herself. "Does Donald feel the same way?"

"No!" The word came out so loud that several customers turned to stare. "I'd die if he even knew. What I'm trying to say is that I'm not innocent in all this. There have been so many days when I wished I were you." She fished a tissue from a small brown purse and pressed it to her eyes. "Nights, too."

Della blanched at the image of her friend fantasizing about her husband. "Why are you telling me this?"

"Because—because I think I might have flirted with him."

"You think?"

Nita nodded. "I tried. But I'm not even sure it registered. That's what I mean, Della. I want you to know what a good

man he is, that never once have I seen him do or say anything disrespectful. He loves you and the children." She
smiled but there was a sadness in it. "He talks about y'all constantly."

Della felt her world come back into focus, right itself again.
But as soon as she realized that Nita was telling the truth, her
own truth slammed her in the chest. She'd accused her husband of being unfaithful. It was unforgivable.

She could lose Donald. Not to another woman, but to her
own stupidity.

"Thank you," Della whispered, standing on shaky legs.

"Della—" Nita grabbed her hand. "I'm sorry. I probably
shouldn't have told you...."

"No." Della squeezed her hand, then began to inch away.
She had to find Donald. "You were honest. Thank you."

She whirled toward the exit, her brain flooded with adren-
aline and indecision. She began maneuvering her way
through the restaurant, realizing with dread just how many
familiar faces had likely seen her confront Donald and Nita.

Fool. Fool.

She clutched her purse against her chest and started jogging. Her breasts jiggled and her thighs rubbed together, but
she couldn't care less. She had to find Donald.

Pasco's was just a block from Main Street, and the main
thoroughfare provided the only real parking in the area. She
prayed that Donald had parked in the vicinity that she was

running toward, in part because her high-heeled sandals were cutting off her circulation with every stride and in part because she didn't know where else to look.

Her prayers were answered when she spotted her husband's truck at the end of the block. Della could see his silhouette behind the wheel and realized that he hadn't yet cranked the engine. She slowed to a walk, uncharacteristically embarrassed for Donald to see her parts jiggling as she ran. Maybe it hadn't occurred to him before that he could abandon their marriage. Great, Della. Give him the idea, then point out how flabby you've become by jogging in heels, she thought.

She approached the truck slowly, unnerved by his stony expression, his fixed stare. She tapped on the window with her nails and Donald turned toward her as if he had no choice. The anger in his eyes made her flinch. She felt as if she was living someone else's life as he rolled down the truck's window and fixed her with a cold stare that made his face look like a stranger's.

Donald had never looked his age. He was one of those men who looked like a perpetual college athlete—blond, tan and still fit after twenty years of marriage. But now she noticed the crinkles at the corners of his eyes, strands of silver mixed in the blond. And there wasn't quite as much of either color as there once had been. She was amazed that she hadn't noticed Donald's hair thinning. Della thought of all the hurried conversations they'd had lately, barely making eye contact over science projects and KFC. Somehow, while they'd been busy raising children and meeting the mortgage, they'd both grown older. This wasn't a lover's spat between two high-school kids. This was grown-up stuff. The kind that left you with joint custody and a broken heart.

And she'd be damned if she'd let that happen.

But before she could beg for his forgiveness, she needed to hear his denial, needed it more than her next breath. A tear rolled down her cheek and she knew that it probably took a clump of mascara with it. She vowed to wear less eye makeup tomorrow. And she would stop wearing heels to work. She'd let her nails go natural and buy some jeans that weren't designed for a nineteen-year-old.

Donald's eyes reflected emotion that she hadn't seen in over twenty years. It was frightening and exhilarating all at once to know that she still had that kind of power over him. "I just need to hear it, Donald. Please," she whispered.

"Hear what?"

"That you didn't. That you and Nita wouldn't…"

He laughed, and the sound was hollow. Dead. Terrifying. "That I wouldn't…" he mocked. "My God, Della, after twenty years of marriage, I need to defend myself? Against what? Your overactive imagination?"

"Please," she whispered.

"Why?"

"Because." She took a step back from the truck and spread her arms. "Because this…" A sob choked her and she swallowed hard. "This isn't what you married." She squeezed her eyes shut. "You married a cheerleader. A size eight with a rack." She dropped her purse and wrapped her arms around her waist. "Not *this*. Not the me I've become."

She was crying now, making a public spectacle of herself, and there wasn't a damn thing she could do to stop. She knew how she must look. A pathetic, overweight, aging bleach-blonde having a nervous breakdown on Main Street in hell. But she didn't care. She just wanted her life back, wanted to return to the mundane, secure cocoon that was her boring little corner of the world.

As if from a distance she heard the truck door open. Hope and dread curled in her gut like some horrible slithering creature.

And then Donald's arms were around her, cuddling her and wrapping her in the scent of him. He dragged her against him and she could smell the brand of soap that she always bought, the same deodorant he'd worn for decades. Della inhaled it like a drug and wrapped her arms around his neck, plunging her fingers into his hair. She couldn't get enough of him, couldn't get close enough.

Then she realized that in that hiccupy, resistant way that men fought emotion, Donald was trying not to cry.

"I love you," he whispered against her neck. "How could you think— I deserve more credit than that, Della." He pulled back to look her in the eye. "And so does Nita. She would never do something like that."

Della fought a laugh. If only he knew. "She's a pretty girl," she ventured. "She's got class."

Donald cocked an eyebrow. "If you call penny loafers and argyle socks class, then okay." He reached around and squeezed her butt until she yipped. "But I don't find that alluring."

Not that Della wanted to pan Nita's appearance on Main Street, but she found that the comment made her feel infinitely better. She wiggled her suit-clad hips against Donald's jeans and felt the bulge of an arousal. She smiled a wicked smile.

"She's thin," Della countered.

"Mmm. She's thin," Donald said. He drew one hand around the front of her suit jacket and slipped it beneath the hem. His hand traveled upward until he found the lace edge of her bra. He dipped his finger under it, teasing her nipple. "But she's missing a few pounds where they count the most."

Della sucked in her breath. Donald took advantage of her parted lips and kissed her, taking his mouth with hers like a horny teenager. She pressed herself against him as his hand kneaded her breast.

"Well, I find this embarrassing," Erica said. "Don't you, Shay?"

Della and Donald jumped apart like two guilty teenagers. Donald wiped at his mouth, liberally smudged with Della's lipstick, while Della righted her suit jacket.

"I think it's a beautiful display of affection," Shay responded. "But I did notice that the crowd began looking a little uncomfortable when the fondling started."

"Oh." Della turned to see a curious gathering of people staring from various directions. Some familiar faces were grinning but a few looked slightly scandalized. Including Reverend Walker from Haddes United Methodist.

"Oh my." She narrowed her eyes at her friends. "Wait. What are you two doing here?"

Erica and Shay exchanged glances. "Well, we were having pizza until we saw you playing with a knife and chatting with Nita. Then we decided to follow you and watch." Her eyes went round with innocence and she shrugged. "Then the groping started and we stayed for the show."

Della put her hands on her hips. "I mean why were you here to start with? At Pasco's?"

Erica bit her lip and gestured toward Shay. "Ask Madame Shay. She's the one that chose Pasco's for lunch."

Shay squirmed a little, fiddling with the crystal around her neck. "It was a coincidence. Honestly."

Della wasn't buying it. There were no coincidences when it came to Shay. She had some kind of psychic honing device in her head that was downright freaky. But you could hardly accuse her of anything devious. She'd simply blame it on the universe. And everyone knew it wasn't nice to blame the universe.

"So…" Shay glanced at Donald, then back at Della. "Is everything okay?"

"More than okay," Della responded, nudging against Donald's side. "We're going on a vacation. The plane tickets were for us. It was supposed to be a surprise, an early twentieth wedding anniversary gift." Shame reddened her face. "Nita helped Donald arrange it."

"Hence the hug?" Erica asked.

"Does everyone know what you thought?" Donald frowned, leveling Erica and Shay with a challenging stare. "I was thanking her, for heaven's sake."

Shay and Erica nodded.

"Well, thanks for nothing. Couldn't one of you come to my defense? You've only known me since the fifth grade."

"W-we didn't think…" Shay stammered. "We— You just never—"

"You're a man," Erica clarified. She shrugged. "Sorry."

"Guilty as charged. I apologize on behalf of my gender for every infidelity ever committed." He tugged Della a little closer to his side. "But I don't need to look any farther than my wife. I've got everything I need," he said, his voice soft.

"Damn," Erica said. "*I* should have married you."

"Your loss." Donald winked at her. "There's just one problem. The kids. I thought I could line my parents up but they've got some kind of stomach flu."

"Oh, no!" Della clutched the crumpled cruise pamphlet like it was a winning lottery ticket. "And my parents are out of town." She shifted her gaze to Erica and Shay, immediately dismissing them both as potential baby-sitters. "I'll call Mattie. I'm sure she'll say yes."

"We've been trying to reach her," Shay commented. "I can't get her at home or at the bookstore. And she's not answering her cell."

"Well, that's odd," Della said. "Mattie is normally so reliable."

"I'll try her at the bookstore again." Shay was already dialing, a worried look on her face.

Della got a strange feeling just noticing Shay's expression. She'd seen that look before. It usually meant trouble. She was about to question her when Shay obviously got an answer.

"Mattie?" Shay practically shouted into the receiver. She looked up, making eye contact with her friends. "Mattie answered. I just can't hear her," she whispered. "There's some kind of commotion in the background."

"Like what?" Erica asked.

Shay tilted her head, listening. "I think it's a police radio. Something's wrong at the bookstore." She held the phone to her ear, her eyes round. "What's wrong, Mattie?" she shouted.

Her face paled as she held the receiver, listening. "Oh, I'm so sorry. Who would do such a thing?"

"What is it?" Della wiggled in between Shay and Erica and leaned her ear toward the phone. "I can't understand her. What's wrong?"

"It's the bookstore," Shay whispered. "Someone broke in and trashed it. Mattie's crying."

"I'll drive," Della announced, fishing in her bag for her keys. She retrieved her key ring—a troll doll with bright pink hair—and found the right key.

"We're coming right over," Shay shouted into the phone. "Just sit tight."

Della gave Donald a quick kiss on the lips. "I'll take the girls. You get Jack and meet us there." She began hustling her friends down Main Street toward her vehicle.

"Wait!" Donald called. "Where is Jack, anyhow?"

Della paused. "I'm not sure. He's somewhere with Eve Dawson looking for a rental office. Call him on his cell."

"I don't have the number."

"I do. It's stored in my cell. Switch?"

"Switch!" Donald yelled.

They both threw their cell phones in the air, catching them on the same count.

"Wow," Shay commented. "That was something."

"What?" Della asked, stashing Donald's cell phone in her bag. "Oh, the phones? We do it all the time. Works wonders at the ball stadium. Let's go," she instructed, heading down Main Street at a Della-jog, which, due to the heels, was only slightly faster than a Della-walk.

"Right here," she instructed as they neared her vehicle, waving at Shay and Erica as they began to get too far ahead of her. She pressed the remote-key and the van gave a *yip*. "Right here. I'm the brown minivan."

Erica and Shay turned to look and Della felt a surge of embarrassment. She really *was* the brown minivan these days: battered, threadbare, boring and invisible. The salesman had called the van taupe when they bought it five years ago, but it was brown, damn it. She was nearing forty and drove a brown minivan. That sucked no matter how you looked at it.

Then she envisioned the faces of her children when they spotted her van in the car line. Della smiled. She might be invisible to everyone else, but they could find her in a nanosecond.

Della decided it was better not to make apologies or excuses for the state of the interior. Shay and Erica didn't have children. There wasn't enough time in a week to explain what one kid could do to a car, much less three. She grabbed a soccer bag out of the passenger seat and slid open the side door of the van. She leaned in and literally threw it into the third row. It landed with a *thud* on what looked to be aging grilled-cheese sandwich on a paper plate. She brightened when she realized that the fat backpack had at least obliterated the sandwich. Della brushed crumbs from the captain's chair nearest her and shoved a *Little Mermaid* videotape beneath the seat.

Shay slid gracefully into the captain's chair without complaint while Erica hopped in the front. Della climbed in, cranked up and headed out with a *screech*. Behind her, she heard Shay buckle her seat belt with a belated snap. Erica did the same.

Della accelerated. Mattie needed her. It was an odd concept, actually. Mattie never needed her, or anyone for that matter. She was staunchly independent, though Della had never actually looked at her that way. Mattie just quietly took care of her own business. There had never been a crisis in her adult life that Della could remember.

Della frowned. Or anything out of the ordinary, for that matter.

But things hadn't exactly been ordinary for any of them in the last few days. Or in Haddes lately, if you considered the break-ins and Christina Wilson's disappearance. The fact that two of her best friends were riding amongst grilled-cheese skeletons in her car after twenty years apart was proof of that. Of course the Donald and Nita incident, which hadn't been an incident after all, had sort of catapulted them through any polite barriers and straight back into the intimate zone. She smiled though tears threatened. It was as if they'd never been apart. Their friendship was still as natural as breathing.

As Della rounded the next corner, a patrol car on a side street caught her eye. She realized the police car had actually been parked in front of Mattie's duplex. "She did say it was the bookstore that had been broken into, right?"

"Right," Shay answered. "Why?"

"Because I thought I just saw a patrol car in front of Mattie's duplex." She accelerated a little more. "I've got a bad feeling about this." She glanced in her rearview mirror. "Shay?"

Shay nodded. "Me, too."

"Jeez, Della, slow down." Erica gripped the dashboard when Della swerved to miss a suicidal squirrel. She glanced around. "You're going to get a ticket."

Della laughed. "You're kidding, right? I'm driving a brown minivan with a PTO bumper sticker. I could have a naked murder victim strapped to my hood and the police wouldn't notice." She rolled through a stop sign. "Honestly. They'd wave and nod."

"You'd better hope so," Erica said, pointing toward a police cruiser as Della screeched to a stop against the curb, a block from the bookstore.

Della swallowed a healthy dose of anxiety at the sight of the police car in front of the bookstore. "I'm telling you, no one will care where I park in this van—"

"That's not what I meant," Erica interrupted. "Isn't that Mac?"

Della took another look. Sure enough, Mac McKay was leaning against his vehicle, police radio in hand. He hadn't noticed them, but one look into the rearview mirror told Della that Shay had seen her ex-husband. Her expression was stony but her body language said it all. She was practically curled into a ball in the rear captain's seat, her arms wrapped around her knees. Her billowy skirt covered her legs like a security blanket.

"Does he know you're in town?" Erica asked, her voice uncharacteristically soft.

"No." Shay shook her head and her loop earrings swung a little too enthusiastically. "Not that I know of."

"Stay here," Della commanded. "You shouldn't have to deal with him right now. The windows are tinted. No one will notice you're even in here." She dug around in the console and came up with a battered mail-order magazine. "Just—just entertain yourself with this while we're gone." She shoved the magazine at Shay, who looked relieved to have something to hold on to.

"Unless you want to come with us." Erica crooked a brow, her stare intense.

"No." Shay glanced at Mac, and for a moment looked as if she would change her mind. Just as quickly her expression changed, and she seemed to resign herself to the situation.

"I'll stay here for now." She laid the magazine in her lap and smoothed the wrinkles from its cover. "Thanks."

"Okay." Erica's smile seemed a little forced.

Della looked at the expanse of sidewalk between her van and the bookstore and made an executive decision. "Erica, feel beneath your seat and see if my flip-flops are down there," she ordered.

Erica looked uncertain, then bent and plunged her hand beneath the seat. Della had a fierce moment of regret, imagining lost marshmallow treats and bubble gum attaching themselves to Erica's sleeve. Or, heaven forbid, her expensive watch. Della had noticed the watch during their first meeting at the Stop-N-Bowl, and had felt a twinge of envy when she'd seen the time-zone rings. Erica was probably one of the few people on earth who actually needed to know what time it was in Bangladesh.

Within seconds Erica straightened with the flip-flops and passed them to her without comment. Della breathed a sigh of relief that nothing disgusting appeared to be stuck to her friend, then toed off her high-heeled sandals. She replaced them with the flip-flops and turned to Shay, who was still clutching the magazine and looking more than a little lost.

"I doubt he'd have the nerve to approach you, even if he knew you were here." She looked over her shoulder at Mac. "But lock the door when we get out and honk the horn like crazy if you need us."

Della and Erica hopped out and began scurrying down the sidewalk toward the bookstore. Mac looked up, no doubt alerted by the *smack-smack-smack* of Della's flip-flops as she jogged.

"Is she okay?" Della called as they passed Mac at the curb.

Mac lowered the radio. "Yeah, she's okay. She's just—" He stopped mid-sentence, literally choking when he saw Erica.

"Close your mouth, Mac," Erica called over her shoulder, leaving Mac to stare after her.

The chime rang as Della and Erica burst through the front door of the bookstore. They came to a breathless stop as Mattie turned to look at them. Her face was pale and tear-streaked, with little smudges of grime here and there. Her eye makeup was long gone and freckles stood out on the bridge of her nose. She looked about eight years old and scared to death.

"Oh, Mat!" Della exclaimed, wrapping her friend in a hug.

Mattie's shoulders heaved beneath her arms but, as far as she could tell, Mattie wasn't crying, just hiccuping like a heartbroken child.

Della looked around her in disbelief. Mattie's normally well-ordered bookstore was in shambles. It was as if someone had gone into a rage, breaking every breakable item in the store and intentionally damaging the rest. Books had been ripped from the shelves, then kicked aside. Every drawer in her desk stood open, the contents spilled onto the hardwood floor. A desk candle was on its side in a puddle of soft wax, its flame miraculously extinguished.

Erica bent to pick up a broken cake plate, remnants of a lemon-flavored dessert still clinging to the shard. "What happened?" she asked, incredulous.

Gerald Randolph came to stand behind Mattie, who was still hiccuping in Della's arms. He had a clipboard in his hand and a grave look on his face. He greeted Erica with a nod. "Good to see you, Erica."

"You, too, Officer Randolph."

The chime rang again, sounding ridiculously cheerful under the circumstances. Della looked up to see her brother striding through the door, his expression stormy. Jack stopped with his hand still on the handle, taking in a broken glass panel at the bottom. His gaze swept the room in one calm, perceptive gesture, before settling on the form of Mattie, still sniffling in Della's arms. Della thought she saw him wince before he finally looked at Officer Randolph.

"Gerald." Jack nodded at the longtime officer.

"Jack Murphy," Gerald responded. "It's good to see you, as well." He narrowed his eyes at Erica, then Jack. "This is a bit of a reunion now, isn't it?"

Jack turned to Mattie, cupping the side of her face before dropping his hand. He looked at Della. "Donald got me on the cell. He'll be here any minute."

"Thanks." Della felt Mattie turn in her arms and she

looked down into her friend's inquisitive stare. Realizing Mattie wasn't up to speed on the Donald-Nita thing, she whispered, "Long story."

Erica cleared her throat. "Can someone please tell me what's happened?"

"A neighbor called to alert us about Mattie's duplex. And while we were investigating the break-in at the duplex, we got the call on the bookstore." He ran a weary hand over his face, then pointed toward the front of the store. "An officer on patrol noticed the broken glass and called it in."

Della stared at the glass door. She'd been in such a hurry when she and Erica first arrived that she hadn't noticed it. In fact, she hadn't noticed it at all until Jack arrived. Her thoughts were racing and Gerald's words were making little sense.

"I don't understand." She shook her head, still cradling Mattie. "Her place was broken into?"

"I'm afraid so," Gerald said. He flipped through the paperwork on the clipboard. "I don't like it, Mattie. Not at all."

"Wait," Erica commanded. She sat the broken piece of cake plate on Mattie's desk, then brushed the crumbs from her hands. "When did that happen? Now? Today?"

Mattie disentangled herself from Della's embrace and nodded, her gaze darting from Jack to Erica to Della. "Can you believe it?" She sniffed, wiping her nose on her sleeve.

"No, I don't," Erica answered. "At least, I don't believe that it was a coincidence. What's going on, Mattie?"

"I don't know!" Mattie gestured toward Officer Randolph, then back at Erica with an exasperated sigh. "Why does everyone keep asking me that? I don't know!"

"Because…" Gerald put his hand on Mattie's shoulder and it had the intended calming effect. "Because the break-in at your home might have been random, and the break-in at your store might have been random. But put the two incidents together within a two- to three-hour span and it's something altogether different."

Jack began pacing the bookstore. "I'd like to take a look at the duplex, if that's okay."

Gerald frowned. "I'll leave that up to Mattie. Now if you'll excuse us, I still need to ask Mattie a few questions."

Gerald and Mattie moved to a quiet corner near the front of the store, and Della, Jack and Erica picked their way through the mess to stand near the back exit.

"I've never seen Mattie cry. Not like this, anyway." Della wrung her hands. "There's just no way I can leave her. I'll have to tell Donald to cancel the cruise."

"You can't do that," Jack interjected. "Donald's been planning it for months."

Della whirled to face her brother. "You knew about the trip?"

He shrugged. "Yeah, so?"

"So nothing." Tears filled her eyes at the confirmation of Donald's innocence. "We'll go another time."

The chime sounded again from the front of the store, and

the threesome watched Mac McKay enter. The tension was palpable. Della had long ago learned to tolerate Mac. He'd managed to stay out of trouble since his marriage to Shay had dissolved, had even started volunteering with the little-league team and attending church occasionally. If there was any violent behavior on his part, she hadn't heard of it. Mac had found tolerance, if not forgiveness, among most towns-people who remembered the incident with Shay. It was as if the passage of time equaled innocence. But Della would never truly forgive him.

Della leaned around a bookcase to get a better look.

Gerald handed Mac some paperwork, then turned back to Mattie. "The big question is…" Gerald paused, glancing over his shoulder as if sensing her eavesdropping. "What has changed in your life recently? Have you started seeing some-one new, for example?"

Della heard Jack release an irritated sigh, and turned to find him listening to Gerald's questioning, as well.

"You go on that cruise," he said. "I'll take care of Mattie."

Della examined Jack's face. She knew that tone. And she knew when her brother meant business. Very interesting. She shrugged off the hope that lodged itself in her chest. She and Donald desperately needed some time away. She had a lot of things she needed to say to her husband alone, not to mention a lot of making up to do. Still, given the circum-stances, it was probably best to let it go.

"No. Even if you baby-sat Mattie twenty-four/seven, I still wouldn't have a sitter for the kids."

"Yeah, you do." Erica picked up a hardback romance from the floor and straightened its rumpled dust jacket. She re-shelved it and met Della's eyes. "I'll do it."

Della burst out laughing, then covered her mouth when Erica looked insulted. "I couldn't let you do that," she said.

"Because it would be an imposition, or because you don't think I can 'do' motherhood?" she asked.

"Okay…" Della cleared her throat and lowered her voice to a whisper when Gerald glared at them over his shoulder. "Don't get mad, but…both."

A hurt look crossed Erica's face. "It's—what—a measly week? Give me a little credit." She shrugged, and the gesture fell just short of looking casual. "I'm staying at Mom and Dad's old place. The kids could keep me company. It would be fun." She fingered the book she'd just shelved. "Kind of an experiment."

Della felt tempted at the mention of Erica's family home. She'd spent a lot of happy times there. It had a long, circular driveway perfect for skateboarding. Maybe Andy could ditch the Goth-poet phase for a week and get his skateboard back out of the closet. The house was surrounded by a couple of acres, dotted with peach and apple trees. Elizabeth could analyze the pollination of semi-migratory butterflies or some other scientific nonsense and Trevor could climb to his heart's content. All in all, the situation could be good.

But Erica? No way. What was she thinking? Della cocked her head, scrutinizing her friend. She wasn't the rebellious eighteen-year-old girl she'd been when they were last together but there was no way she could take care of three kids out of the blue. Yet…there was something different in her eyes. Maturity, no doubt, but something else. She seemed to *want* to do this. But…

"Besides," Erica added. "How hard could it be?"

Ha!

Della looked at Jack, who was watching Mattie like a hawk and hadn't appeared to have heard a word they'd said. Very interesting indeed.

She turned back to Erica, who had assumed her "I'll take that dare" posture—hands on her hips, chin in the air.

"Well, old girl," Della said with a zen-smile, "I think you're about to find out."

CHAPTER 7

Shay felt like a trespasser, digging through Della's console in search of a sheet of paper. She shoved aside a half-dozen oil-change receipts and a crayon drawing of a princess. At first she'd assumed the drawing was a precious keepsake, but after coming across four others just like it, she decided to nab one. She found a purple marker and scribbled a note on the back: *Walking back to the inn. I'll be in touch.* Then, in smaller letters, *I'm sorry. Love, Shay.*

She propped it on Della's dash, then cringed when she caught sight of herself in the rearview mirror. *Coward.*

The words weren't a lie, just a huge omission. But what could she say? *I'm frightened. I've always been weak and likely always will be. Forgive me. Love, Shay.* Well, that seemed a little deep for a note left on the dashboard of Della's van. But it was the truth. The horrible, ugly truth.

Shay had waited while her friends went inside to comfort Mattie. Hiding in the shadows of the van, she'd watched Mac like a rabbit eyeing a wolf from the safety of its hole. She'd been trembling since the moment she laid eyes on him. But when she felt a familiar constriction in her chest, she knew she was in for a full-blown panic attack. Every horrifying memory of her life with Mac seemed to slam into her brain at once. Her body reacted, phantom pains shooting through the old wounds, unable to grasp what was memory and what was real.

Damn him.

No, her mind whispered. She'd forgiven him a long time ago. It had been the only way out of the darkness and she refused to unravel the peace she'd found. But the sight of Mac in his officer's uniform hadn't helped. She could think of nothing more disgusting than Mac promising to protect and defend. He'd lingered outside the bookstore for what seemed like an eternity, and all the while she'd lain on the floorboard, gasping for breath and praying the attack would stop. She'd finally unlatched the van's sliding back door and pressed her face against the crack, sucking in air like a prisoner.

She was still hunkered down in that position when she heard the patrol car crank. Shay hadn't been certain it was Mac's vehicle, but the hope that it was had caused the attack to wane. When she finally lifted her head, damp with sweat and shivering, the panic attack over, he was gone.

The thought that he could return was the only thing that drove her from the vehicle now. But it was enough. She couldn't survive being trapped like that again.

Shay slipped from the van, closing the door as gently as possible behind her. She forced herself to move away and toward the sidewalk. She controlled her breathing, forcing herself to walk rather than run.

Little League baseball fields flanked Main Street, and Shay would bet her last dollar that there was still a red-dirt path winding from the rear of the ball field back to Freeman Street, and from there to the inn where she was staying. She was counting on it. Shay could see the edge of a chain-link fence and a small patch of grass a block away, and she focused all her energy on getting there.

She, Mattie, Della and Erica had spent their share of summer nights at the ball field, eating hot dogs and checking out the boys in their baseball uniforms. And they'd walked those dirt paths a thousand times, feeling independent as they ventured away from the crowd and into the cool shelter of the woods.

Shay clung to the memory as her skirt tangled around her ankles and sweat dripped into the V of her bra. Her long auburn curls caught in the breeze, waving like a flag behind her. She wished for a ponytail holder to contain it, to hide it somehow. It was like a red flag, a flashing neon sign that said, *Notice me, I'm Shay Chambers.*

Back in town. Still half crazy. Still adrift.

The patch of green grass grew larger and Shay breathed a sigh of relief when she reached the edge of the fence. She slipped around the side, her mind racing as she finally reached the shadowed dugout and empty concession stands. She flattened herself against the side of a cinder-block building and breathed in the cooler air. She could do this.

Shay visualized the inn, then the winding path that would take her there. It was the closest thing to home she had at the moment. It was a restored turn-of-the-twentieth-century Victorian that, if memory served, used to belong to a pair of spinster sisters. The elderly sisters had likely died, and Shay hadn't recognized the new owner, a fact that relieved her from playing "catch up with an old acquaintance." In fact, she'd managed to avoid seeing anyone she knew so far except her friends.

Which would have been great if things had worked out as she'd imagined.

She felt a stab of disappointment, but she refused to give in to it. Shay shoved away from the dugout and searched the wooded area behind the ball field. The path was all but obscured by brambles, but it was there. Thank God. She gathered the hem of her skirt and tied it in a knot on the side of her hip to avoid ripping it on the underbrush, and began walking. Her sandals dusted themselves with red grit as she entered the woods, and the tension in her shoulders relaxed slightly. She was safe. No one would spot her until she emerged across the street from the inn where she was staying.

Disappointment surged again. Her friends hadn't thought to ask her to give up her room and stay with them. Della and Mattie still had homes here, and Erica had returned to her parents' old place. But Shay had nowhere to return to. Her aunt and uncle had retired to a Florida condo right after she left town. And no matter how many years separated her from that move, thinking of it still left her feeling like the orphan that she was. Maybe Della and Mattie hadn't wanted to intrude. Or maybe the years that had divided them had truly divided them.

What had she hoped? That Mattie would take her into her home to repeat teenage nights filled with giggling and cookies? That Della would offer to put her up, jump at the opportunity to have her get to know the kids? Shay shoved a branch aside and worked her way up the incline. Yes, in truth she'd pictured herself tucking Della's children in at bedtime, catching up with Mattie over a glass of wine, maybe seeing a movie.

But it hadn't happened that way. It hadn't happened at all.

And soon what little money she'd stashed for the trip would be gone. Then she'd be homeless. A gypsy, her Aunt Danielle had once called her. The comment hadn't been intended to be cruel, yet it fit in too many ways to deny. She certainly looked the part, both then and now. Yet she'd wanted to be anything but. What she'd wanted is what she didn't have: a family, a home, a place to belong. But in the end, the comment had turned out to be a self-fulfilling prophecy.

Shay topped the small incline and heard the traffic on Freeman Street. She leaned against the trunk of a tree, not yet ready to emerge from the shelter of the woods. A dog barked and a lawn mower buzzed in the distance. She could smell the freshly cut early-summer grass and the wood smoke from the local barbecue joint. She'd lived in Phoenix for the past fifteen years, yet everything about Haddes whispered *home*.

In truth, she'd never wanted to leave.

As an adult, she could see that her aunt and uncle had let her down. As her guardians, they should have helped her escape Mac's abuse. But they hadn't, and the hurt child that lived inside her still wept at the betrayal. It was as if they'd merely tolerated the ten years she'd lived with them, and her marriage to Mac had ended their tenure.

They hadn't wanted to see the abuse at first. Mac's parents were longtime residents of Haddes, his father an old hunting buddy of her uncle's. But eventually they were forced to acknowledge it. Even so, they simply told her to work harder at her marriage. It was clear that they hadn't wanted to step back into the role of parents any more than they'd wanted that role when she was eight.

Of course she hadn't chosen to work at her marriage. She'd likely be dead now if she had. But her aunt and uncle had been scandalized by the divorce. They'd packed their bags for Florida and made it clear they were going alone. Shay had packed her beat-up Honda and, with nowhere else to run, headed west. She'd lied to her friends, telling them that she had a cousin in Arizona. They'd agreed that she had to get away from Mac, and she had assured them it would be temporary. Shay had imagined Arizona as a place of acceptance, a place where her psychic intuition could flourish in the open.

She hadn't flourished, though she had managed to build a life for herself, however imperfect. But after twenty years of working as a clerk in a New Age bookstore, she wasn't any closer to understanding why things were the way they were than on the day she left Haddes. Her job gave her a sense of affirmation, but it only kept her a paycheck away from financial doom. Add a string of bad relationships to the mix, and she was on the same path she'd been on when her aunt and uncle abandoned her.

She breathed deeply, trying to clear the negative thoughts, but they circled back with a will of their own. It was the ultimate irony that the universe had put her together with her aunt and uncle. They'd been gifted with an overdose of religious enthusiasm that had little to do with God and everything to do with feeling superior. And she'd been gifted with an intuition that they considered inherently evil. They simply hadn't known what to do with her, much less how to love her.

Maybe it was time she stopped blaming them. Most days even *she* didn't know what to do with herself.

She honestly didn't know what she would have done growing up had she not had Mattie, Erica and Della. They were her real family. Only with them had she ever found acceptance. They loved her for who and what she was. The only other time she'd known that kind of unconditional acceptance was with her parents. And memories of them had faded to the point that she no longer knew what was a true memory and what was a fabrication of how she'd wanted things to have been.

Shay untied her skirt and felt it blow around her ankles. But she would never deny the memory of them sitting beside her hospital bed, holding her hand as she recovered from the accident. Only later had she learned that the accident had taken their lives instantly. It hadn't been real, her aunt and uncle had assured her, only a figment of her traumatized mind or the medication. But she knew they'd been with her. And that day had marked the beginning of her abilities—a gift, she always felt, from her parents.

No matter what the rest of the world thought.

Shay walked the short distance and stood on the side of Freeman Street, still unnoticed in the shadows. Coming together again with Mattie, Erica and Della was bittersweet, disorienting and familiar at the same time. It seemed everyone had found their life but her, even if their lives were less than perfect.

She stifled a laugh. No one did less-than-perfect better than she did. Her friends, especially Erica, had been incensed that she'd tolerated Mac's abuse, that she'd tried to stay in the marriage, even for a short time. They were understandably angry that she hadn't turned to them for help.

If they knew that she'd repeated the cycle again and again, she could never live with the shame.

Shay watched the traffic go by without really seeing it, her gaze fixed on the inn. She wished she were already inside, that she didn't have to step out into the open or maneuver the traffic. But she did. And that fear wasn't entirely Mac's fault. There'd been more than one Mac in her life. She ran her hands over her arms. Her last failed relationship was with a man named Bruce. His violent nature had turned physical the night she left for Haddes.

She shivered. And he'd threatened to find her no matter where she ran. He'd made a million threats, but only one had stayed with her. *I'll see you in hell,* he'd said.

Well, that may be, but she had friends there. And this time she intended to lean on them.

"That's not funny," Mattie scolded. She snapped her fingers at the dog. "Drop it."

Buddy just stared at her, the tampon string dangling from the corner of his mouth.

She'd only left the dog for a moment, but in that moment

he'd managed to discover the box of spilled tampons. Somehow he'd removed the wrapper and plastic case from one—which she actually thought was rather talented of him—before she'd taken the box away. But now he was staring at her, refusing to drop the last remaining prize.

"Now!" she commanded. "I will not pay to have a tampon surgically removed from your gut." She made a serious face and pointed at him. "Drop it!"

Buddy made an asthmatic, snuffling sound, then opened his mouth, shifted the tampon to the front of his tongue and spat it out on her carpet.

She threw her hands in the air. "Now that's just gross."

It had been a long night, but she'd actually felt pretty optimistic this morning. She looked at the wet wad of white cotton sitting atop her usually pristine beige carpet and decided that maybe her headaches weren't over yet.

Once the police report had been filed, she'd turned the bookstore's welcome sign to "Closed," locked the broken front door and walked to her car, shaken and weary to the bone. Jack had driven the land barge for her, then had searched every crack and crevice of her duplex, in case the intruder had returned. Mattie had been right behind him, the back pocket of her jeans bulging with used tissues, her flashlight clutched in strike mode. She'd almost hyperventilated when he'd come to her closet, torn between fear and embarrassment. She'd finally wormed her way between Jack and the closet door, insisting on checking it herself. Mattie figured that, between her metal flashlight and Jack nearby, she'd take her chances rather than expose yet another part of herself.

Had the break-in only involved the bookstore she would have been comforted by the fact that she was home. But there was no real sanctuary, no safe place in which to retreat. She felt naked, stripped bare. And the thought that she might never know who had been in her home was more unnerving than the violent act itself. Would she always search the faces of strangers and acquaintances, weighing their sanity and motivation?

Della and Erica had arrived shortly after Jack brought her home and had helped to right furniture and begin the awful process of cleaning up. Mattie hadn't completely stopped crying until Shay arrived, carrying a pair of dollar-store rubber gloves, her Bible and some sage incense.

And—best of all—an offer to spend the night.

Della and Erica had stayed for a few hours before leaving, Della to prepare for her trip and Erica to prepare for Della's brood. Mattie had had to practically shove Jack out the door, promising to lock it behind him and keep her cell phone on her hip. She'd only found the courage to let Jack out of her sight because of Shay. Together they'd managed to put the duplex back in workable order pretty quickly. It turned out that most of her personal belongings were scattered rather than broken. But that was little comfort, considering that a stranger's hands had touched her things.

Two words kept rolling through her head: *Why* and *who?*

They'd finally taken a break around midnight. Exhausted and heartsick, Mattie had fixed them both a glass of red wine and together they'd collapsed on the sofa to watch a rerun of SNL. She'd traded in her jeans and grimy blouse for an oversize football jersey and a pair of fuzzy slippers. The break had been so therapeutic that it had accidentally lasted all night. They'd woken up on the sofa this morning, wineglasses empty and the television still on.

She'd put on a pot of coffee while Shay showered. Mattie had been halfway through her first cup when Eve Dawson rang the doorbell, Buddy by her side. Eve had had the good taste to take Buddy by the groomer's for a flea-dip and deodorizing bath, but the bad taste to tie a yellow bow around his neck. Mattie couldn't help but think that the bow was the exact color of American cheese.

Instead she'd thanked Eve, carted in the fifty-pound sack of dog food—not an easy task in fuzzy slippers—and tried to pick up where she left off last night. Her efforts could now be focused on things that one person could do, such as scrub face cream from the tile grout and suck crushed potpourri from the pile of her carpet. So that's what she'd been doing. At least until the tampon incident.

Mattie headed for the kitchen for a towel, but froze when

Buddy made a deep-throated noise. She looked over her shoulder. Was that a growl? It was impossible to tell, since the dog never changed expressions. He just stared at her, making sounds that could either be the heralding of her imminent death...or gas.

"Wow." Shay's voice sounded from the hallway. "Who is this?"

"This," Mattie answered, her voice tight, "is Buddy. Eve Dawson brought him over while you were in the shower. He was part of Ralph Barnes's estate. And now he's going to be my watchdog." She flinched when Buddy began sniffing the air. "Watch your extremities."

Shay breezed into the room, smelling like ginger shampoo and looking like a dew-kissed Celtic princess in sweats, a towel still wrapped around her shoulders. She cast her gaze upward at Mattie, smiling. "You're joking." Her expression grew serious and she dropped to her knees in front of the dog. She cocked her head, looking into his eyes. "You won't hurt me." It was a statement, not a question.

"He's very protective," Mattie added, mimicking Eve's original sales pitch. "That's a very admirable quality in a dog."

Shay looked skeptical, then began rubbing Buddy beneath the ears. He closed his eyes and moaned. Not a threatening moan, but a pleasurable moan so heartfelt that it was a little embarrassing. Mattie looked at Shay, whose eyes were closed, as well. She shuffled off in search of more coffee.

She'd just topped off her mug when Shay's voice rang from the den. "Is this a tampon?"

Mattie smiled. "A gift from Buddy."

The doorbell rang and Mattie looked down at her sleep garb. What the heck. A lot of things seemed a lot less significant today. She tossed the dish towel to Shay, who used it to scoop up Buddy's gift.

"Be careful. See who it is first," Shay called as she used the yellow ribbon to lead the dog off down the hall.

Mattie tiptoed to the door, coffee in hand, and looked through the peephole, something that never would have occurred to her to do before yesterday.

Jack stood on the other side of the door, his hands shoved into the pockets of his jeans as he glanced suspiciously around the front lawn.

Mattie opened the door a crack. "Jack, hi. What are you doing here?"

He leaned his arm against the door frame and examined her through the crack. "Checking on you." His hair was disheveled, in a roll-in-the-hay kinda way that made her knees go weak. "Everything okay?" he asked.

Mattie was glad that only a portion of her puffy morning face showed through the crack, then remembered that it didn't make any difference. No matter how she looked, Jack would never be anything more than a friend.

A friend that looked suspiciously like he'd slept in his car.

She bent her knees to see around his arm, looking for his truck. Erica had driven Jack's truck over last night and had left it at a haphazard angle against the curb. It was still at that angle. Her heart skipped a beat when she realized that Jack had kept watch through the night. She was immensely grateful, even if the motivation wasn't what she'd once hoped for.

She decided to look at the situation as a liberation. The fact that Jack was gay allowed her to be herself. She didn't have to worry that she wasn't fully dressed or that the dog had just used one of her tampons for a chew toy. It was a relief, actually, especially in light of all that had happened. She could use another friend, and the fact that he was six-two and knew how to use a gun was a definite plus.

Mattie opened the door and motioned him in, lifting her mug. "Coffee?"

He stepped over the threshold, his gaze traveling over her slipper-clad feet, bare legs and football jersey, finally resting on the coffee cup. "Sure." He smiled. "You look comfortable. I take it last night went okay?"

"It did," she answered, heading off in the direction of the coffee. "We almost had fun."

Jack shut the door and locked it. "You had fun? I left you crying and cleaning yesterday and now you tell me you had fun?"

Mattie took a mug from the cabinet and filled it. "Okay, *fun* is an exaggeration, but it was nice having Shay here. She cleansed the place by burning some sage." She extended the coffee with a shrug. "Cleansing in the spiritual sense. It got rid of the negative vibes."

He looked around, then accepted the coffee. "It looks like y'all cleansed it with more than sage. You made a lot of progress."

She leaned back against the counter. "Thanks."

"Listen." Jack hesitated, taking a sip of coffee. "I don't want to scare you, but it's going to take a lot more than sage to make me feel better about this."

The knot that had loosened in her gut tightened again. "I know. I can't make sense of it."

"I've been thinking, there has to be some catalyst for the break-ins." Jack sighed. "I know that Gerald asked you this yesterday, but you need to concentrate on any changes in your life, business or personal. For instance, have you borrowed money? Who did you go out with last? Are you seeing anyone new?"

Mattie felt her cheeks flush. She wasn't in a hurry to admit to any man, gay or straight, that she hadn't been on a date in months. She chose her wording carefully. "No, I haven't borrowed money since the bookstore first opened. And I told Gerald the truth. I'm not seeing anyone new."

Jack sat the coffee mug on the counter. "But that's not true. You agreed to go out with me. That's the kind of information Gerald was looking for."

"That's not the same thing." Mattie felt herself blush again with misplaced embarrassment. He was doing that flattery thing again, and it was so much like flirting that it left her disoriented. "We're just friends."

"Okay." He drew the word out, frowning as though he were lost in thought. "Since I'm not a factor, what about Shay and Erica?"

Mattie was caught off guard. "What about them?"

"They've suddenly made a reappearance in your life. Maybe you should have mentioned that to Gerald."

Mattie eyed him over the rim of her coffee mug. "You're kidding, right?"

"Not entirely." He lowered his voice. "What do you know about either of their lives since they left Haddes?"

"They're my friends, Jack." Mattie felt genuine anger. "Since when have you become so jaded?"

"PI work will do that to you," he answered, looking down. "I couldn't help but notice…"

Mattie felt her blood pressure rise a notch. "What?"

"Shay's car." He gestured toward the driveway. "It's the Toyota Corolla in the driveway with an Arizona license plate, right?"

She nodded.

"Did Shay happen to say anything about moving back to Haddes?"

Mattie felt a stab of guilt. She didn't know what Shay's

plans might include. She'd hardly asked her friend anything about her life. Mattie had been too caught up in her own. "No, she hasn't."

He shrugged. "It's probably nothing, but I noticed that her car is crammed full of stuff."

"Meaning…?"

"It just looks like she threw it all in, like she packed on the run. There's even a wire dish drain in the back seat."

Mattie pictured Shay showing up out of the blue with her rubber gloves and willingness to help, and was instantly defensive. "A dish drainer? We should call 911," she said sarcastically.

Not only had her misguided crush on a gay man faded seriously in the last sixty seconds, but she was getting really mad at him.

Jack straightened. "I don't mean any disrespect. I just noticed, that's all. People don't typically pack belongings like dish drainers unless they're planning on moving permanently. It just struck me as odd."

"Well, Shay isn't one to do things by the book." Mattie pictured Shay holding the smoldering sage in front of her as she walked from room to room through the duplex, praying without hesitation or embarrassment. Not everyone could look at her friend and see her for who she really was. Apparently Jack was one of those people. "She's just open to ideas that other people can't imagine."

"Being eccentric isn't a crime." Jack ran his hand through

his hair. "But that kind of openness can be dangerous. It's a door, so to speak, and there are plenty of kooks willing to walk through it. I've seen case after case like that. And instead of just inviting trouble into their own lives, they invite it to destroy the people who are trying to help them."

"Well, Shay wouldn't let that happen." Mattie shook her head. "She learned that lesson with Mac."

Jack turned to look out the kitchen window, leaning his arms against the counter. Mattie watched a muscle in his jaw tighten while the silence stretched.

"I remember," he said.

"Good." Mattie glanced over her shoulder, making certain Shay wasn't within earshot. "Because there are days when I think I'm the only one in this town who does."

Shay buried her fingers in Buddy's fur and fought back tears. She'd tugged the reluctant dog as far as the laundry nook in the hallway, then had watched to make certain Mattie was safe as she answered the door. She'd started to take him the rest of the way to the bedroom once she realized it was only Jack, but before she knew it, Mattie and Jack had been deep in conversation.

Intuition told her that there was something intimate between the two of them and she'd felt instantly trapped. Rather than interrupt, or look like an eavesdropper, she'd stayed put.

And now she'd give anything to be anywhere else, to not have heard Jack's words.

Shay's hand stilled when she felt a zigzagging scar beneath Buddy's thick fur. She followed the thick scar tissue with her fingertips until it met his left ear. Her chest tightened in sympathy. "No wonder," she whispered to him. No wonder she'd felt such an immediate connection with him.

He was a victim. And a survivor.

She swallowed hard. Jack had hit the nail on the head, had managed to sum up her life in a few offhand sentences. She'd invited trouble all her life, yet had managed to stay one precarious step ahead of it. But maybe, with her latest failed relationship, history was threatening to repeat itself.

Was it possible that Bruce had followed her here? Could he have discovered that Mattie was her friend and reasoned that he could find Shay here? She closed her eyes, envisioning the violent chaos that had been Mattie's home, and faced the truth.

It was possible.

That kind of evil was like a vine. It wound through the darkness, entwining other people as it reached for the light, searching to destroy the goodness. Shay buried her face against Buddy's neck and felt him lick her ear.

She'd put her friends in danger. It was unforgivable.

No. The word built up inside her like a living thing. No.

Her friends were the only real light she'd ever known. She'd be damned if she'd let anything harm them.

She wouldn't stay another night at Mattie's, wouldn't put her in danger. And if Bruce was in Haddes, she'd make certain that he knew where to find her.

Shay Chambers was through hiding.

CHAPTER 8

"Did you know that piranha can strip the flesh from a plucked chicken in less than one minute?"

Erica pulled her head from the fridge to stare at Elizabeth. Della's middle child looked like an angel with her brunette curls and cat-shaped green eyes, but she delivered her facts like the Angel of Doom.

"No," she answered. "I absolutely did not know that."

The Angel of Doom grinned, obviously pleased that she'd yet again one-upped Erica with a little-known fact. The smug look on her face was exactly like Della's. In fact, Erica thought she'd seen that exact expression on Della's face when she told Elizabeth not to forget to pack her *Big Book of Little-Known Facts*.

Elizabeth, perched on the edge of the kitchen counter, was drumming her heels against the cabinet as she flipped the pages. "Did you know that the ancient Egyptians removed the organs from the bodies of the dead before they began to mummify them?"

Erica reluctantly retrieved a package of ground beef from the refrigerator as her stomach gave a sharp twist.

"Ew," she countered, trying not to sound affected. "I think I may have known that one but tried to forget it. Hey, are there any *cheerful* facts in there?"

"Hmm…" Elizabeth chewed the nail on her index finger and stole a peek at Erica over the top of the book. "Not really."

Erica took a gander at the size of the volume and seriously doubted that answer. You could kill somebody with the darn book. Or at least a chicken. That is, if the piranha hadn't gotten him first.

Elizabeth checked her watch, looking pleased that the little white lie had gone unchallenged. "It's time for my homework," she announced, jumping from the counter.

"Good." Erica smiled sweetly to cover how relieved she must have sounded. "I mean, it will be great to get it over with, right?"

Elizabeth, who was in the process of dragging a backpack toward the kitchen table, froze mid-stride. "Do you think homework is a chore?"

Erica straightened. She knew a loaded question when she heard one. "Not a chore, exactly. Just, well, necessary."

Elizabeth crossed her arms over her chest. "Like a necessary evil?"

"No, that's not what I meant." This child was eight? She was a diabolical genius. Erica had no intention of going toe-to-toe with her. "I—I'm going to make some spaghetti while you get on that homework, okay?"

Elizabeth looked disappointed, then finished dragging the backpack to the table. She unzipped it and pulled out an array of textbooks, then a large binder. Erica blinked at the title written neatly across the front in black marker: *In Case of Emergency.* It was at least an inch thick. How many emergencies could there be in the life of an eight-year-old? She decided not to comment.

Elizabeth sat the binder in the middle of the table, then stacked her textbooks in alphabetical order near her elbow. She pulled her long curls into a ponytail and situated her notebook at a perfect diagonal. Erica watched as she licked the tip of her pencil and began writing. She looked like a miniature accountant. But just as she began writing, she paused, an odd expression wrinkling her brow.

"Where's the Terrier?" she asked.

"A terrier?" Erica repeated. "I don't have a—"

"No." Elizabeth stood, knocking over her notebook. "Not a dog. Trevor. Mama calls him Trevor the Terrible—" Her voice cracked. "The Terrier, for short."

"Oh God." Erica dropped the package of ground beef into the sink.

Elizabeth snatched up the emergency binder and clutched it to her chest. "Oh no!" She began to flip through the pages at dizzying speed.

"Wait," Erica said, trying to sound calm. "I'm sure he's around here somewhere."

"Wash your hands," Elizabeth shrieked.

"What?"

"You've been handling ground beef. *E-coli.* Wash your haaaands!" The last word ended on a wail that would make a hyena proud.

Erica did as instructed, then dried her hands on a dish towel. She placed her now-sanitary hand on Elizabeth's shoulder. "Trevor was just right here, honey," she soothed as Elizabeth found a binder tab labeled TREVOR. Her heart thumped in her chest. She'd managed to lose one of Della's children in less than a day. And Trevor had his own tab in the emergency binder? Oh Jeez. This was not good. "He was playing with his little car. Remember? Come on, we'll find him."

"We need to call 911."

"No." Erica threw down the dishrag and offered Elizabeth her hand. "Let's look for him first. Then, if we can't find him, we'll call—" panic burrowed into her chest "—then we'll call the police."

To her shock, Elizabeth relented. She placed her small hand in Erica's and Erica was surprised to feel how soft and small it felt within her own. She was still a little girl, and right now, she was scared.

"What types of things does Trevor like to do?" Erica asked. "I mean, where do you think he might want to go?"

"He climbs," Elizabeth said. "He climbs things."

That didn't sound good. "What types of things does he climb?" *The roof? Mount Everest?*

Elizabeth looked at her like she'd lost her mind. "Anything," she answered sincerely.

Oh!

"Trevor!" she called. No answer.

"He won't answer you," Elizabeth explained.

"What? Why?"

"He doesn't talk." Elizabeth shrugged. "Well, not to anybody but Mama."

"But your mom is on vacation. How can we find him if he won't answer us? Surely he'll talk—"

Elizabeth shook her head. "He only talks to Mama."

Oh, great. Mama was on a floating dessert bar somewhere in the Caribbean and she'd managed to lose her youngest child. Erica dragged Elizabeth down the hall. Her parents' house was big, a multilevel with enough closets to hide a cell block of fugitives. She began to tremble and dropped Elizabeth's hand so that she wouldn't suspect. Together they dashed from room to room, calling Trevor's name just in case he decided to answer. No Trevor.

When they came back full circle to the kitchen, Erica felt a sense of dread. "Elizabeth, where's your brother?" she asked.

Elizabeth shook her head. "I don't know. We're looking for him, right?"

"No, no." Erica took a deep breath. "Your other brother. Andy."

"Andrew," Elizabeth corrected.

"Right. Where is he?"

"Last time I saw him, he was outside in that old shed."

"The shed?" Erica glanced out the window at her father's workshop. What in the world would the boy be doing out there? She had visions of him making a bomb or rolling a joint. Well, he was just going to have to put the bomb-making on hold and help her find Trevor. She kneeled down next to Elizabeth. "I'm going to get Andrew to help us look for Trevor. Can you start looking in all the closets?"

Elizabeth's expression was uncertain for a second, then she nodded. "Yes. But are there any guns in them?"

Guns? The bottom dropped out of her stomach.

"Mama says I can't play hide-and-seek in Sissy Barkin's closets because her daddy keeps guns in them. He hunts deer." She wrinkled her nose. "I don't like that."

Erica felt her heart pound in her chest. Guns? Of course she should have checked for guns. Her father had kept an old rifle around when she was growing up—and hadn't he inherited an antique handgun from her grandfather? Oh God, she didn't know. How could she not know? How could she have invited children into her home and not thought of something as important as this?

Erica pressed her hand against her abdomen and fought tears. In her mind she saw the plus sign in the window of the pregnancy test. She'd actually felt joy, excitement. Stupid, stupid. She wasn't cut out for this. Who had she been kidding? Six hours into temporary parenthood and she'd put Della's children in mortal danger. Her heart cried out, ached for John. Erica closed her eyes. "Please come back," she whispered. "I can't do this alone."

"I'm right here," Elizabeth answered.

Erica opened her eyes and forced a calm expression. "Just…just open each closet door and look inside. Don't go in there." She patted Elizabeth's shoulder, then gave her a forward push. "Go. Call his name, even if you don't think he'll answer you."

Elizabeth dashed off down the hall, and Erica headed for the backyard. "Andy!" she yelled, when she was within earshot of the shed. "Andy, Trevor is missing."

The door to the shed opened slowly and Andy stuck his head out. His expression was dead calm and he was chewing a wad of gum. A baseball cap was turned backward on his head. Her hope for semi-adult help faded. "Yeah? He's with me." He blew a bubble and looked around. "At least he was. He was right here just a minute ago."

Hope surged, then plummeted. "Where?" she insisted. "Where was he last?"

Andy took a step back into the shed, and Erica followed.

"I was right here, messing with these old tomato cages, and he was bugging me."

Erica's gaze fell on the wire cages that had once surrounded her father's tomato plants. Spiderwebs clung to the wire, and rust had all but eaten through in places. The sense that time was passing made her head swim. A pair of her father's gloves lay on the workshop bench and a painful longing nearly knocked her to her knees. If he were here, he'd know what to do.

Erica forced herself back to Andy, and she noticed that fresh wire had been twined around the cages in strategic places. Andy had been repairing them. But why?

"I told him to take the truck outside—he was playing with a toy truck—and play on the grass." Andy frowned and looked at his watch. "That was only about five minutes ago."

It took far less time than that for a child to disappear. "Help me, Andy." She heard the panic in her voice but no longer cared. "He's outside somewhere. We've got to find him."

"Right."

Andy straightened, and Erica realized his height matched hers. He suddenly looked older. And concerned. Erica was relieved to have his help.

"I'll search around the shed. You search from here back toward the house. Elizabeth is looking inside."

"Got it," Andy answered as he jogged off.

Erica began searching around the back of the shed, over-whelmed by the number of places a four-year-old could hide. The shed was supported at the back by concrete cinder blocks, and Erica tried to reason whether a child would enter such a dark, dank place. She kneeled down, wishing she'd thought to bring a flashlight.

"Trevor?" she called. "Are you in here?"

No answer. But, of course, she hadn't really expected one.

She flattened herself, chest down, against the ground and tried to get a better look. Was it her imagination, or did something move in the shadows? She inched farther underneath the shed, feeling the damp soil embed itself beneath her nails and cling to her T-shirt. "Trevor, buddy, are you in there?"

"Is this what you're looking for?" a masculine voice said behind her, unexpected.

Erica jumped, hitting her head on the underside of the shed. She rolled to a sitting position and blinked against the sun. "Trevor!" she shouted. She snatched him into a hug with her good arm.

"I take it he belongs to you."

"No. I mean, yes." Erica smiled, brushing the caked mud from her hands, then stood to thank the man. Her breath caught in her chest and her smile faded. She shielded her eyes from the sun to get a better look. It was the neighbor she'd watched from her bedroom window, she realized. She tugged

Trevor against her side, remembering the man's angry tantrum with the garbage can.

The man took a step toward Trevor. "Is this your son, or not?"

"I'm baby-sitting," she explained. "He's not my son." Erica pressed her hand against her abdomen, dizzied by the fact that she might have a son at this time next year.

The man frowned, wrinkling his forehead. His eyes were a light, flinty blue color that intensified when he narrowed them, standing out in contrast to his tanned skin. The effect was startling, if not a little scary. "You can't do that," he stated.

You're right, she thought. *I don't have a clue how to be a mother.* She blinked, realizing that her train of thought had jumped its track. "Excuse me?"

"You can't let him wander off like that."

"I know." She studied the man's angry expression, thinking there was something familiar about him beneath the scowl. "It's just that we didn't know he'd taken off and—"

"There's a creek just down the hill that swells after a rain."

He shifted, and Erica got the distinct impression that he felt Trevor was better off in his care. She lifted the boy into her arms, wishing she weren't alone.

"The creek," he stated as if she were dense. "He could have gotten swept away. It's dangerous."

Of course she knew about the creek. She'd grown up here. Erica felt both irritation and guilt as an image of Trevor near the creek's edge implanted itself in her brain. She shivered and pressed his soft little body even tighter against her shoulder.

"Lock him in if you have to. A mistake like that could cost you."

The irritation grew. This was her home. He was a stranger. And she wasn't a complete idiot, even if she felt like one at the moment. Who was he to lecture her?

"Erica?" Andy's voice came from the house, sounding grown up and a lot like his father's.

She marveled for a moment that the photo of the infant she still carried in her wallet had turned into a nearly grown man. One she was immensely relieved to have around at the moment.

"You found him?" Andy asked.

"Yes!" she called, taking a step backwards from the man, but never taking her eyes from him. "I've got him now."

The man nodded, then turned and began walking away.

"Thank you!" she called, forcing a lighthearted lilt into her voice.

He waved, if you could call it that, then disappeared into the scrubby patch of overgrown crepe myrtle bushes that separated the two properties.

"Trevor James Murphy, you are in sooo much trouble." The squeaky voice rang from the house, and Erica looked up to see Elizabeth standing on the back deck, one hand planted on her hip, the other clutching the emergency binder.

Erica glanced at Trevor, who was totally unaffected by his

sister's scolding. "What do you say we make another break for it?" she asked.

Trevor only grinned, then grabbed two handfuls of her hair, holding them out like pigtails on either side of her head.

"Okay, we'll stay, but you have to deal with your sister. She scares me."

Trevor nodded, and Erica had to wonder how much he understood. She had a feeling it was the last sentence he was agreeing with.

"Thank you!" Shay forced herself to sound cheerful as she waved over her shoulder at Eve Dawson.

"Stay in touch," Eve called.

She pushed open the door to the real estate office and stepped out onto the street. Mission accomplished. Shay made an intentional show of dropping the key to Ralph Barnes's estate in her purse, took a deep breath and smoothed her sweater over her hips, wiping her sweaty palms in the process. She'd chosen the sleeveless red sweater on purpose. It was her "notice me" sweater.

Or, in her case, a moving bull's-eye.

The real estate office was on Main Street, and small town hustle and bustle hummed around her. She'd intentionally parked a few blocks away, to increase her chances of being seen. She'd even paired the red sweater with a pair of skinny jeans and sleek boots, and had tied her long curls up with a red scarf. The outfit was a far cry from the natural linen skirts and flat sandals she usually wore, and the change was almost exciting. In a horrifying, exposed kind of way.

Shay scanned the street. She recognized Mary Lou Jensen, the local florist, as she swept the sidewalk in front of her store. She gave a small wave before she realized that the elderly Mrs. Jensen likely didn't recognize her. Or even remember her, for that matter.

But that was beside the point.

She'd vowed to make herself as visible as possible, get the word out that she was back in town. And that meant she was going to have to completely change her ways. No more shrinking. No more invisible. No more fear. *Eye contact*, she told herself. *Speak up.*

"Hello, Mrs. Jensen!" she called. "How are you?"

The older woman paused from her chore, shielding her eyes from the sun. "Very well," she answered. "And you?"

"Wonderful," she lied, walking toward her. "You probably don't remember me. I'm Shay Chambers. I used to live here in Haddes."

Mrs. Jensen frowned, her face drawing into a road map of wrinkles, then brightened. "I do, indeed." She smiled and patted Shay's arm. "You're that little orphan girl that Jackson and Danielle raised."

Shay's stomach took a one-two punch and she felt blood rush to her face. *That little orphan girl.*

Yes, that was her.

Shay forced a smile and disentangled her arm. "It's wonderful to see you again," she said as she began walking away.

"You back to stay?" Mrs. Jensen called after her.

Smile, she commanded herself as she turned around. She shielded her eyes from the sun and tried to look nonchalant. "Yes, at least for a while. It's great to be back," she lied.

Mrs. Jensen shook her head and made a few brisk swipes with her broom. "This town ain't what it used to be," she muttered. "Kidnappings, robberies. I'd watch my back if I was you. And my pocketbook, too."

"I'll do that," Shay answered. She hesitated, but when the old lady continued to sweep without further comment, Shay decided she'd been dismissed.

Shay continued down the sidewalk, focusing on the sound of her boot heels as she caught a stray tear with her knuckle. She forced herself to slow down. She'd been running from the little orphan girl for twenty years. There was no running this time. This was where she needed to be.

In hell, in all its glory.

She considered stopping off for groceries, but decided to drive straight to the Barnes estate. If Bruce was watching her, she wanted him to get a good look at where she'd be staying. Shay forced herself to linger on the sidewalk, adjusting imaginary items in her purse, then headed to her car. As soon as she slipped into the driver seat, her fingers began to tremble.

She shoved the key into the ignition and forced herself to drive. Heading slowly down Main Street, she rolled down her window, ignoring the voice inside her that begged her to hide behind the tinted windows.

Not this time. Not anymore.

She checked her watch, surprised that only a few hours had passed. She'd accomplished a lot in a short time. Not only did she have a rent-free place to stay, but she'd landed a meager income, as well. When she'd asked about Ralph's place becoming available for rent, Eve had offered to hire her to clean out the remainder of his estate. It was perfect, really. She would no longer be a danger to Mattie, and the modest salary would at least keep her in peanut butter and jelly for a month or two.

Shay felt a shiver of apprehension as she pulled into the driveway of the Barnes house. It was welcoming, in a gothic, mysterious sort of way. But there was also something that made her want to turn away from it. She shoved the gearshift into park and switched off the ignition, staring up at the house. Shay closed her eyes and allowed the energy of the place to flow over her. Chaos filled her mind, a static that never fully came into focus. She recognized it instantly. That was how Ralph had been. A kind, benevolent soul who couldn't escape the chaos of his own mind to find his place in the world.

Shay felt her breath catch in her throat. That was her, as

well. An image of herself living in Ralph's estate popped into her head—aging and alone, eccentric and misunderstood. She swallowed hard and straightened. That was a fate she was willing to fight.

Shay slid from the car and marveled at the brush of denim against her thighs, the snug fit of the boots against her ankles. She'd dressed only to be noticed, but there was something empowering about the simple outfit. She recalled the way her skirt had tangled about her legs as she'd escaped Della's van, how the yards of fabric had threatened to snag on the underbrush and her bare feet had felt exposed in the flat sandals she wore. Today was different.

She took her time unlocking the hatchback and removing her suitcase. She'd left a few pieces of old furniture behind in Arizona, but most everything she owned had made the trip with her. And it all fit in the hatchback of a Toyota. As much as she hated to acknowledge negative thoughts, that realization was just downright depressing.

Shay slammed the hatchback and noticed that she'd parked with her license plate facing the road, something she wouldn't normally do. She shivered. This time she wanted to be found. It might be suicide, but at least Bruce wouldn't go through her friends to find her.

The door to the Barnes place swung open with a creak as she unlocked it, and Shay stepped inside. It was musty, but homey. She sat her suitcase down in the foyer and locked the door behind her. Box after box lined the walls and mounds of newspapers dotted the floor. She didn't know whether to laugh or cry. The job she'd taken was monumental.

It would also keep her employed for longer than she'd imagined. Whether that was good or bad remained to be seen.

Shay sat her suitcase down and decided to explore a relatively clear path to her left. It led to a kitchen that appeared to have been carved from the chaos, its floor clear and its counters scrubbed. A coffee maker was the only sign of domestic life in the room and sparkled like a beacon. Shay grinned, imagining Eve clearing a small place for the coffee maker and working her way outward. You couldn't argue with that logic.

She found filters and a small sack of coffee in the overhead cabinet and fumbled around with the unfamiliar machine until she had a pot brewing. Shay leaned against the counter and watched the dark liquid bleed into the carafe with a steamy hiss.

Fear began to seep into her, finding her in the stillness of the room. She gripped the counter to keep from running. She might be forced to run again at some point, but not today.

Today she was busy doing the only thing she knew to do—exposing herself to keep her friends safe.

Shay looked around at the disheveled old house that was now her home, however temporary. The mere sight of it would scare the daylights out of most people. It was marked by insanity and abandoned, cluttered with memories and ghosts that no one understood.

Well, she was hardly most people.

She crossed her arms and rubbed at the sudden chill bumps that dotted them.

Truth be told, they were a perfect match.

CHAPTER 9

Mattie picked up the phone. It was over. Time was up. There was only one thing left to do.

She had to call her parents.

There was no judging what her mother would say when she learned of the break-ins. She was as likely to say "Isn't that interesting, dear?" as she was to scream and faint dead away.

And her father, God love him, would be of no use. The man couldn't find an inroad to fatherhood if he had a map. It was simply unnatural to him. She could predict the scenario. He'd call endlessly to see what her plan of action was. He'd never offer to help, mind you; he just wanted to hear her plan repeated ad nauseam. And in the end, she'd handle the situation alone.

She sighed. No wonder she'd put this off for twenty-four hours.

She dialed her mother's work number. "Haddes Animal Clinic. Joan speaking."

"Mom, hi, it's me."

"Hi, sweetheart," she answered. "Are you okay?"

Mattie digested that question for a moment before answering. Had her mother already heard about the break-ins?

"Mattie?" The *tap-tap-tap* of fingernails against a computer keyboard filled the silence. "Are you still there?"

Mattie envisioned her mother at the front desk of the animal clinic, bifocals shoved to the tip of her nose, telephone clutched to her ear, and her focus on the computer monitor rather than her daughter. Her hair would be in a curly strawberry-blond halo, the ends sheared within an inch of her scalp to contain it, and she'd be wearing scrubs with little kittens dotting the aqua fabric.

Sometimes she imagined that she'd been switched at birth. Or, more accurately, she hoped this. But Mother Nature was a twisted soul.

"Yes, I'm still here."

"I heard there was a little problem down at the bookstore."

Good grief.

"Uh, yes. Someone broke in." *I must have been out when you rushed right over.* Weren't only children supposed to be the center of their parents' world?

More tapping on the keyboard ensued, and she heard a dog barking in the background. "That's terrible. What was taken?"

"Nothing, really. That's the odd thing—"

"By the way, I heard you got a new dog."

"Uh, yes." *To fend off my deranged stalker.*

"Eve brought him by yesterday evening for a dip."

Mattie took a deep breath and held it, trying not to be hurt by her mother's lack of concern. Her mother was simply a ditz. Mattie had come to that conclusion at the age of eight, when she'd started signing her own field-trip permission forms and reminding her mother to put gas in the station wagon.

"Listen, Mom, the duplex was broken into, as well."

"Goodness." There was a long pause, then the sound of a receipt being torn. "So I heard Jack Murphy is staying at your house," her mother commented as if they'd been discussing the issue—or anything coherent, for that matter.

"Yes. No." She shook the handset of the phone as if she could shake some sense into the disjointed conversation. Apparently Eve had dropped a few hints when she dropped off the dog. She put the receiver back to her ear. "He kept an eye on the house last night." She chewed her lip, trying to guess her mother's train of thought. "From his truck."

"So are you two seeing each other?"

"No."

"He's quite handsome, don't you think?"

"Yes, he is, but…" She chewed her lip some more, wondering whether to shut her mother up at the risk of opening a new dialogue about homosexuality. "Jack is gay."

"I heard that but it can't be true. I remember when he and

little Marsha King got caught by Reverend Walker on that hayride. Jack got caught with his hand up Marsha's skirt, as I recall."

Mattie felt faint at the image. "I don't remember that," she answered.

"Oh, of course you wouldn't. Your father and I tried to shield you from such things."

Oh, yeah, they only allowed her to witness the non-traumatic things. Like messy divorces.

"Marsha always was a little on the easy side. But I hardly think he'd have had his hand up her skirt if he was gay."

"Mom, I'm going to go now. I'll talk to you soon, okay?"

"Oh, okay. Let me know if you need anything."

Hope surged in Mattie's chest, but was shot down by her mother's next words.

"We just got in a new shipment of Iams."

Jack eyed the old Barnes house and decided that the brick exterior was the only reason it was still standing. He doubted the trim had seen a coat of paint in forty years. His gaze fell to the dinged-up old Toyota in the drive and he wondered if Shay had any intention of telling Mattie that she wouldn't be staying the night at her place. He took a sip of coffee and watched as she carried more belongings from her car. It was none of his business, but the fact that she would take off without a word left him a little irritated.

Not to mention suspicious.

Suspicion was exactly what motivated him to drop in on Eve after he'd seen Shay leave the real estate office. He'd pretended to ask a follow-up question about a commercial office for rent, but he'd actually learned everything he needed to know about Shay in five minutes. God bless small-town gossip.

What he didn't know was what the hell was going on with Shay. Or with Haddes, for that matter.

He glanced at the folded newspaper on the front seat of his truck and shook his head. A high-school photo of Christina Wilson was on the front page, the caption "Local teen missing" emblazoned below it. He'd read the article more than once, had memorized the details of her controversial disappearance. He picked it up again, staring at her photo. Damn. Things like this weren't supposed to happen in Haddes. And they weren't supposed to happen to good people.

Jack had been at the hospital the night Christina was born. Rand, Jack's best friend, had been as proud as any new father. He'd also been nineteen and scared half to death. And Jack, of course, had been totally out of his element. He'd congratulated his friend and then abruptly left for college the next day. When word reached him that Christina's mother had taken off a few months later, he hadn't known what to say to Rand. So he'd avoided the whole mess, which had been easy to do while he was away at school.

Familiar guilt settled on his shoulders. He and Rand had

once been inseparable, like brothers. But while he was at frat parties and football games, Rand had been at home caring for Christina on his own. And when they might have come together again years later, the differences in their lives had seemed too great to bridge. So they simply hadn't tried.

Jack had spent time with Christina on a couple of occasions over the years, once on her third birthday, and once when he'd been home for the Christmas holidays. She'd been about ten that last time, with bony knees and crooked teeth. It was hard to reconcile the image of the beautiful teenager in the photo with the child that had been conceived when he and Rand were practically kids themselves.

He wasn't a father, but he could imagine what hell Rand was going through right now.

Jack straightened as Shay made another appearance. She grabbed what appeared to be the last box from her car, then slammed the hatchback shut and locked it. She looked around, as though she expected someone to be watching, then hurried back into the house.

He didn't know why Shay had suddenly moved out of Mattie's house, but he knew one thing: if she wasn't staying at Mattie's tonight, he was.

The closet wasn't working. For one thing, her back was to the door while she tried to write. That wasn't good. In every scary movie she'd ever seen, the big dummy that got the ax had had his back turned. Mattie looked over her shoulder, re-assured herself that no one was about to attack, and tried again.

Freddie the Frog Prince and Lucy Lillipad Lou, the title read. The cursor blinked at the first line. She closed her eyes, leaning back in her office chair. The once crystal-clear vision of the book was now a blurry mess.

And the manuscript wasn't the only thing that was a mess. She'd actually scared herself by looking in the mirror earlier. The sun she'd gotten while washing her car had faded to a blotchy, peely mess. Dark circles lined her eyes and her hair looked as traumatized as she felt. Mattie hit the delete key on the keypad, then spread out her hand, staring at the ring she'd found. So much had happened since that day, it seemed weeks in the past. Mattie sighed. She vaguely remembered feeling attractive as she'd first slipped it on her finger; she'd felt on the verge of some unrealized change. Of course, that had had more to do with seeing Erica and Shay again than it had any sort of personal change.

Personal change wasn't her expertise. If you didn't count double breaking-and-entering.

She squinted at the cursor, willing the words to flow.

Jack got caught with his hand up Marsha's skirt....

Jeez. There it went, again. Her mother's comment kept popping, uninvited, into her brain. Not an image you wanted in your head while trying to write a children's book. She shook her head to clear the thought and tried again.

Mattie was determined to get her life back on track. The daily schedule that had once seemed monotonous now was a pot of gold at the end of the rainbow. And she was determined to reach it, starting with bringing five manuscript pages to her weekly writer's meeting. She thought of the disarray that stood between her and the ability to host the meeting at the bookstore as usual tomorrow night, and cringed. She could do it. One garbage bag at a time and one word at a time. Right now she was tackling the words, since being at the bookstore alone at dusk wasn't something she was ready to do. She would tackle that tomorrow when she had ten hours of daylight ahead of her. And lots of witnesses.

Speaking of which, where was Shay? She looked at her watch, frowning. She'd taken off without a word, leaving a note that she was running some errands, slipping out the side door while Mattie talked to Jack. Mattie hadn't heard from her all day, which had taken her by surprise. But then, Shay wasn't the most predictable of people. Her free-spirited nature was as maddening as it was charming.

Freddie the Frog Prince took off his crown while Lucy Lillipad Lou hopped right down…

Okay, that was better. It wasn't Seuss, but she was at least putting words on the screen. She reread the sentence, frowning. Of course, it would read a lot better if she wasn't picturing Freddie Prinze, Jr. and Lucy Liu. And it would be a whole lot better if she'd stop picturing Freddie the Frog Prince with his hand up Lucy Lillipad Lou's skirt. The temptation to put the children's book aside and write one of her short stories was overwhelming. She put her face in her hands and spun in the office chair, moaning.

The sound was instantly repeated behind her.

Mattie froze, listening. Another deep, blood-curdling moan sounded behind her. She turned slowly in her office chair. Buddy. The dog was watching her from the doorway with the intensity of a serial killer.

This was her protection?

"Hey there, Buddy," she called, using her best preschool-teacher voice. "Good dog."

He lowered his head and began to drool.

Maybe she could rub his ears like Shay, make friends. Yeah, that was the ticket. She leaned forward and extended her hand. "Come here, fella."

His lip curled and a throaty growl echoed through the closet. Mattie pulled her hand back and reached slowly for her cell phone, a fake smile plastered on her face. Dogs could smell fear, she reasoned. So maybe the stupid grin would off-set the obvious. She kept one eye on Buddy while she dialed Shay's cell-phone number.

"Hello," Shay answered. She sounded like a breathy sex-line operator.

"Hey," Mattie whispered, trying not to hyperventilate. "I'm in the closet." She hesitated, not sure where to begin her explanation.

"Mattie?"

"It's the dog." She spoke up, but kept her voice low and even. No sense making the big guy nervous.

"He has me trapped in the closet."

"Trapped?" Shay sounded skeptical. "You mean he's acting aggressive?"

Mattie checked Buddy's rabid expression before she remembered that eye contact was a sign of challenge. She averted her eyes, having no desire to become the alpha male, and stared at the boxes of her shoes instead. She actually had a fleeting moment of satisfaction, thinking how she'd re-boxed, re-stacked and arranged her shoes by color. Then she remembered why she couldn't currently leave the closet, and stole another peek at the dog out of the corner of her eye.

"Aggressive… Yep," she answered. "That's it."

"Put him on," Shay responded casually.

Mattie held the line. Put him on? My God, her friend really was nuts. And to think she'd wasted so much energy defending her over the years. "Huh?"

"Lay the phone near him," she commanded. "Gently."

Or she could stand back and toss it. Maybe bean him between the eyes with it. That could actually give her a head start. It sounded better than death by New Age stupidity.

"You're serious?"

"Yes, I am. And I'm coming right over."

That was good news, considering plan A. Mattie heard a car door slam and an engine crank over the cell connection. "Where are you?" she whispered.

"Five minutes away," Shay answered. "Now let me speak to Buddy."

Oh, good grief. Mattie took two baby steps toward the dog and bent her knees enough to slide the phone in his direction. The dog sniffed the phone, then cocked his head, listening. Mattie could hear the squeaky sound of Shay talking to Buddy over the phone.

She stared, dumbfounded, as Buddy began wagging his tail. When he plopped down on his stomach next to the phone, she began breathing normally again. But when he started licking her cell phone with his eyes half closed, she decided it was time for a new cell phone.

And maybe plan C.

Mattie spotted her winter coat hanging in the back of the closet, and gently removed it from its hanger. She slid it on over the knee-length football jersey she wore, reasoning that the calfskin leather was more easily replaced than her own skin. She found a pair of fuzzy gloves in one pocket and a ski cap in the other, and slid them on. Easing forward, she plastered on another fake smile, avoided meeting the dog's eyes, and squeezed her body sideways between Cujo and the door frame.

Sweet freedom.

Mattie grasped the doorknob to the closet door and swung it shut. It slammed with a *thud* and latched. She leaned against it and started laughing. When the doorbell chimed, she was still laughing. She pushed herself off from the closet door and walked to the foyer, peering through the peephole of her front door. Shay waited on the other side, still holding her cell phone to her ear.

Shay lowered the cell phone, confusion in her expression as she eyed the winter attire. "Are you okay?"

Mattie peeled off the ski cap and gloves, realizing she looked like a nut. She turned that thought over in her head. Maybe her mother wasn't the only ditz in the family, considering the current events in her life. "Yeah." She gestured over her shoulder. "I trapped Buddy in the closet."

Shay returned the cell phone to her ear. "I hear him. He sounds like he's eating something."

"He's licking my cell phone," Mattie explained. "I think he has a crush on you. Come on in."

"No, I don't think that's it." Shay looked as if she was seriously considering the idea as she shut and locked the door behind her. "We're more like kindred spirits."

"That's scary." Mattie shrugged out of the coat and dropped it over her sofa. She turned toward Shay, a lot more irritated than she had a right to be. "Where did you go? One minute you were here, and the next you'd disappeared."

"You didn't get my note?"

"Yeah, I did." Mattie tried not to sound hurt. "But you said you had an errand. That was hours ago. I was beginning to get worried."

"No reason for that." Shay waved her hand, but there was something that didn't ring true about the dismissive gesture.

Mattie eyed her, sensing something was up. "You look different," she commented. "Great, but different."

And she did. There was a confidence about Shay that Mattie hadn't seen in a really long time. Her cheeks were flushed, her hair pulled into a high curly ponytail and topped with a flowing red scarf.

"I found a place," Shay announced.

"A place?" Mattie parroted, a sinking feeling in the pit of her stomach.

"I'm going to be staying at the old Barnes place. Eve hired me to clear it out."

Mattie was shocked. It was juvenile of her, but she'd assumed that Shay would want to stay at her place again tonight. Without realizing it, she'd actually counted on Shay to be there. A kernel of disappointment lodged itself at the base of her throat and she swallowed back tears. Maybe she'd invested too much in the bond she'd felt between the two of them last night.

"Oh." Mattie worked to fix a supportive expression on her face. "That's great. So you're planning on staying in Haddes for a while?"

"I think I will." Shay looked pleased. "Now that this opportunity has come up."

Mattie bit her lip to keep from saying something she'd regret. Clearing out Ralph Barnes's smelly old estate was low on her list of things she wanted to do, if not dead last. It was hardly a golden opportunity. She couldn't imagine Shay trading the life she'd built for herself in Arizona to work in a place that smelled like sneakers and mold. But that was Shay's choice. And since when had Shay made logical choices? She'd broken free from the bond they all had shared a long time ago. Resentment threatened, and Mattie rubbed her chilled upper arms

"I'm glad for you," she said softly.

Shay looked uncomfortable, as if she sensed Mattie's disappointment and didn't quite know what to do about it. She fidgeted with the crystal around her neck, then lifted the cell phone to her ear again. She frowned. "It really does sound like he's eating something."

"No." Mattie shook her head. "He's just licking—" She pressed her hand to her chest. "He wouldn't!" Mattie ran toward the closet and flung open the door.

Buddy looked up, a black high-heeled boot dangling from his mouth.

"You…" Mattie flung the word at him as she marched, fearless, into the closet.

He dropped the boot, now a slobbery blob of rawhide.

Mattie felt tears spring to her eyes. She had never gotten to wear the boots and now it was too late. Her gaze swept over the rows of pristine cardboard boxes filled with pristine shoes and she had the undeniable urge to wear them all before it was too late.

She turned her frustration on Cujo. "That was a pair of four-hundred-dollar Via Spiga boots, you horrible beast." She picked up the boot, hugging the wet, shredded leather against her chest. "I surfed the Internet for days to find these wholesale and it took six weeks for them to be delivered." She growled at the dog between clenched teeth. "You are so outta here!"

"Mattie, don't…" Shay squeezed by her, kneeled beside Buddy. "He didn't mean to."

"Didn't mean to?" Mattie glanced at the dog, then the boot, then back at Shay. "He hates me."

"He does not hate you."

"Yes." To her horror, Mattie's lip began to tremble and tears threatened. "He does."

Shay stroked Buddy's fur. "He didn't mean to hurt you. I think he was just looking for some comfort." She tilted his head to look into his eyes. "I think he still feels a little lost." She glanced at Mattie over her shoulder. "He just needs to find his place in the world, that's all."

Mattie hesitated, sensing that the weight behind Shay's words included more than Buddy. She raised her chin, not yet ready to forgive either of them. "Take him," she sniffed. "Before one of us kills the other."

Shay stood, tugging on Buddy's collar until he stood beside her. He had the good grace to tuck his tail between his legs. "If that's what you want, I will."

"Well, he's obviously not happy here."

"I'm sure he's happy here," Shay whispered. "It's just probably best for him to go."

Mattie swallowed hard and fought the urge to dig deeper. Whatever was happening in Shay's life was obviously none of her business. And she'd made it clear that she wasn't staying. "Will you keep him, then?"

"No," Shay answered quickly, frowning as she shook her head. "I can't have a dog. But I'll find him a home for you."

Mattie wrapped her hands over her arms. *Maybe you can find me one, too,* she thought. Her own home had felt strange since the break-ins, like it no longer belonged to her. It felt soiled, tainted, as if someone else had worn her favorite housecoat and returned it unwashed.

"Are you sure?"

"Yes." Shay cast her gaze downward and began inching Buddy toward the door. "I'll take care of everything."

Mattie bit back the caustic comment that came to mind. Shay had never taken care of the details. That task had always been left to her or Della. Shay and Erica had always managed to shirk the mundane.

And yet she couldn't imagine anything more mundane than clearing stacks of yellowed newspapers from a deteriorating old house. Unless it was caring for a mentally unstable dog.

"Thanks." She shrugged, trying to distance herself from the rejection. "I'll bring you some dog food tomorrow."

"You don't have to—"

"No." The word sounded so harsh that Mattie tried to inject a cheerful note into her next comment. "I want to." She sighed. "Mom just got in a new shipment of Iams."

Della watched the little boy jump off the side of the pool for about the hundredth time. He was about Trevor's age and, with his wet hair plastered around his face, could have been her son. She fought a surge of homesickness, then glanced down at her cell phone, nestled between a melting margarita and her chaise longue. She'd promised Donald that she wouldn't call home while they were on the cruise, and Erica had sworn on all that was holy that she'd call if there was an emergency.

She sighed, and the nagging feeling she'd been fighting since leaving Haddes began nibbling at her subconscious again. There was something important that she'd left undone, she was certain of it. She'd long ago learned to listen to the nagging inner voice that said she'd forgotten something. It was always right. Sometimes it was as insignificant as her deodorant, but on other occasions it was major—the eye of the stove left on, or almost forgetting Trevor at the baby-sitter's. She adjusted her bathing suit and stretched out on the lounge. It would come to her eventually. She slid on her sunglasses and laid her head back, going through her mental checklist: she'd paid the neighbor kid to feed the hamsters and had boarded the dog at the veterinarian's; she'd paid the bills that would come due in advance, and had rescheduled her clients at the salon. So what was it? She'd alerted the parents of Andy's teenage friends to help Erica keep an eye on him, and had remembered to pack Elizabeth's soccer uniform....

But there was still something.

Della gave up on the checklist and fumbled around at the side of her lounge chair until she found her margarita. She took a long sip and glanced beside her at Donald. The trip was the most—well, okay, the *only*—romantic gesture he'd ever made, yet she found herself annoyed with him. Of course, his appearance at the moment wasn't exactly appealing. He was sleeping on his back in a chaise longue identical to hers, his mouth slightly parted. His chest was becoming an alarming shade of red and his feet were pointed upward in a duck-like posture.

But she loved him.

So why was she still thinking about that one fleeting moment when she'd thought they were over, that moment that had offered her freedom, a chance to start fresh?

She should be ashamed of herself for even letting the odd-ball thought resurface. She loved Donald and their life together. But the idea of starting over had tripped something in her psyche that wouldn't seem to fade away.

Donald made a startled, snuffling noise and Della jostled his arm. It had become a poolside ritual. She had to poke him every five minutes or so to keep his snoring from becoming embarrassingly loud. He cracked an eye open, and smiled a lazy, sensual smile that made Della's heart do a little teenage flip-flop. God, he was still so handsome.

"Can you ask the waiter to get me a beer?" he muttered.

Then it hit her.

She'd done everything necessary to get them on this trip. All he'd done was have a grand idea. Well, grand ideas weren't worth a piss unless you put some muscle behind them.

When he'd told her about the trip, she'd been consumed with guilt for suspecting him of having an affair. So consumed, in fact, that she hadn't pointed out the fact that no real arrangements had been made for the children. She hadn't wanted to ruin the moment, so she'd tried not to be annoyed that he hadn't thought to drag the children's suitcases from the attic. Of course someone had to prepare the laundry that needed to be put inside the blasted suitcases. And cancel the bug man. Della felt her face flush. He hadn't even thought to put gas in the car for the trip to the airport.

Yet this had to be a true milestone. He wanted *her* to ask the waiter to bring *him* a beer.

In her next life she was going to be a man. And then she could have a grand idea, do nothing but board an airplane, and then be rewarded for her efforts with hotel sex.

Life was so unfair.

CHAPTER 10

Jack watched Shay tug a big-ass dog to her Toyota, then coax him inside. She jumped behind the wheel and took off so fast that he doubted he could tail her. But this time he wasn't going to try. All he cared about was that she wasn't planning on staying the night at Mattie's. And that he was.

The problem was how to break the news to Mattie.

He glanced around, as if the answer to the puzzle of all that had happened would be in plain sight. It was too easy to look around Haddes and decide that whatever or whoever had committed the break-ins was long gone. The late afternoon was picturesque. The sun was setting, and the evening breeze had picked up, mixing the aroma of azalea blossoms and freshly cut grass. A baseball game could be heard in the distance, the lights from the field glowing.

Yet every instinct he possessed told him not to let his guard down, and not to let Mattie spend the night alone. He shifted against the hard seat of his truck, then tugged the keys from the ignition as he made his decision.

He would be a hell of a lot more comfortable on her sofa. Closer, too. Which would make him immensely happy if she either stopped parading around half dressed, or stopped treating him like a brother.

If Haddes had an honest-to-goodness hotel where no one knew who she was, Mattie would have already checked into it. Fear and pride were at war, and so far pride was winning. But it was hanging by a thread. *Chicken, chicken*. She'd done everything she knew to try to get comfortable in her own home since Shay and Cujo had pulled away. She'd tuned her television to a Mayberry marathon on some obscure cable station, turning up the volume to a cheerful roar. She lit a vanilla candle, zapped a bag of microwave popcorn and warmed some apple cider on the stove. It was very Norman Rockwell. If it weren't eighty degrees outside, she'd have built a fire in the fireplace.

Her father had called twice in the last hour—having heard about "the trouble," as he referred to it. He hadn't offered to come over, of course, and for a moment she'd actually been tempted to ask him. If the intruder returned, her father could always bore him to death with questions.

So what is your plan, Mat? Where will you take it from here? Truth was, she had no clue where to take it from here, and her only plan was to stay up all night and watch *The Andy Griffith Show*.

The doorbell rang, and it occurred to Mattie that perhaps she'd telepathically summoned her father. She sidled up to the door as if she were being watched, though she'd already tugged every curtain and blind in the house into place, even stuffing a few loose corners with cotton balls, just in case. She rose on her tiptoes and looked through the crack.

Jack. Her heart did a little happy dance. He was like a walking, talking reprieve from her fear. His presence made her feel safe. She looked down at the yoga pants and tank top she wore, and then decided it didn't matter. She was going to stop second-guessing and accept the fact that Jack was gay. At least she didn't have to run and put on a bra, or worry that she wasn't wearing makeup or that her ponytail was crooked. She could just *be*.

She unfastened the chain and opened the door, feeling herself grin from ear to ear. "Hey, there."

"Hey." He frowned, looking her up and down. "Did you check to see who was at the door?"

"Of course." She gestured for him to come in. "I'm glad to see you," she said honestly.

"Good." He dropped a duffel bag at his feet, then shut and locked the door behind him. "Because I'm staying."

"Oh." She barely kept from cheering. Shay's rejection still stung and her parents' oblivion left her cold. The fact that Jack cared enough to show up again after a sleepless night was staggering. She bit her lip when gratitude threatened to turn to tears. "You would do that for me?"

"I would." He looked her up and down for a second time, then shook his head slightly as if puzzled. "And I'm going to."

"Thank you." She hugged him, but when Jack failed to hug her back, she wondered if she'd overstepped some boundary. Just as she was about to pull away, he put his arms around her and drew her against him, his hand pressing between her shoulder blades until she felt her breasts flatten against his chest. She felt a little heady, and had to keep herself from forgetting certain unalterable facts about his sexuality. She blinked, smiling as she pulled away. "I know I should try to talk you out of it, but honestly, I'd love it if you'd stay with me tonight."

"Sure." Jack still held her by her upper arms, and his thumbs rubbed slow circles over the delicate skin.

The microwave beeped and Mattie took a step toward the kitchen. "I just popped some popcorn. Want some?"

Jack ran his hand through his hair, blew out a pent-up breath and stared at her for a moment before answering. "Yeah, why not?"

He plopped down in a kitchen chair and watched as Mattie ripped open the bag and poured the popcorn into a bowl. She retrieved two mugs from the pantry and poured herself and Jack a mug of cider. She slid his toward him, then sat down at the table.

"Thanks." He grinned, glancing around. "It's sort of, well, Christmasy in here."

Mattie laughed, pulling her legs to sit criss-cross in the chair. "I know. It's stupid, isn't it? But I was scared. I was trying to think of anything that would make it feel homey in here again."

"You don't have to be scared." He ignored the popcorn and cider, leaning his elbows on the table. His eyes met hers. "I'm not going to let anything happen to you."

The intensity of his gaze made Mattie's pulse quicken, and mentally she dashed around, looking for a topic that didn't make her wish Jack was available. "Hey, speaking of homes, did you and your partner ever find a house?"

He let the silence lapse for a few pauses, then narrowed his eyes and leaned back in his chair, crossing his arms over his chest. "Why do you keep putting it that way?"

"I'm sorry." Mattie bit her lip. She was pretty sure she'd made some politically incorrect reference. But for the life of her, couldn't put her finger on it. "Put what that way?" she ventured.

"'You and your partner…' The way you say it makes it sound like we're a gay couple."

"But you are." She pressed her knuckle to her mouth, realizing the first thing that had popped into her mind had just popped out of her mouth.

"Mattie…"

She stared at the tabletop, then the cider, her mind in a frantic rewind.

"Mattie, you know I'm not gay," he said slowly and evenly, as if speaking to someone who wasn't very bright. "You've known me practically my whole life."

Mattie stared at the popcorn

"Mattie, look at me."

She tilted her chin slightly but couldn't quite meet his eyes.

"You're kidding me, right?" He shifted uncomfortably. "Why on earth would you think I was gay?"

"Uh…" The word left her mouth in a sort of guttural groan, like a calf separated from the herd. "Uh…" There went that awful sound again. She was capable of actual words. She was a college graduate. *Magna cum laude*, in fact. Sooner or later she'd manage a word.

"Did—did you think I was gay this entire time?" His eyes narrowed. "Della did fill you in on why I looked the way I did that night at the bowling alley. *Didn't she?*"

"You mean Kimee." It was more of a statement than a question.

"Yes."

"No, she didn't." Mattie finally met his gaze, looking into eyes that were still that gorgeous shade of flint gray, and her skin tingled. But she could still see a trace of bronzer at the corners of his eyes. Hey, her assumptions would hold up in court.

Jack's face turned an odd shade of red. He clenched his fists and glanced around as though he wanted to upturn the kitchen table, but instead started laughing.

Mattie sat frozen, embarrassed, mortified. Excited.

Jack leaned closer until his mouth was near her ear. When he spoke, his voice was low, nearly a whisper. "Della told Kimee that I needed to get a head shot made for the chamber of commerce," he said, as though he was telling her a secret.

Little shivers of delight scattered across her arms. He was simply explaining the situation, but his method of delivery had her mind headed straight for the bedroom.

"She, uhm, went a little nuts." Jack chuckled, and the vibration sent chills down the length of her body.

He was so close that Mattie was afraid to look up at him. And she got the distinct feeling that he was doing it on purpose. "She wanted to fix you up for the photographer?" she asked, still looking down and trying for all the world to seem unaffected.

"Uh-huh." He leaned back, then lifted a strand of hair that had escaped from her ponytail. "And when I refused, she cried. That's when I gave in. I'm a sucker for a woman in distress."

"Oh." Mattie nodded, thinking she was feeling a little distressed.

"You ought to be ashamed of yourself."

"I'm…sorry?" she offered, completely absorbed by the fact that he held a strand of her hair.

He released the tendril, then grabbed the edge of her chair and, in one swift motion, faced it toward his. "What am I going to do with you?" he asked.

"I—"

Jack grabbed her knees, his hands strong and warm beneath the thin fabric of her yoga slacks, and uncrossed her legs as if unwrapping a present. In an instant, he'd slid her across the wooden surface of the chair and had draped her legs over his thighs. Her hips bumped his and her eyes closed as she felt his arousal. She was very close to fainting.

Then he kissed her, and it was twenty years' worth of fantasy exploding in their contact. Every sexual nerve ending in her body jumped as his tongue slid into her mouth and found hers. He didn't wait for her to respond; he expected it.

And she did respond. It was as if she were in a dream, alive in someone else's body, as she pressed her hips against his, desperate to feel him against her again. His hands found her breasts through the thin fabric of her shirt and her nipples puckered as if they'd been waiting for his touch. She felt his thighs tighten beneath hers, and he moaned into her mouth.

"I've been wanting to do that since I walked in the door tonight and saw what you were wearing."

Oh. Wait. What she was wearing? Her mind withdrew slightly from the haze of lust and she looked down at herself. Like being dashed with cold water, she realized how horrible she must look. Before it hadn't mattered, but now... Oh

God. Had she even shaved her armpits this morning, let alone her legs? Face to face, he must have seen her crow's feet, the dark circles under her eyes. She leaned back, wondering how to disentangle herself from Jack without his getting an even better look. She couldn't do this.

Even under perfect conditions, she couldn't handle a man like Jack. And this… This wasn't what she had scripted twenty years ago. In her fantasy, everything had been perfect. Her mind reeled. Jack *had* been perfect just now. But she wasn't. In her fantasy, she was supposed to be just as perfect as Jack.

She would never have paraded around braless if she'd known he was straight. Oh… And this morning she'd answered the door straight out of bed. She'd had on that horrible football jersey and had had coffee breath….

"And this morning," he whispered. "That thing you were wearing kept inching up. I wanted to touch you, Mattie." He tugged the strap of her tank down, threatening to expose her breast. "You don't know how much I wanted to do this."

"Oh…" One minute she was about to die and go to heaven and the next she'd managed to disentangle herself from Jack and was standing beside him, adjusting her clothing. "Jack." She shook her head. "You are not gay."

He was not only straight, he was crazy. Crazy if he'd wanted her this morning looking like she'd looked.

He seemed momentarily confused, then leaned back in the chair, his stare intense. "I know that."

"And we're…" She shook her finger as if she were scolding him, which only made him smile. "This is way different. Tonight…"

He stood and walked toward her. Mattie took a step backward, still holding her hand up. This wasn't her. This couldn't be happening. This wasn't the sentimental, romantic seduction she'd written about twenty years ago. This was hot. This was like an encounter in one of her short stories. This wasn't her.

Or was it?

The thought made her freeze, and Jack caught up with her in that span of time. And then he was so close that his thighs brushed hers. She still didn't move. He lowered his head and took her mouth, tugging at her lower lip with his teeth. She still didn't move.

"Tonight I want to keep you safe," he whispered. "But when you're ready, I want *you*. Over and over again."

Erica froze, egg beater in her hand, as another wave of nausea hit. Elizabeth had informed her, at the ungodly hour of six a.m., that Saturday was bacon-and-egg day. So she'd rolled her butt out of bed, wrapped up in her mother's old housecoat, and had staggered into the kitchen, determined to find at least one domestic, maternal gene somewhere in her body.

"*Can we fix it? Yes, we can!*" a cartoon voice taunted from the family room. Erica could see Trevor's silhouette as he sat cross-legged in front of the television, mesmerized by a talking tractor. Or was that technically a front-end loader? She squinted to get a better look when the talking tractor did a ballet move on a mound of dirt. Whatever happened to Mr. Green Jeans and Captain Kangaroo, anyway?

She thought of Andy, sound asleep in her brother's old bedroom upstairs, and had a definite moment of teenager envy. Erica was accustomed to early mornings and late nights. War was hell as an office environment. But since the pregnancy had kicked in, she found she'd rather sleep in than face the inevitable morning sickness. She lifted the stainless steel mixing bowl and the eggs sloshed in the bottom, their yolks staring up at her like slimy, lifeless eyeballs. Oh God. She swallowed hard. It was just a matter of time. The only question left was when and where she was going to barf.

"Aunt Erica, are you okay?"

She closed her eyes so that she was no longer looking at the eggs, fixing a smile on her face before she glanced over her shoulder at Elizabeth.

"Sure," Erica replied. Elizabeth still looked skeptical, so she tried again. "So how do you like your eggs cooked?"

She brightened. "Poached."

Oh, great.

"You know, the kind that when you pop the white bubbly part it squirts out the sticky yellow juice and—"

"Yeah, I got it—poached," Erica interrupted, focusing on

the fact that Della's daughter had started calling her Aunt Erica. It had a nice ring to it, and made motherhood seem a little less abstract. And she could use all the validation she could get.

But the kid still wasn't going to get a poached egg.

Erica turned her back on the bowl of eggs and headed for the coffeemaker, which had finally hissed the last of its liquid into the carafe. She found the largest mug in the cabinet and filled it to the brim. Surely this would work some kind of morning sickness voodoo. She inhaled the steam that rolled off the coffee and knew instantly that she'd made a terrible mistake.

Everything about the brew was normal, but her gut roiled and the back of her throat contracted, rejecting the smell for some reason known only to her pregnant body.

"Oh," she muttered, dumping the cup in the sink with a *thud*. She gestured illegibly to Elizabeth. "Wait here," she squeaked before she ran to the hall bathroom.

And puked her guts out.

"Aunt Erica!"

In the haze of her sickness, she heard Elizabeth call her name more than once. But every time she tried to answer, another wave would hit and the words would be lost in the depths of the toilet bowl. She heard the unmistakable *thump*, *thump*, *thump* of Elizabeth dashing up and down the hall, but couldn't find an opening to reassure her that everything was okay.

She finally laid her forehead on the toilet seat, which normally would be gross, and wondered if other pregnant women suffered to this degree. Surely not. Mankind would have died out millions of years ago. Erica gave one final heave, flushed and collapsed on a fuzzy white bath mat. She tugged a dry towel from the edge of the tub and laid it over her shaky shoulders. It was seven in the morning and she felt as if she'd run a marathon. How was she ever going to survive another eight months of this?

She closed her eyes, content in the simple fact that she was no longer throwing up. And then she welcomed the sweet darkness.

"You'd love Indiana, Erica."

John pulled her against him in the darkness and she felt the temptation in his words as surely as she felt the temptation of his hips against her backside. They'd just made love, and yet she wanted him again. The man was like a drug.

He nuzzled the back of her neck. "Let's go for it. The picket fence and whole nine yards. Let's get the hell out of this desert and make a life."

"You know I don't do picket fences." Erica smiled, teasing, but beside her John went still.

The tension continued for a few beats, then John began stroking her arm in slow, distracting circles. "What's so terrible about picket fences?" he asked.

Erica closed her eyes, willing her old determination to return. She'd fought to escape small-town life, to make something for her-

self that was more than ordinary—that meant something. No matter how much she cared for John, it would be insane to give up all she'd worked for.

"They fence you in," she finally answered.

"But they fence out the bad stuff," he countered.

"Hmm... I'm pretty sure terrorists have figured out a way around them," she teased.

"I'm serious," John whispered.

The smile left her and she twisted in his arms to face him. "So am I," she answered.

"I have a feeling," John whispered, "that it's now or never. If I don't get out of here soon, I may never get out of here."

"Erica?"

"*John!*" The voice inside her head pleaded for him to stay as the darkness faded. "*John, don't leave me! I've changed my mind, I've changed...*"

"Oh my God!" The shrill voice echoed off the tile walls of the bathroom and penetrated her skull.

"Is she okay?" Another voice followed, softer, but equally startling.

"Oh. What?" Erica struggled to sit up, her body stiff from lying on the bathroom floor, reality replacing her dream in a painful rush. "Me? I'm okay..." She squinted at the figure dashing toward her. "Mattie?"

"Yes, I'm here." Mattie dropped to her knees on the bath mat, her face drawn into a pinched frown. "What happened?"

"I, uh…" She wiped her damp eyes, realizing she'd only been dreaming. "I wasn't feeling good."

"You're just sick?" a masculine voice asked.

Just? Erica blinked against the glaring light from the overhead fixture. Shay and Jack stood in the bathroom doorway, looking at her as though they'd seen a ghost. Erica caught a glimpse of Elizabeth peeking around Shay's hip, the child's tear-streaked face swollen and red. She blinked, getting a better look. Elizabeth was clutching the emergency binder. Oh, Jeez.

"You're not hurt, then?" Jack asked.

"No." She sat the rest of the way up. "I'm sorry. I was sick to my stomach. I lay down…" She glanced at the bath mat, embarrassment flowing over her. "Maybe I drifted off."

A thousand what-ifs hit her at once. What if she'd left the bacon on the stove? What if Elizabeth had panicked? What if— The last what-if made her blood freeze in her veins.

"Trevor!" she gasped.

"He's still watching television," Shay reassured her.

Elizabeth inched farther around Shay's skirt, eyeing Erica as if she'd been betrayed. "I thought you were dead." Her eyes held blatant accusation, as if Erica would have died intentionally just to frighten her. "I activ—" She hiccuped on a small sob. "I activated the emergency call tr-tree."

Erica looked again at the white-knuckle grip the kid had on the binder and knew she was about to lose it again. She looked up at Jack, mentally pleading.

He nodded, putting his arm around Elizabeth. "Everything's okay now. Hey, why don't we go check on the Terrier?" he urged, easing her down the hall.

With Elizabeth safely out of the picture, grief and the sheer impossibility of her situation hit Erica all at once. Her parents were gone. John was dead. She would be raising this child alone. The emotions balled in the back of her throat, then ripped from her in a feral cry. She whirled toward the toilet and lost it again, this time in front of her friends. She flushed without looking up, the embarrassment her final defeat. Then the tears started again, falling against the Tidy-Bowl-blue surface with a steady rhythm.

"I'm pregnant," she whispered.

The words were too soft, lost in the confusion of her tears. Another sob tore from her, and she barely recognized the sound as her own. She couldn't face this alone.

She needed her friends.

Erica lifted her head. "I'm pregnant," she whispered, this time loud enough to be heard. She felt the tears go cold against her cheeks and knew she must look desperate. And she was. Erica met Mattie's eyes briefly, then Shay's. There was no judgment, only concern. And a lot of shock. She shook her head. "I don't know what I'm going to do."

"Oh, Erica…" Mattie inched a little closer and looped her arm over Erica's shoulders.

Shay grabbed a washcloth from the counter, dampened it and kneeled to press it against Erica's forehead.

Shay and Mattie looked at each other, smiled fragile smiles, then looked back at Erica. "Congratulations," they said in unison.

"No." Erica ran the washcloth over her face. "It's not like that. The baby's father is dead."

Mattie and Shay's expressions both fell.

"How?" Mattie asked. "What happened?"

"He was a journalist." Erica brushed the tears from her cheeks. "He was covering a story on a humanitarian relief effort in Afghanistan. The lead supply truck tipped a land mine." She lifted her injured arm. "The same explosion that injured me killed him and part of the humanitarian crew he was with." She blinked. "John. His name was John."

When Shay nudged Mattie aside and drew Erica into a hug, the tears started again. She sank into her friend's familiar embrace, limp and exhausted.

She lifted her head from Shay's shoulder a few minutes later. "Damn, I hate crying."

"I'm so sorry, honey," Shay whispered.

"Me, too." Mattie reached over them to pull a wad of toilet paper from the roll. She handed it to Erica. "Blow."

Erica blew her nose, thinking it felt as swollen and round as a red rubber ball. She dragged more tissue from the roll and was blotting her eyes when Jack returned.

"Is everything okay?" he asked, looking hesitant.

She had to admire him, since Erica was pretty sure that three crying nearly-middle-aged women in a bathroom wasn't the most welcome sight to a man. She finished blotting, then smiled up at him. "I'm almost forty, pregnant, relatively unemployed and single," she answered.

His only reaction was that his eyebrows shot up. "Wow," he said.

"Oh, and I lost Trevor yesterday and pretty much passed out in the middle of making breakfast this morning. It's a little late to learn that I'm really bad at this parenting thing, don't you think?"

He winked at her. "Once when I was watching Trevor, he ate cat food and shoved a bead up his nose."

She laughed, feeling better. "You'd better watch it. I'm pretty sure Elizabeth has the Child Abuse Hotline number in that binder."

"Speaking of which," Jack said, a serious expression on his face, "I'm last on the emergency call list behind Mattie and Shay. What's with that?"

"Maybe the cat food incident?" Shay offered with a rare smile.

"That can't be it." He shook his head. "I never told Della about that one."

"Uncle Jaaack!" Elizabeth screeched.

The foursome exchanged glances, then hopped to their

feet. Erica was shaky, but managed to make it out of the bathroom before Mattie and Shay. She trailed Jack to the family room, where Elizabeth was standing.

"He's gone," she announced with more irritation than panic. "I went to the bathroom." Elizabeth screwed up her mouth. "I had to go to the one downstairs because y'all were in the other one."

Erica began frantically glancing around, knowing the *he* meant Trevor and the *gone* was bad news.

"And?" said Jack.

"And when I got back…" Elizabeth shrugged. "He was gone."

"That's how it was last night," Erica added, her voice tight. "One minute he was here and the next he was gone."

"Where did he go? Yesterday, I mean."

"Oh, to the neighbor's house." Erica snapped her fingers. "Yes, the neighbor's!"

They all headed for the back door at once. He has to be there, Erica thought. Calm. Stay calm. He does this all the time, she reassured herself. It's only been a few minutes. But the thought of the neighbor's condemnation still rang in her ears, as did his warning about the creek.

She was out the door behind Jack and literally flew down the back stairs. They all started calling Trevor's name, though she'd learned from experience that he wasn't about to answer. Her mother's old housecoat bunched around her knees, and she hiked it up as she jogged toward the neighbor's. She found a tangled opening in the wooded area that separated the two properties, and fought her way through, feeling disoriented as she came out the other side.

Erica had seen little more than glimpses of the neighbor's house since she'd been home, and was surprised by the changes that had been made. It had obviously been remodeled and would have been beautiful if it hadn't looked so neglected. The grass was long, weeds popping up in undignified clumps here and there. A small blue car sat in the driveway, with an airbrushed tag on the front that read: *Christina*. An SUV was parked in the grass, with deep ruts indicating that someone had driven around the car rather than move it. Bits of trash still clung to the grass where the neighbor had emptied the garbage can. All the lights appeared to be off, which made a shiver of fear run down her spine.

Why Trevor was so determined to come over here was beyond her. "Trevor!" she yelled.

Jack was right behind her. He stopped, surveying the area as she'd done. He frowned. "Who lives here?" he asked.

"I don't know. We met yesterday when Trevor came over, but we didn't introduce ourselves. It says Wilson on the mailbox."

Jack jogged to the door and pounded on it.

A few seconds later the door flew open and the neighbor stepped out on the stoop. His jaw was unshaven and his dark hair disheveled. He looked like he'd been on a week-long drinking binge, and, worse, Trevor wasn't with him.

Then again, that might be good news.

"Rand," Jack said, his voice low.

Erica went still. Rand Wilson? She realized, then, why the neighbor had looked familiar. Rand and Jack had been ahead of her in school, but she should have realized who he was. But the Rand she recalled had been carefree, a prankster. The scowling, unkempt man who'd behaved so strangely was far from the handsome young basketball player she remembered.

"Jack," Rand responded. He extended his hand. "How are you?"

"Good." The two men shook hands. "I didn't know you lived here," Jack said.

"About three years now."

"I just learned about Christina. Man, I'm so sorry. I wish I'd known sooner—"

"Don't." The other man held up his hand, then shook his head. "You don't need to apologize."

"I'd like to help," Jack said.

Erica glanced at the car with the personalized tag. She had the distinct feeling that something important was at stake, but she had no idea what they were talking about. And that wasn't her concern at the moment. Trevor was. She was growing more frustrated by the minute. She didn't know whether to stay and listen to them exchange pleasantries or start searching the property. She knew firsthand how fast Trevor could travel. And time was ticking.

She jogged to the stoop and took matters into her own hands, trying not to be daunted by the fact that she was still in her mother's old housecoat and had just pulled her head from the toilet.

"Hi. Listen, the little boy who came to your house yesterday. He's missing again."

Jack nodded. "My nephew. Della's youngest."

Rand straightened. "That was Della's son? I had no idea."

"Yeah," Erica said, preventing them from taking another stroll down memory lane. "He's taken off again and we were hoping he showed up here. Have you seen him?"

"No. But I'll help you look. He was in the back yesterday."

Erica nodded, then noticed Mattie and Shay making their way through the wooded area. She frowned. "Where's Elizabeth?" she called.

"With Andy," Mattie answered. "Back at the house."

That was a relief. At least two out of three were accounted for. "Help me check this way!" she yelled, waving to Mattie and Shay as she headed for the backyard.

As soon as she rounded the corner of the house, she heard an odd, rhythmic sound: *eek, eek, eek, eek.* She glanced around, searching for the source, until her eyes fell on an old trampoline surrounded by black netting. She squinted to see inside the tattered netting. Sure enough, Trevor was in the center. He was attempting to jump, but his feet were so firmly planted that he was only making the trampoline sway. Erica covered her mouth with her hands, unsure whether to laugh or cry.

Mattie and Shay came to a breathless stop beside her, and Erica pointed to the trampoline.

Mattie breathed a sigh of relief, then laughed. "The little guy was on the trampoline all along."

"Thank heavens," Shay added.

Jack and Rand joined them. "Did you find him?" Jack asked.

Mattie smiled, then pointed again. "Right there. On the trampoline."

One minute all eyes were on Trevor, and the next they were on Rand. He snatched Mattie's hand and spun her around.

"Where did you get that?" he snapped. Rand's words ripped through the moment like a knife. He jerked Mattie's hand toward him, and she gasped.

"Back off." Jack stepped in, putting himself between Mattie and Rand. "What's going on?"

Rand's face was drawn in an expression of fury, his eyes glowing like a wolf's. He examined Mattie's right hand, then stared at Jack. "This is Christina's ring."

CHAPTER 11

"What?" Jack wrapped his hand over Rand's and freed Mattie's wrist. "That can't be right. There's probably a million rings like—"

"No, there aren't." Rand pointed. "I had that one made for her on her sixteenth birthday." His voice was ice cold. "There's not another one like it on the face of the earth. Now tell me where you got it."

"I found it." Mattie's hand trembled as she worked the ring from her finger and offered it on her open palm to Rand. "In the back seat of my car."

Rand took the ring, emotion etched on his face as he slid it onto the tip of his pinkie. He finally looked up, his eyes damp. "In the back seat of your car?" The words were laced with disbelief.

Mattie nodded. "I just bought the car." She looked to Jack for support. "I don't understand."

"The police cruiser?" Jack asked, his expression stony.

"Yes. The day you saw me washing it."

"You drive a police cruiser?" Rand asked.

"A retired one." Mattie shook her head. "I bought it at auction. The city just replaced a few of them with new vehicles."

Rand straightened and a muscle in his jaw jumped. "Do you know what officer your vehicle was assigned to?"

Mattie nodded. "Mac McKay."

All eyes went to Shay, and she felt the blood drain from her face. "Oh God," she whispered.

"What?" Rand demanded, glancing between them.

"You probably don't remember me." Shay took a deep breath and tried to still the trembling that was weakening her legs. "I'm Shay Chambers. I was married to Mac a long time ago."

Of course that was only half the story, and it must have showed in her face.

"There's more?" Rand asked, his eyes narrowed.

"I haven't been in touch with Mac in almost sixteen years." Shay's hand instinctively went to her crystal. "But when I was married to him, he was a violent man." She took a deep breath, trying to allow the memories to surface without sinking herself. "Small-town divorce is never easy, but my accusations against him made it harder for both of us, but especially me. I left town rather than press charges. It was just easier at the time."

"I'm sorry." Rand's emotions practically flowed beneath the surface of his calm as he looked at Mattie, then Erica and Shay. "I do remember you now. You were all friends with Jack's little sister Della."

Erica stepped forward. "I'm sorry I didn't recognize you yesterday, Rand. It's been a long time." It was obvious Erica sensed something was wrong, since she appeared to be using uncharacteristic tact. "I'm afraid I don't fully understand what's going on here."

"My daughter, Christina, is missing." Rand paused, coughing, and Shay suspected that it was to cover the pain. "She's eighteen. She's been gone for just over a week now."

"I'm sorry," Erica's expression registered shock, then compassion. "What do the authorities say?"

Rand threw back his head and laughed, then stopped abruptly, as if his emotions had carried him up a crest and back down. He wiped away tears that had nothing to do with the laughter. "They say she's a runaway."

"The paper said there was a note," Jack said.

"Yeah, there's a note. And it doesn't prove a damn thing except that Christina was forced to write it." He stared at the ring as he spoke. "My daughter isn't a straight-A student, but she writes. Poetry, music. The note was a joke. It was mechanical, simple. Christina was more eloquent at six years old. And we've had our problems, but if she wanted to leave, she'd tell me straight out. She wouldn't leave a note."

"How can you be certain?" Jack asked.

Rand shifted, his eyes suddenly tired. "Christina's mother left a note when she ran out on us." He straightened. "She always said that her mother took the coward's way out. So Christina wouldn't just leave a note. No way would she do that to me a second time."

Jack clamped his hand over Rand's shoulder. "I told you before that I want to help. I meant it."

"Then help me get to the bottom of this." He looked in Jack's eyes, imploring him. "No wonder the police won't help me. They know something. Mac McKay knows something. Or they're covering for him."

Shay tried to stay silent, but couldn't. "You can't go to the authorities about the ring." She wrung her hands. "You don't know Mac. He's violent. If he is involved somehow, you need to be careful."

Rand went still, his gaze knowing. "What used to set him off?"

Shay felt her breath catch in her throat. No one had ever asked her that before. In fact, she wasn't sure she'd ever allowed herself to analyze it. But she knew. The answer had popped in her head the instant Rand had asked.

"It was when I...knew things," she answered.

Mattie moved beside her, touching her arm. "You mean your abilities?"

"Yes," she answered. "But not just that. Mac would become enraged if he thought I knew more than he did where *anything* was concerned."

"Abilities?" Rand asked, echoing Mattie.

"I have an intuition." Shay recited the answer she'd formed a long time ago. "It borders on psychic ability."

Rand nodded, not questioning. "So the son of a bitch hurt you because you were smarter than he was?"

Shay nodded, a dam of tears building behind her eyes. Rand's anger toward Mac wasn't for her defense alone, but it felt good. Mac had never had to pay for what he'd done to her, or to their child when she'd miscarried. Shay had convinced herself that the punishment that waited for Mac in the afterlife was enough. But Rand's rage called to her own, summoned it. And to her surprise, she found the anger was still right below the surface, right where she'd left it.

"Your abilities…" Rand stepped forward, his face drawn. "Could you use them to help me find Christina?"

Shay's first instinct was to withdraw, to run from what she might see. But she felt herself moving forward, reaching out to Rand. "I'll try," she said. She held her hand out for the ring. "May I?"

Rand hesitated, possessively turning it over in his hand.

"She sometimes gets vibes from objects," Erica explained.

Rand shrugged slightly and dropped the ring into Shay's palm. She wrapped her fingers around it, certain that she could help. She felt the energy immediately, felt the ring jump in the palm of her hand as if it were a living, breathing thing.

"Someone has been desperate to find this," she whispered, voicing what she instinctively felt.

"Christina?" Rand interrupted.

"No." Shay shook her head, certain that it wasn't the girl who needed the ring. She looked at Mattie, her gaze falling to the hand on which she'd worn the ring.

Mattie drew her hand to her chest. "The break-ins?" she whispered.

"That would explain it," Jack said, suddenly alert. "Who knew you had the ring?"

"I don't know. I slipped it on my finger the day I found it. I showed it to Eve Dawson, asked her if it could have been part of the Ralph Barnes estate. Other than that, no one really, except for all of you, of course…" Then she gasped.

"What is it?"

"The day I was washing my car…" Mattie went pale. "I hadn't thought about it until now, but Mac stopped by."

"What do you mean 'stopped by'?" The tone in Jack's voice was cold.

"He saw me and stopped to ask how the car was running." She shook her head. "We barely spoke. He knows I hate him, but for some reason he likes to pretend that I don't."

"Did he see the ring?" Rand asked.

"I don't know. It was on my hand. But the whole conversation probably took less than five minutes."

"Long enough," Jack added.

"What do you think?" Mattie asked Shay.

"I—I don't know." She took a deep breath and closed her

eyes. She wanted to leave the speculation about Mac to the others, wanted the ring to take her where she needed to go. To Christina.

But it didn't.

Instead, she went inward, seeing her own circle of friends—Mattie, Della and Erica—as they'd been at eighteen. And then her own life, as it took a downward spiral with Mac. She felt the physical pain, the layers upon layers of emotional scars that had began with her parents' deaths and had been compounded by the death of her unborn child. The memories were like static, a jumble of confusing emotions that assaulted her, keeping her from connecting with Christina. Yet the girl was there. She could see flashes of her through the confusion, but she couldn't hold on to the image. She finally opened her eyes, dizzy with the effort.

"I'm sorry." She shook her head, then offered the ring back. "I could sense her, I just couldn't connect. I'd like to try again later, see if I can get something more."

Rand only nodded, slumping as if he'd added the burden of disappointment to the load he already carried. Shay's heart ached for him, and she almost wished she hadn't tried.

"I'll search Mattie's car," Jack offered. "See if we come up with anything."

Rand's eyes sparked with fresh anger. "But if you do find something, don't take it to *them*." He ran his hand through his hair and shifted, his body alive with tension. "They're hiding something. I know it."

The trampoline resumed its squeaking, and everyone turned in unison as Trevor dropped from the side and ran like a flash toward Erica's house. "Oh no you don't," Erica whispered, then took off at a dead run after him.

"I think that's our cue," Mattie said. Her gaze fell on Rand. "Please let me know if I can do anything."

He nodded. "Thank you. Keep her in your prayers."

Jack touched Mattie on the arm. "I'm going to stay and talk to Rand for a few minutes."

Shay absorbed the intimate gesture, then felt a fresh burst of envy. There was an intense emotional connection between Jack and Rand, and a fairly obvious one blossoming between Jack and Mattie.

And she, as always, was odd man out.

Jack's first instinct was to turn on some lights, but this was Rand's home, so he shoved his hands into his pockets and waited for Rand to close the door behind them. Though the house had probably been built in the sixties, the interior was as fresh as any new home. White Berber carpet lit by the morning light that slanted through the wooden blinds muffled their footsteps as they entered the family room. A pair of zebra-striped house shoes sat next to a new navy sofa, and a teen magazine lay on the floor next to them.

"I haven't touched anything since Christina disappeared," Rand explained. "But I combed the place for clues—for anything that might lead me to Christina. I even searched the garbage. Nothing.

"Damn!" the word exploded through the room. Jack whirled to face Rand, and found him staring transfixed at a blinking answering machine across the room. Rand jogged to it, then glanced over his shoulder at Jack.

"Let me give you some space," Jack offered.

"No." Rand held up his hand in protest, but the gesture ended up looking a lot like a plea for Jack to stay. "I always take the handset if I go outside. Or my cell. This morning I forgot." The last words were muttered like a heartsick apology.

As Rand pressed the play button, the machine beeped, then began to replay the message. *"Rand, this is Lieutenant Robertson, down at the precinct. I thought you'd like to know that we picked up the Houser kid for questioning. I'm sorry I missed you. I'll check back with you if there's anything we feel you should know."*

Rand looked over his shoulder at Jack. "Chad Houser is Christina's boyfriend," he explained. "Christina's best friend came forward two days ago, claiming that Chad roughed Christina up one night last month." He shook his head, staring at the answering machine. "I never even knew that."

"Why are they just now picking him up?"

"They couldn't find him. His family was supposedly on vacation, but that sounds mighty convenient to me."

"So you think it's true—you think he could have something to do with Christina's disappearance?"

"Maybe." Rand shrugged. "I can't say I like the boy, but it's hard to like any of the boys Christina sees. You look at them all, try to decide if there's anything physical going on." He shook his head. "Honestly? You want to kill most of them half the time."

Jack smiled. "Payback is hell."

Rand nodded, almost smiling.

"What do you say we head down to the precinct?"

Rand looked surprised. "You don't have to."

"I want to."

Rand grabbed his keys and a cell phone from a nearby coffee table. "Let's go."

They took Rand's car rather than hike the distance back to Erica's house. Rand shoved aside a mound of papers as Jack slid into the passenger seat of the truck. "I've been trying to dig up anything I can. I searched the Internet for hits on Chad or any of his family members."

"Find anything?"

"No." He shoved the truck in reverse and managed to back through the grass and around Christina's car without hitting it. "Not a thing. Not other than the fact that his father is a deacon in the Baptist church."

"Have you hired anyone to investigate?" Jack asked.

"No." Rand hesitated as he took the truck out of reverse,

thumbing a few pages into the pile of papers. He held the corner of one sheet back for Jack to see. He'd printed the home page from Jack's Web site. "I was about to get in touch."

Jack smiled, and a few of the years that separated their strained friendship seemed to melt. "Glad I could save you the call. My partner, Cal, is the best in the business when it comes to background investigations."

"I've, uh, heard his name mentioned around town."

Jack got a bad feeling about that. "Yeah? In what way?"

"Just that he was your partner." Rand put the truck in gear and skidded out of the drive. "I wasn't sure what that meant."

Jack wanted to scream. So far he'd taken the assumptions where Cal was concerned with pretty good humor—after all, Cal was a great guy and his closest friend—but the last person you want to believe you're gay is a friend who'd once seen you in super-hero pajamas. Jack balled his fists and told himself that Rand had bigger concerns at the moment.

"All that means is that Cal is my partner in the PI firm. He's gay and proud of it, but I'm still playing on the same team I've always played for, if that's what you're wondering."

"I gotta admit, I was wondering." Rand commented as he rounded a corner and narrowly missed a mailbox. Rand slowed as he reached town, finally making the turn that led them to the police precinct.

Jack immediately spotted the gangly kid who was leaving the building. Before he knew what was happening, Rand had accelerated, then skidded to a tire-screeching halt in front of the boy, narrowly missing a man in a suit who flanked him. Jack groaned. It was really bad form to scare a lawyer, but even worse to try to run over him.

The man in the suit slapped the hood of Rand's truck with his hand. "What the hell do you think you're doing?" he yelled, his words muffled by the glass that separated them.

Jack ignored the man, watching the kid instead. The boy just stared through the windshield at Rand, his dark eyes tired.

Rand was out of the truck within seconds and had grabbed the kid by the front of the T-shirt, trapping him between his body and the bumper of the truck.

"If you've hurt her, I'll kill you."

The man in the suit slammed his briefcase on the hood of Rand's truck. "That's a direct threat." He looked over his shoulder at a gathering crowd. "With witnesses. Be careful, Mr. Wilson."

Jack stepped forward to stand beside Rand, who hadn't budged. "Calm down," he urged.

Rand shot him a lethal look. "You have no idea what hell I'm going through. And this kid hurt Christina once. Maybe once wasn't enough for him." He shoved the boy harder against the hood. "Is that right?"

"I didn't have anything to do with her disappearing!" Chad fought back with surprising strength. "I lost it once, okay? She was talking some trash about givin' it up to some old dude. I just lost it. I didn't mean to hurt her."

Rand loosened his grip but never took his eyes off Chad. "What the hell are you talking about?"

"Nothing. My client has nothing to say to you. And if you don't take your hands off—"

"We had a fight," Chad continued, ignoring his fuming lawyer. "She said she'd been seeing some guy behind my back. Someone older. I don't know." The pained look on his face seemed sincere. "I was pressuring her to have sex, okay? She said if I didn't back off she was gonna give it up to him."

Rand dropped his grip on Chad's shirt, stepping back. "Who? Who was this person she was seeing?"

"Don't say a word, Chad," his lawyer warned.

"I don't know." Chad shook his head, ignoring his lawyer. "She wouldn't tell me. I don't even know if he really existed. I swear to God, I'd tell you if I knew."

"Rand," Jack said.

"I know." He turned away, his shoulders slumped. He took a step toward the cab of the truck, then stopped, running his hand through his hair. He turned back to Chad. "If I find out you aren't telling me everything you know, I'll kill you."

"Rand," Jack warned again, placing his hand on Rand's arm.

Rand jerked his arm away, then scanned the faces of the crowd that had gathered. He stopped when he saw Mac McKay staring from the steps of the station house. He leveled a deadly stare at the officer, then raised his voice to be heard. "This is not over. I know more than you think. And if you've hurt my daughter, I'll make you wish you were dead."

"Are you okay?" Erica asked.

Shay smiled, then suppressed a yawn. "Yeah. I'm fine. Do I smell coffee?"

Boy, that was a loaded question. "Yeah." Erica nodded. "Let me fix you a cup. You still like it black?"

She nodded. "Thanks."

Erica poured the coffee, at a loss for words. She'd always been secretly jealous of Shay's psychic ability. It had made her an easy mark for Erica's put-downs and one-liners, but the truth was that Erica thought it was pretty damn amazing. And she'd never seen it in action like she had today, at a time when it really mattered.

"Did you not sleep well at the new place?" Mattie asked, interrupting Erica's thoughts.

Erica spun, coffee cup in hand. "New place?" She shot Shay a look, admiration suddenly gone. Shay was like quicksilver, taking one form, then another, sliding from place to place. And about as reliable. "I thought you were staying with Mattie."

"I was. But I'm going to be staying at Ralph Barnes's place from now on. Eve Dawson hired me to go through the estate, to get it ready to go on the market."

Erica bit back at least a dozen snide remarks about Shay's erratic choices. She sat the coffee on the table. "You left Mattie alone?"

Shay turned slowly toward Mattie.

Mattie squirmed. "No, I, uh…" She hopped up, suddenly interested in washing her hands. "Jack volunteered to stay the night," she said over the running water. She dried her hands on a dish towel before facing her friends. "No problem."

Erica smiled, crossing her hands over her chest. "Safe *and* warm?"

"Just safe." She smiled, then sat down at the table, absent-mindedly pulling Shay's coffee toward her. "For now."

"The big brother," Erica teased. "Now isn't that every best friend's fantasy?"

A strangled sound came from Mattie as she took a sip of Shay's coffee. "Hot," she explained, fanning.

Erica and Shay exchanged smiles. "I'll bet," Erica muttered."

"Hello!" Elizabeth's voice split the giggles that followed. "I *am* in the room. Can we keep it PG-13?"

The three women spun to face Della's middle child. If the kid ever fell asleep, Erica was going to search her for a zipper. She was pretty sure that there was a forty-year-old hiding inside the eight-year-old somewhere.

"Yes, ma'am," Erica answered. She rolled her eyes when Elizabeth looked away. "It's like living with my mother again," she muttered under her breath.

"Speaking of that," Shay said, "you gave me a start in that housecoat." She smiled, shaking her head. "It was your mother's, right? I remember it. She used to make us pancakes the mornings after we'd spent the night. Your mother was so great. The resemblance between you two is startling."

Tears threatened as Erica looked down, suddenly transfixed by the faded pattern of the flowers that dotted the cotton fabric. And the memories. It was hard to be mad at Shay.

"I once prayed that your mother could be my mother," Shay whispered. "And then, of course, I prayed for God to forgive me."

"Oh, Shay." Erica reached down and hugged her.

"I miss her," Mattie added, sighing.

Emotion hit Erica like a fist. "Me, too. There's a lot I'd like to ask her right now."

"Like how to find Trevor?" Elizabeth asked.

"He's not...?" Erica whirled to face Elizabeth, who was smiling.

"Nope. He's in the shed with Andy."

"What's he doing out there, anyway?" Shay asked.

"I found him repairing my father's old tomato cages yesterday." Erica shrugged. "Maybe it's just a guy thing to tinker."

"I think he feels a connection to your father out there," Mattie added.

"My father?" Erica was confused. "He knew my father?"

"Of course." Mattie frowned. Della used to bring the kids over to visit. "Your dad and Andrew were close."

She was dumbfounded. How could she not have known this? Because she was halfway around the world most of that time, she realized. The thought that Andy had spent time with her father made her feel both jealous and grateful.

"Della said Andy has become a coffee drinker in his old age," Erica said, peering out the window at the shed. "Maybe I'll take him a cup."

"Make sure Trevor's out there while you're at it," Shay added. "That kid is like quicksilver."

Erica paused, coffee carafe in her hand. Shay often did that, echoed a thought or phrase that had just run through Erica's mind. Shay really was tuned in to the world around her in a way that the rest of them would never understand. If only she could perfect that gift and find Christina Wilson.

She felt an undeniable urge to find the girl. Maybe it was her budding maternal instinct, but her mind kept turning the situation over, sifting through scenarios. None of which were anything but conjecture. And heaven knows, she wouldn't be much help. Della's brood was all she could handle right now.

Erica stole a glance at Shay. Maybe this time Shay's abilities would prove to be the answer. She finished pouring the coffee, amazed that so much had remained the same while the world had changed so drastically around them.

Mattie stood and walked to the sink, peered down at the bowl of eggs. "You want me to make the kids some breakfast?" she asked.

"I'm hungry," Elizabeth added, tagging along behind Mattie.

"That would be great," Erica answered, blinking back gratitude. She was ridiculously weepy today.

"I'll put some bacon on while you do the eggs," Shay added, joining them.

Elizabeth scrambled to sit on the counter, then smiled at Erica as if she'd orchestrated the whole thing.

"I'll just take this out to Andy, then." Erica gazed around at the circle of friends, then ducked out the back door before the waterworks started.

She found Andy and Trevor in the shed. Andy was repairing what appeared to be the last tomato cage, while Trevor watched, perched atop a tall stool her father had kept in there. Trevor had kicked off his tennis shoes, and his feet were crusted with dirt, but since all his toes appeared to be accounted for, she didn't complain.

"Coffee?" she asked, holding up the mug.

"Hey, thanks," Andy said, tossing the pliers on the old wooden counter and accepting the coffee.

Erica's gaze stilled on a plastic nursery flat filled with young tomato plants. "Where did you get those?" she asked, pointing to the counter.

"My mom." Andy took a sip of coffee, grimaced, then

nodded toward the plants. "She thought it would be good if I helped you get them started."

Erica was touched by the gesture—even more touched that Della had kept in contact with her parents. She suddenly couldn't remember why she had been so determined to leave Haddes in the first place. She walked to the shed door and stared out at the garden spot that had always been the host to her father's tomatoes. The dirt was freshly upturned. "You did that?" she asked.

Andy looked pleased. "Yeah. The garden tiller was so rusted out it probably wouldn't work, even if it had gas in it, so I used the old push plow." He shrugged. "Your dad used to let me do that when I was a kid."

Erica rested her hip against the door frame. "I didn't know." She turned and faced Andy. "I didn't even know you two knew each other."

"Mom visited a lot. And somehow I always wound up out here with Mr. Donovan. I'm about to plant them," he said, pointing to the tomato vines. "You want to help me?"

Erica looked down at her bare legs protruding beneath her mother's housecoat, then at the pair of old flip-flops she wore. Her hair was sticking out in a crazy ponytail and she could really use a hot shower. But, honestly, she couldn't think of anything she'd rather do at that moment than plant tomato vines in her father's garden.

"Sure."

She helped Trevor down off the counter and followed Andy as he scooped up the flat of tomato plants and trudged off toward the garden. He dropped to his knees in the middle of the patch of tilled soil, and Trevor ran to join him, automatically plunging his hands into the dirt. Erica kicked off her flip-flops at the edge of the garden and felt her own toes sink into the sun-warmed soil.

She was a child again. And she was home. And it all felt so right that she wanted to cry.

"Loosen one of the plants and pass it to me," Andy instructed. He slid his hands into her father's leather gloves and dug a generous hole, obviously pleased to be in charge.

Erica did as he instructed, memories welling up inside her. She turned the vine upside down, loosening the roots from the tiny plastic pot that had incubated it. When she sat it upright in the palm of her hand, she smelled the familiar spicy scent of the tomato plant and saw that the tiny white roots had curled against the container, looking for a way out. She swallowed back emotion as she offered the plant to Andy.

"Just one sec," he said. "I've got to make the hole a little deeper." He measured the hole with the length of his gloved hand, just as she remembered her father doing, then smiled. "That ought to do it."

As Erica held the tender plant, she looked at Andy and marveled that the connection she'd thought was lost was found again through Della's firstborn.

"That's right." She took a deep breath. "My father always said that you had to dig the hole deep enough."

Andy grinned and took the plant with gentle reverence. He placed it in the hole, then scooted aside.

Erica leaned forward, feeling the warmth of the soil beneath her fingertips as she buried the exposed roots. "Because if you don't get the roots deep enough, the new plant won't survive."

CHAPTER 12

It seemed ridiculous to be in a good mood, considering she was surrounded by destruction, so Mattie forced the smile from her face. She picked up yet another ruined book and tossed it in the industrial-size garbage can, remembering to scowl. The sight of lemon cake stomped into the bookstore's carpet was supposed to make her frown, so she did. But as soon as she began vacuuming, she thought of Jack and the smile returned.

When you're ready, I want you. Over and over again.

Every time she remembered his words, her knees went weak. He couldn't know what a turn-on it was for her that he'd put the ball in her court. Just knowing that he wanted her to come to him set off a million fantasies in her head. And she'd gotten good at fantasizing about Jack over the years.

He had no idea that he'd unleashed the beast.

They'd made out on the sofa like two horny teenagers until they'd fallen asleep in each other's arms, exhausted from the frustration of wanting and waiting. It was obvious that they'd both wanted to take it all the way, but Jack had made it clear from the start that it wouldn't happen the first night. Which had just heated things up more.

But tonight was fair game. And so was tomorrow night.

Mattie eyed her computer as she continued to vacuum. She often worked on her children's books at the store when business was slow. But never *her* stories. She'd never written them outside of her closet. Right now she wanted nothing more than to slip into a pair of leopard-skin pumps and go at it. But she couldn't.

She was determined to host her writers' meeting at the bookstore tonight, and in order to do that, she had to put the place back in some semblance of order. The majority of the other writers in her group were rather, well, geriatric. And southern women over the age of sixty weren't likely to let carpet laced with lemon cake go without comment.

She turned off the vacuum and parked it in a corner, then switched on her desk fan and stuck her heated face in front of it, closing her eyes. The things she wanted to do to that man… The things she *planned* to do to that man.

Mattie felt a sort of redemption for the years spent alone, considered it an affirmation that the one lesson she'd learned from her parents' divorce had been a worthy one. Her parents' marriage had had no passion. Not once, when they were still together, had she seen them kiss on the lips. They operated like roommates. They were parents, not lovers.

Married but not sexual mates. So in her own life she'd waited on the passion, had refused to settle for less.

And now she'd waited long enough.

The door chimed and a voice called "Yoo-hoo!".

Mattie jumped, opening her eyes. And then wished she hadn't. Her mother had breezed right past the "Closed" sign Mattie had hung on the door. Of course, such things shouldn't apply to your mother. But then again, a lot of things should apply to her mother that didn't.

"Hi, Mom."

"Hello, sweetheart." Her mother plopped a plastic grocer's bag on her ransacked desk as if nothing were out of the ordinary. "I brought your dog a rawhide bone."

"Oh." Mattie switched off the fan. "I actually don't have him anymore."

"What?" She snatched up the sack. "Who does?"

"Shay. She's going to find a good home for him."

"Shay…" Her mother twisted the sack, as if in deep thought. "I heard she was back in town."

Mattie was surprised. "You did?"

"Mmm. Stirring things up, is what I heard."

Her mother had never really approved of Shay. Like a lot of people, she was suspicious of Shay's abilities. Never mind that Joan Harold had recorded every episode of *The Pet Psychic* ever produced. Apparently, telepathic communication was a-okay between people and poodles, but not people and people.

"Stirring things up, how?" Mattie asked.

"Oh, never mind. You know people. They talk."

Yes, they do, Mattie thought.

"So?" her mother added cheerfully. "I heard you and Jack spent the night together. Was I right?"

"Right?" Mattie tried not to stutter. "About what?"

"About him being gay, silly." Her mother began drifting from aisle to aisle as if looking for a book, stepping over the carnage from the break-in as if it didn't exist.

Mattie closed her eyes and counted to ten. It was only fair to Jack to help clear up the question of his sexuality. On the other hand, she hated to fuel her mother's fire. She decided on the short, sweet, no-details approach. "You were right, he's not gay."

"Ah. Good. So how was it? You two are opposites." She winked. "Like your father and me."

Her mother *winked*? Oh, Jeez. Mattie saw the train wreck coming, but still had to ask. "What's that supposed to mean?"

"Just that there was never a dull moment between your father and me." She widened her eyes and smiled. "At least, not in the bedroom. Opposites attract, you know."

The earth shifted, and when it did, something was way off kilter. Never a dull moment in the *bedroom*? Between her *parents*?

"That can't be right," Mattie said. And then she hated herself for speaking out loud.

"Oh, but it was." She winked again. "And still is. From time to time."

Still is? From time to time? Mattie wanted to run screaming from the room. If she'd had ear-lids she would have closed them. And to make matters worse, her mother was still talking.

"…always did burn up the sheets," her mother continued, as she fanned herself with her hand. "Lordy, that man was blessed with bedroom skills…."

Make her stop. Make her stop. Mattie was one step away from sticking her fingers in her ears and chanting, when her mother's words stopped her cold.

"…it was when we weren't in the bedroom that we had trouble." She laughed. "Big trouble. Big boring trouble."

"What?" Mattie couldn't seem to stop herself. "What are you trying to say?"

"That we would still be married if we could have had sex twenty-four/seven."

Mattie could barely breath. Her mother was talking in teen-age slang about having sex with her father. And worse, she got the distinct feeling that it was something she needed to hear.

"Mother…" She cleared her throat. "I never saw you and Dad so much as hold hands when you were married."

"You don't see us hold hands now, either, do you?" Her mother winked.

That was it. No more. "Okay, Mom, I get your point." Mattie held up her hand.

Apparently, Mattie had gotten the lust gene from her mother. And while her mother had been in the closet doing it with her ex-husband, Mattie had been in the closet writing about it on her computer. Neither seemed particularly healthy.

"Well, I certainly didn't mean to make you feel uncomfortable." Her mother tugged a book from the shelf and clutched it to her chest. "I thought your generation was free to discuss such things."

"Mother, you never told me the facts of life." Mattie looked her in the eyes. "I think maybe going from zero to sixty is a little much for me."

"Whatever, dear." She plopped the book down on the counter, then leaned to peer into the garbage can. "I don't suppose you have this one in a damaged copy?"

Mattie opened her mouth to speak, but no words came out. Ten minutes ago she'd been looking forward to a physical relationship with Jack. But now she knew that any relationship with Jack was doomed. She may have inherited the lust gene from her mother, but she had a horrible suspicion that she'd inherited the boring gene from her father.

The Mattie that Jack knew was free-spirited and relaxed, not uptight and inhibited. And the only reason she'd given him that impression was that she'd thought he was gay.

But now she knew the truth. And once he knew the truth, it would be over with before it ever began.

She looked down at the book: *Raising a Happy, Healthy Pet*.

Her mother had yet to acknowledge the break-ins in any reasonable way. And now she wanted a cut-rate price on a damaged book?

She pushed the corner of the book toward her mother. "No, Mother, I don't. But consider it on the house."

"That's very nice of you, sweetheart." Her mother smiled, oblivious to the fact that Mattie was on the verge of strangling her. "I'll tell you what…" She set the bag with the bone inside it on Mattie's desk, then patted it. "I'll leave this with you after all. I'm sure I can trust you to get it to Shay."

Mattie tented her fingers against the top of her desk and counted backward from one hundred until the door chimed and her mother left the store. Then she opened the sack, took out the dog bone, and threw it as hard as she could against the glass door. It made a solid cracking sound, and Mattie smiled when she noticed that the damaged panel was a little more damaged.

Just like her life.

Shay folded the newspaper over and scanned the want ads. She needed to write an ad twice as good as the best one in there to stand a chance of placing the dog in a good home.

She scribbled a few thoughts on a sheet of paper, then scratched them out. Beside her, Buddy moaned in his sleep, then rolled over on his back and farted.

It needed to be a really, really good ad.

Shay stared at the dog's comical pose and grinned. He was a good dog. It was a shame that all he'd been through had only made him more unappealing to the rest of the world. Life was unfair that way. Shay recalled the rigid scar tissue beneath his fur, and the instant connection she'd felt with him at Mattie's.

If only she could keep him.

The simple idea was so startling that her breath caught in her throat. Why *couldn't* she? It would be her decision. There was no one to stop her. Shay looked down at the ad she'd attempted to compose and the words swam as tears filled her eyes.

She'd begged for a dog as a child, but her aunt and uncle had steadfastly refused, claiming it was one more mouth to feed. Shay swallowed hard. They hadn't needed to explain that they had one mouth too many already. That had been pretty evident.

And then there was the stray puppy she'd found one Christmas, not long after she and Mac married. He'd refused to let her keep it. Shay shivered and hugged herself. He'd taken the poor little thing by the scruff of the neck and tossed it out the kitchen door. It had been cold that night, a rare dip into the teens, and she'd found the puppy dead the next morning, huddled next to the foundation of their house. She hadn't had the courage to stand up to Mac that night, and the image of the poor frozen puppy had haunted her since.

So at what point had she decided that she was undeserving of a pet? Shay looked down at the gangly old dog and realized she didn't have to deny herself anymore. Besides, if not her, who would take Buddy? And the way she saw it, she was actually in *his* home, not the other way around.

She wadded the paper into a ball. "I'm going to keep you," she announced into the silence of the room. "And no one can stop me."

Buddy cracked one eye open, took a deep breath and fell over on his side, never fully waking.

Shay stood, tiptoeing through the kitchen in her socks, and filled an old copper teakettle with water. She decided to focus on the fact that this was Buddy's home and that, as his friend, she would be welcome here. Truth was, she still felt nervous in the Barnes house, continually looking over her shoulder.

Shay hadn't been able to sleep last night. In all honesty, she'd been too afraid. So rather than fight it, she'd gone to work, sorting the debris until she was too tired to continue. She'd finally given in to sleep just as the sun rose, curling up on a musty old sofa in the parlor. The world always seemed a much safer place to her when all the corners were lit and the shadows had been chased away.

She had just drifted off to sleep this morning when Elizabeth called, saying that Erica was ill. Shay had smiled, despite the fact that the call had scared her half to death. She'd actually felt needed, had felt like she belonged. But that emotion fled once she learned that Mac might be connected to Christina Wilson's disappearance.

If only she'd had the courage to stand up to Mac all those years ago, this might have been avoided.

Shay drifted to the parlor's bay window and stared out into the darkness. Tonight was going to be different. Tonight she was going to get some sleep rather than cowering in the shadows until dawn. The kettle whistled, and she jumped, pressing her hand against her pounding heart. She tugged the old velvet curtains closed, stirring up a cloud of dust, as she blocked out the darkness. Buddy sneezed in his sleep, then raised his head to study her, one round tuft of eyebrow raised.

"Okay, so I'm still working on the bravery thing," she said. "Give me time."

Shay returned to the kitchen and set the kettle off the eye of the stove before she began searching a box filled with her belongings. She was pulling an envelope from the depths of the box and unsealing it when the aroma of blended herbs reached her nose. The smell of lemon and sweet basil was familiar, reminding her of home. Her life in Arizona hadn't been perfect, and Lord knows it hadn't always been easy, but it was a cakewalk compared to the volcano of emotions she was experiencing right now.

She dumped the little pouch of herbs into a coffee mug, then filled it with boiling water. The potpourri simmered, filling the kitchen with the soothing aroma. Shay carried the mug to the parlor, placing it on a coffee table that she'd cleared earlier. She then retrieved a candle and centered it on the coffee table, next to the potpourri, and lit it.

Shay grabbed a blanket from the back of the sofa and wrapped up in it. Then she sank down to the hardwood floor and leaned her elbows against the coffee table, watching the flame as it began to melt the wax. Hating Mac was no use. She'd learned that a long time ago. And she couldn't change the past any more than she could control the future. So she did the only thing she knew to do.

She closed her eyes and prayed for Christina Wilson to come home safely.

Mattie tugged the turtleneck off and threw it on the floor. It landed in a pile of other shirts she'd discarded, all of which made her feel matronly or frumpy. She glanced over her shoulder, feeling vulnerable in only her bra and panties as she walked the length of her closet, scanning the row of clothes for inspiration. She was beginning to wonder if she'd ever feel safe in her own home again, but considering her closet had been ransacked and occupied by a mad dog as of late, fear was probably a logical emotion. She'd considered putting a sign on the front door of her duplex that read *I no longer have the ring*, but she figured that was taking it a notch too far.

Besides, in a town the size of Haddes, that was probably common knowledge by now.

The clothes swayed as she ran her hands over the hangers. She was acting ridiculous, considering her writers' group was made up of a handful of little old ladies who had seen her every day of her life. What she wore tonight shouldn't matter. But last night with Jack, she'd felt like a different person. She'd felt pretty, sexy, desirable. Heck, she'd felt powerful. Was it wrong to want to feel that way every day from now on? And why was everything she owned so damn boring, anyway? There wasn't one low-cut anything in her possession, unless you counted a camisole.

Mattie's gaze dropped to her suitcase. Inside the front pouch were four CDs with *her* stories on them. No frogs. No turtles. No children's characters. No boring turtlenecks. There were main characters with names like Roxie and Alexia, women who weren't afraid to wear skintight jeans and four-inch black silk pumps, fishnet hose and thigh-high boots. She would settle for having even a small part of those women in her.

And then it hit her. She stared at the suitcase, blinking. She did have those women in her. She had created them. So how boring could she be?

She reached behind her and popped open the clasp to her bra, letting it fall to the floor. She stood there for a minute, allowing the cool air to pucker her nipples, feeling her bare toes curl into the thick pile of the carpet. She forced herself to not scurry for a housecoat or reach for a shirt. Instead she embraced the feeling, allowed her senses to come to life.

She wasn't too old. She wasn't too boring. And it definitely wasn't too late.

Mattie scanned the boxes of shoes. She was going to take it slow. She was going to start small. But she was going to start.

She bit her lip as she considered her options, then slid a box from the stack. Opening the lid, she pulled out a pair of cotton-candy-pink sling-back pumps with three-inch heels. Her mouth watered as she ran her hand over the supple suede. The shoes had never been worn. She'd tried them on the day they'd been delivered, but had never worn them outside of her closet.

She sank her right foot into one shoe, her left foot into the other. And there she stood, wearing only a pair of silk panties and a killer pair of pink heels. She was three inches taller and infinitely sexier. She plunged her hands into her hair and lifted it on top of her head, feeling her bare breasts rise and the air kiss the back of her neck. She imagined Jack doing the same.

It was almost a shame to get dressed.

Mattie moved to her dresser, feeling her breasts sway and her butt dip and rise in a provocative little rhythm as she walked in the heels. She opened a drawer and pulled out a silky lace camisole, slipped it over her head. It dropped into place, looking vastly different without a bra underneath. She kicked out of the shoes just long enough to slip on a pair of jeans that fit perfectly five pounds ago, then pulled the shoes back on. She stood, looking in the mirror, and barely recognized herself.

She actually looked good. And way too provocative for her children's book circle.

She returned to her closet and chose a pink summer sweater that buttoned up the front, tugged it over the camisole. She buttoned it halfway, allowing the lace to peek from beneath the front closure and her nipples to draw against the fabric. When she looked in the mirror, she decided it was the perfect marriage between Roxie-Alexia, her erotic story characters, and Mattie Harold, bookstore proprietor.

But an hour later, as the ladies of the book circle filed into the store, she wasn't so certain.

Mattie greeted them at the door, where the ladies seemed torn between assessing the bookstore's broken glass door and staring at her shoes. One by one, they gaped at her camisole and then, with thoroughly stunned expressions, began glancing around the bookstore as if they expected the perp to come swinging from the rafters on a vine. It was the most excitement the writers' circle had seen since Mattie substituted coffee for the Earl Grey tea.

Mattie sat down in her usual chair situated in front of the cash register, with a half-moon of chairs encircling her. She curled her manuscript pages in her hand and shifted her feet, tucking her pink pumps against the wheels of the chair as she waited for everyone to take their seats.

She could do this.

Donna-Jo Moore took a seat, one cashmere-brown eyebrow even higher than it was normally painted as she looked Mattie up and down.

Janet Cummings whispered, "Oh my," beneath one cupped hand as she took her seat next to Mildred Hampton, who had pasted a mannequin-smile on her usually tranquil face.

Only Estelle Ashworth, who was sporting a rather punkish new hairstyle, had the nerve to inquire about Mattie's new attire. She plopped her considerable weight down in her chair, crossed her legs as gracefully as any marine and asked, "What the hell are you wearing?"

Mattie cleared her throat. Estelle's honesty was actually welcome. "I'm trying something new," she said, extending her foot and lifting the hem of her jeans. "What do you think?"

"They're certainly high-heeled enough," Donna-Jo whispered in a shocked tone.

Mildred squirmed, her cherubic face lit up. "My daughter gave me a pair that color for Christmas. But the heels aren't so high." She fanned her face, giggling. "I've always wanted to wear them."

"Why, you'd look ridiculous if you did," Janet scolded. "Just ridiculous, Mildred."

"Well," Estelle said in her commanding monotone. "I think change is good." She touched the razor-clipped ends of her hair. "And it's about damn time. You've been dressing like a Sunday school teacher for years. That's no way to get a man."

Mattie opened her mouth to object, ready to argue that she didn't need to attract a man, then closed it. Estelle was right. She did want to get a man. And she wasn't about to apologize for it. Besides, she didn't want to argue with Estelle, who was a little scary, even when she was on your side.

"I heard she already did," Janet whispered to Mildred, whose face turned red.

"She's not deaf, Janet," Estelle scolded. "If you've got something to say, then say it."

"Well…" Janet muttered, then began digging through her briefcase, eventually pulling out her manuscript. "I just think with all the quality bras on the market these days…" She let her words trail, waving her hand in the air.

The door chime rang and all eyes went to the front of the store.

"Speak of the devil." Mildred giggled and her round cheeks went as red as apples.

Jack entered, smiling as he scanned the circle of women.

Mattie heard them sigh in unison. Apparently there was no age limit on Jack's charm.

"Jack…" Mattie tucked a lock of hair behind her ear and tried to look casual. She gestured toward the circle of women. "This is my writers' group. Would you like to join us?"

Jack frowned slightly. "What do y'all write?"

"Children's books," Mattie answered.

"So…" Jack took a seat next to Janet, who scooted her briefcase to one side and looked scandalized. He looked directly at Mattie. "And that's what you write, as well? Children's books?"

Estelle sighed and cast him an irritated look. "Yeah. Once upon a time… Children's books. Remember those?"

"Yeah, I do. Vaguely." He leaned back in his chair, crossing his legs, and grinned at Mattie. "I just never pictured Mattie writing children's books." His gaze hovered on her braless chest, then dipped to her shoes.

"Are you here to take Mattie home?" Mildred asked, her face flushed with excitement.

"Honestly, Mildred." Janet swatted at Mildred's arm. "What a question."

Mattie straightened, an odd awareness settling in her chest. It was as if he knew something that he wasn't telling. It was as if he *knew*. She crossed her leg and ran her hand over the soft suede of her right shoe. "And what would you envision me writing instead, Jack?" she asked.

He uncrossed his legs and leaned forward, resting his elbows on his knees. "I don't know…maybe something more provocative?"

Mattie's breath caught in her throat. He *knew*. Her heart pounded. She had no idea how he knew, but he did. She could see it in his eyes. And to her surprise, she found it exhilarating. "And why would you think that?" she asked.

He narrowed his eyes and a muscle flexed in his jaw. "I read something not long ago. The pages were damp and the ink had smudged, but I was pretty certain that your name was on it."

Little vibrations of shock flowed over her and Mattie fought for control. "You know it's against the law to read other people's work without permission."

One corner of his mouth lifted in a grin. "Not if it's been discarded. Say, for instance, in a ditch."

She recalled ripping the fantasy letter and letting the pieces fall into the ditch. Jack must have retrieved it. But how? Why? She felt her mouth go dry.

Once her heart slowed a little, she decided it was her turn to play. She uncrossed her own legs, then mimicked Jack by separating her legs and leaning one palm on each knee. "And was it provocative?" she asked.

Jack's eyes were smoldering. "Extremely."

"Well, I never!" Janet exclaimed. "What is going on here?"

"Hush!" Estelle hissed.

Mattie ignored them. Everyone but Jack had ceased to exist. She trailed her fingertips over the soft denim of her jeans. "Were you surprised to find your name on it, as well?"

Now it was Jack's turn to look shocked. He stood abruptly, frowning. "The ink was smudged in places."

So he hadn't known.... A feeling of self-satisfaction flowed over Mattie. She licked her lips and cocked her head, relishing the power. "Then it must have been smudged in all the wrong places."

"Oh," Donna-Jo Moore sighed.

"This is simply uncouth!" Janet exclaimed.

"No." Estelle crossed her arms over her chest and smiled as if she'd scored a front-row seat. "This is great."

"Are you going to take her home now?" Mildred repeated, clasping her hands together.

"Yes." Jack moved to stand over Mattie, then tugged her to her feet. He tilted her chin up and took her mouth with his in a kiss so deep and warm that Mattie felt faint. When he finally lifted his mouth from hers, he glanced around at the other women. "Yes, I'm going to take her home now."

CHAPTER 13

The first thing Shay was aware of was the scraping sound coming from the bay window. She blinked, suddenly realizing that she'd fallen asleep on the floor. The sound came again, and this time she heard Buddy respond with a deep-throated growl. She turned her head slightly and saw that Buddy was beside her on the floor, fully alert and staring at the window.

She hadn't been dreaming.

Still cocooned in the blanket, she fought the urge to disentangle herself. Instead she held perfectly still, listening.

Nothing.

She had no real sense of time, but the small candle still flickered on the coffee table and no daylight shone through the portion of curtain that she could see. Just when she was about to move, the sound came again, more intense this time. A knock, then a soft curse. There was no mistaking it. Someone was attempting to jimmy the lock.

Panic flowed through her, and Shay jumped up, knocking over the coffee table. She clawed the blanket from her shoulders and tossed it aside. As if in slow motion, she watched the blanket land beside the toppled candle, igniting the fringe like a hungry wick.

And then he was crashing through the window.

Shay heard herself scream over the sound of breaking glass, watched in horror as a hooded dark figure rolled to the floor then stood, hunched and glaring at her. She backed up, colliding with the sofa as the flames grew.

"You witch," the figure shouted, raising a finger to point at her.

Shay couldn't make out the features of the man beneath the hood of the jacket, but she knew the voice. Mac. And lit by the growing flames that separated them, he looked exactly like the devil she knew him to be. He made a move toward her, then stopped. Shay felt a nudge beside her, then Buddy began barking furiously.

"Stay out of this!" Mac yelled. He made another move toward her then stopped when Buddy lunged. He raised his finger again, pointing. "Keep your damn black magic out of this or I'll kill you. And I'll do it right this time, woman."

Woman. The word pierced her consciousness like a poisoned thorn, immobilizing her. It was what Mac had called her, when he beat her. Never before, and never after, but only when he was hitting her. *Shut up, woman. I ought to kill you, woman.* The memories slammed into her, and she felt herself stagger as she stumbled around Buddy to get away. And Mac saw the weakness, knew he had an opportunity.

It all happened at once. Mac came charging through the flames and Buddy attacked. She heard the sound of the dog's ferocious attack mixed with Mac's scream of pain as Buddy knocked him back through the flames and against the window. She watched Mac scramble toward the broken glass pane, then lunge back through it, leaving Buddy frantically clawing to get to him.

As if from a million miles away she heard the electronic screech of the fire alarm. And then the trembling began. Shay's knees buckled as she tried to move, and she gripped the arm of the sofa in desperation, coughing as she tried to gain control. Flames now engulfed the blanket and were beginning to trail across the hardwood floor. Smoke spiraled through the room, siphoning through the shattered window.

Shay staggered forward, grabbed a throw pillow from the sofa and began pounding at the flames, coughing. She continued to beat the charred fabric even after the flames had been extinguished. Buddy circled her, barking nonstop as she kept up the frantic beating.

Sirens could be heard in the distance and Buddy began to howl, pacing the floor. Eventually the sound became deafening, and Shay realized the sirens were for her. Then the tears began. She grabbed Buddy around the neck, whispering thank-yous as he licked the tear-stained side of her face.

"Fire Department!" a deep voice yelled from the other side of the door, and was followed by pounding. "Is anyone inside?"

Shay stood long enough to stagger to the front door, open it and collapse into the arms of a firefighter.

"When Officer McKay didn't report for duty yesterday, we grew suspicious. But we didn't have anything concrete to go on until today." Chief Wells nodded toward Shay. "Thank you, Miss Chambers, for coming down to file charges."

"You're welcome," Shay whispered. She signed the last of the paperwork, then leaned against Mattie's shoulder. Mattie wrapped her arm around Shay and they stood, facing a grim-faced Gerald Randolph.

Officer Randolph shook Jack's hand, then Rand's. "I wish we had more to go on at this point. Every available officer has been dispatched. We'll find McKay."

"Find my *daughter*," Rand said, gripping Gerald's hand.

Chief Wells stood. "That's our first priority, Mr. Wilson, rest assured."

Erica entered the room, carrying a cola in her good hand and holding Elizabeth's hand with the tips of her fingers that peeked from beneath her cast. Elizabeth glanced around with wide eyes, as if she were absorbing every detail of the police precinct. Andy followed, carrying Trevor in his arms.

"Are you okay?" Mattie asked as Shay took a sip.

"Thanks to Buddy," Shay responded.

Shay and Mattie exchanged glances.

"I must have mentioned that," Shay said, glancing between her friends.

"About a million times." Erica smiled and squeezed Shay around the shoulders. "But that's okay. He was your hero."

"I haven't had a hero since my father died," Shay whispered.

"Then you're overdue," Rand said. "Thank you for everything you did today."

"I should have done this twenty years ago." She met Rand's eyes. "If I had, maybe Christina wouldn't be missing. I'm so sorry."

Rand tugged Shay's shoulders to face him. "You are not responsible for that monster. Do you understand that?"

Shay nodded, dropping her head. "I'd like another chance." She met Rand's eyes. "With the ring."

Rand dug his hand into the pocket of his jeans and pulled out the ring. He dropped it into Shay's hand, then curled his fingers over hers until her hand was closed. "Keep it until we find her," he said.

Shay closed her eyes and a wall of cold cinder block flashed before her. Her eyes flew open, excitement flowing through her, but she realized she was facing the exact wall she'd hoped was a vision. Disappointment settled over her.

She wanted so much to find the girl that she was jumping at every clue her subconscious might stumble across.

"What is it?" Jack asked.

"Nothing." Shay shook her head, then glanced at Rand. "Are you sure about the ring?"

He nodded.

Rand and Jack stayed behind at the precinct while Mattie and Erica loaded Shay into Della's van. Erica buckled Trevor into his car seat, situated the rest of the crew, then cranked the vehicle. She turned the air conditioner on full blast, took a deep breath and pulled out onto Main Street.

They'd been traveling for a few minutes when Shay pointed to a street sign. "Turn here," she directed. "It's the best way to get back to the Barnes place."

"No," Erica stated calmly. "You're staying with me and the kids until this is all over with."

"No, I'm not," Shay said. "I won't hide from him or anyone else anymore."

Mattie frowned. "What do you mean, anyone else?"

Shay glanced at Della's children, then back at Mattie, obviously not willing to impart too much. "Just that I'm tired of being a victim."

"Then I've got something that I want you to have," Erica said, heading toward her parents' place.

"What's that?"

"My father's rifle."

"No." Shay shook her head. "No way. No guns."

"You'd be doing me a favor." Erica glanced in her rearview mirror at the children. "I need it out of the house."

"Every hour four Americans are killed by a firearm," Elizabeth stated.

Shay frowned from the back seat. "Okay, I'll store it for you, if that's what you want. But I won't use it."

"Deal," Erica said, turning into her parents' long driveway.

As soon as they rounded the corner, Erica's parents' house came into view. As did a buxom blonde sitting on a pile of suitcases.

"Della?" Mattie and Erica said in unison.

"Mommy!" Elizabeth squealed, unbuckling her seat belt and jumping up and down.

Trevor clapped but didn't say a word.

"What's today?" asked Andy.

"Tuesday," Mattie answered. "When were Della and Donald supposed to be back?"

Erica frowned. "Not until Thursday."

"Uh-oh," Shay whispered.

Erica pulled the van to a stop near a smiling Della, who looked tanned and relaxed. The children were out first, and Della scooped them, one by one, into a bear hug.

"Where's Daddy?" Elizabeth asked.

"Oh, he'll be along in a few hours. He's taking care of a few details. Hey…" She pulled a giant plastic bag from behind her luggage. "There are some cool gifts in here for some great kids. Why don't y'all take these inside and open them up?"

"Yeah!" Elizabeth squealed. "Keys, Aunt Erica?" she asked.

Erica dropped the house keys in Elizabeth's palm. "Keep an eye on your brother," she whispered.

Della looked at Erica. "*Aunt* Erica?"

She shrugged. "We bonded."

Andy lingered, looking a little suspicious. "Did you have a good time?" he asked.

Della handed the sack of gifts to Andy with a wink. "An awesome time," she answered.

He smiled, looking relieved, and followed his siblings up the walkway to the house.

Erica approached Della when the kids were out of earshot. "Is everything okay?" she asked.

Della wrinkled her nose. "I forgot something," she said.

Mattie shook her head. "You *forgot* something? You don't come home from a Caribbean vacation because you forgot something."

"You do when the thing you forgot is to remove the pepper from your husband's briefs."

Shay gasped, clapping her hand over her mouth. "You didn't!"

"I did." Della sat back down on her luggage and, smiling, swung her feet back and forth like a child. "Shay, do you remember telling me that if I sought revenge it would find me again, and when it did it would come back uglier than before?"

Shay nodded.

Della snickered. "Trust me, Donald's…" She fell into an all-out laugh, holding her sides and wiping her eyes as she nearly toppled off the luggage. "Well, it was uglier than before!"

"That's—" Shay tried to suppress a laugh "—awful, Della."

Mattie also bit her lip to keep from laughing. "Poor Donald."

"You're enjoying this," Erica said. "What gives?"

"Mmm…" Della wiped her eyes on the hem of her blouse, then looked Erica in the eyes. "What gives is that we had a long talk on the MedEvac ride."

"MedEvac?"

"Yeah." Della wrinkled her nose again. "It was very dramatic, but it was the only way to leave the ship. And, oh, the pilot was sooo cute."

"Della," Erica prompted.

"Oh, okay." She shifted. "We had a long talk and let's just say that Donald is going to learn the children's teachers' names and figure out how to pack a lunchbox."

"Amen!" Mattie held her hand up for a high-five and Della slapped it.

"Amen!" Della added, then narrowed her eyes at Mattie. "Hey, what's with you? You look different."

"She got laid," Erica said, laughing.

Della leaned back, staring at Mattie. "Looks good on you. Who's the donor?"

Mattie chewed her lip. "Uh…"

Della's expression was suspicious. "You're glowing *and* you look guilty. You're not pregnant, are you?"

"No…" Mattie glanced at Erica, as did Shay.

"What?" Della asked, narrowing her eyes at Erica. "What's going on? And where were y'all at this morning anyway?"

Erica, Mattie and Shay exchanged looks.

"It's a long story," Shay answered.

Shay scrubbed at the charred spot on the hardwood floor and wondered what Eve would have to say about the damage. She looked at her watch. She probably had only another hour or so before word of last night's attack made its way to Eve. She picked up the garbage sack that contained the ruined blanket and hesitated at the back door. She peeked out the door's window. The garbage can was only a few feet away, but she couldn't force herself to go outside. Instead, she double-tied the handles and laid the sack at the threshold. Maybe later.

She turned and eyed the rifle that was propped next to her refrigerator. She'd argued with Erica on principle, but the truth was the minute Erica mentioned the gun, her heart had leaped with relief. Of all the things there were to hate in the world, violence and weapons were at the top of the list.

And yet she still wanted it.

Shay walked over and picked up the rifle, unzipping its padded storage case. Ironically, she knew how to use it. Her uncle had seen to that. An avid deer hunter, he'd insisted that Shay learn how to use a rifle. She'd hated everything about handling the weapon: the scent of gunpowder and oil, the noise and the recoil that bruised her shoulder. But most of all she'd hated the sight of the dead deer that her uncle would bring home from his hunting trips. Her aunt would force her to view the animals, saying that she should be proud of her uncle. The sight of the carcasses with their glassy eyes and lifeless bodies made her violently ill, but she'd hidden her repulsion. She hadn't needed another mark against her.

But today the sight of the rifle seemed to draw her. Shay pulled the weapon from its case and brought it to her shoulder, peering down the sight. She drew her hand across the polished wood and cold metal and felt her pulse leap with an emotion she didn't recognize. She lowered the rifle, frowning. It was power, and the sweet temptation of revenge.

She sat the rifle down and took a step backward. "No," she whispered out loud.

An image of Mac, as lifeless as the deer carcasses, entered her mind. She envisioned his eyes glassed over, his brutal fists limp. And she wasn't repulsed.

"No," she said again, shaking her head. She had transcended that emotion a long time ago. The only way to cope with what she'd endured was to forgive Mac, to love him as his Creator did in spite of what he'd done. The ability to do that made her a better person.

So why was it suddenly so hard?

Shay whirled, frantically searching for her belongings. She had to leave. She wouldn't compromise her values, and if staying meant doing that, then she had no choice. She would go. Today.

But where?

She looked at Buddy, curled up on the doormat and sleeping. Maybe they could return to Arizona. She could deal with Bruce, ask him to take her back. He'd threatened her, but he hadn't actually hit her. She rubbed her upper arms where the bruises had finally faded. It hadn't been so bad. Maybe she could even make it better, turn things around.

Shay grabbed a handful of plastic grocery bags and began filling them with her belongings. She was suddenly alive with energy, desperate to gather her things and be gone. That was all she wanted. To be away from this place. From the memories and from the temptation.

She was packed in less than an hour, the back of her tiny car overloaded so that Buddy could fit in the front. She'd left the key to the Barnes place and a note for Eve on the kitchen counter. Regret stabbed her, but it would have to do. She couldn't stay for explanations. She couldn't.

But she did have two things left to do: she had to return Christina's ring to Rand, and the rifle to Erica. Shay removed the ring from her pocket, thinking to drop it in a little box she'd found among her packed belongings. But as soon as her fingers touched the gold band, she was hit by the image of a cinder-block wall. She leaned back against the seat of her car, trying to hold on to the vision, wanting desperately to see more. But as quickly as it had appeared, it was gone.

Shay blinked, returning to her surroundings. The wall had been the same as yesterday, only this time there was a distinction. Yesterday she'd thought the cinder blocks were painted, as they were in the precinct, but today the image had been clearer, and the cinder blocks had been bare. She closed her eyes, remembering. They had been seeped through with moisture, little bits of earth and moss clinging to the cracks.

Clearer, yes, but no more helpful than yesterday. She cranked the car and shoved the gear into drive. Still, she would tell Rand everything she saw in her vision. It was all she could do.

Shay forced herself to drive at a normal speed toward Erica's house. Buddy hung his head out the window, but periodically looked at her and whined, as if he questioned the sanity of her plan. Well, join the crowd. Running wasn't exactly a plan, but she was damn good at it.

Erica's family home was on the outskirts of town, and Shay was bombarded by memories of her time in Haddes. She gripped the steering wheel as she passed a convenience store, remembering the nights that Mac would wake her, forcing her out of bed to buy him more beer. Why hadn't she just bought a tank of gas and left town instead?

But there were other landmarks that triggered good memories: the side road that led to her high school, the farmland that had been host to hayrides and bonfires, the church that had helped to hold her faith. Shay fought tears at the sight of the painted white steeple. Her aunt and uncle had attended the same church, but while they'd attended, she'd worshiped. The little orphan girl who had been forced to hide her gifts had managed to find her faith, while the adults had been too filled with pity and obligation to notice.

She took a deep breath as the landscape turned to countryside, carved from pine-laden mountains and valleys that were green with pastureland.

And then she saw it.

Shay felt her gaze drawn to a barely visible dirt road that led upward. She hit the brakes, coming to a stop at the mouth of the road. The jagged ribbon of sandy dirt road disappeared into the shadows of the mountain, seemingly swallowed by the branches of low-hanging trees. She shivered. It was familiar, yet she had no real memory of the place. Beside her, Buddy shifted, then pulled his head into the interior of the car and whined.

"Wait," she whispered, as much to herself as the dog.

Shay took a deep breath, then pulled the ring from its little box. She held it, turning it over in her hand as she prayed for Christina. Memories crept in, threatening to block her concentration: her uncle with a deer carcass strapped to the back of his truck, Mac with a rifle on his shoulder. And then she knew. The memories weren't blocking her—they were guiding her.

Her heart pounded as she understood the significance of the dirt road. It led to an old cabin, one that the McKay men had used as a hunting lodge over the years. Shay had never been there, but Mac had often spoken of it, pointing out the road as they'd passed. He'd complained of the cabin's primitive cinder-block structure, grumbled about the dampness as if he'd been a prisoner there himself, forced to take part in the hunt.

And Shay knew. She held the ring against her chest and closed her eyes. No revelations came, but she knew with everything in her being that Christina was in that cabin.

Her fingers trembled as she searched for her cell phone in the car's clutter. She located Mattie's number and hit dial.

"Hello," Mattie answered.

"Mattie, it's Shay. I think I know where Christina is. Is Jack with you?"

There was no comment, only a shuffling. "This is Jack."

"Jack, it's Shay. Get in touch with Rand. I think I know where Mac has Christina. There's an old hunting cabin." She forced herself to slow down. "It's somewhere on Pikes Mountain."

"Pikes," Jack repeated. "Got it. Where are you?"

"I'm almost there now."

"Stay put," Jack commanded. "Do you hear me? I'm calling the police and Rand. We'll be there soon."

"Okay," Shay whispered.

"Promise me," Jack said.

"I promise."

It was the only lie Shay Chambers had ever told.

CHAPTER 14

Shay pulled the rifle from the back seat. She slipped it from its case, feeling the slick weight of it in her hands as she made certain that it was loaded, then released the safety. Unlatching the car door, she eased out, then urged Buddy to do the same. He seemed to sense her need for stealth as he followed soundlessly behind her. Shay instinctively hunched down, picking her way across fallen leaves and branches, until she was able to flatten herself against the cinder-block exterior of the cabin.

She steadied her breathing. Logic told her she could be at the wrong place. Or she could be wrong altogether. But her heart and every instinct she possessed told her otherwise.

She glanced around. Barely visible behind a stack of decaying firewood was a red pickup truck with empty beer cans scattered around it. Shay squinted to read a small sticker in the back window of the cab: *Fraternal Order of Police.*

Bingo. Shay had no idea how the shelter might be laid out, but there was only one visible window. She crept toward it, keeping her body flat to the exterior wall. When she reached it, she held perfectly still, listening. There was no sound. Shay leaned forward slightly and peered through the window.

A lanky brunette girl lay on an old iron cot, her ankle shackled to its frame by a pair of handcuffs. Shay's breath caught. The girl looked like Erica, her dark hair fanned out over the filthy mattress. Shay blinked, horrified. No, it wasn't so much that she looked like Erica. It was that she represented all of them—the young girls they'd once been, the victim she never intended to be again.

And she was about to be set free.

Shay risked a better view, scanning the dank little room for some sign of life. There was none. But when Christina lifted her hand to her face, Shay's heart soared. The girl was alive.

Shay clutched the rifle. She had no idea where Mac was, but now seemed as good a time as any to try to go in. Shay inched along the wall until she reached the door, then swung it open. Christina jumped, then scrambled into a sitting position on the mattress, the handcuffs clanking against the bed frame, her eyes wide with fear.

"It's okay," Shay soothed. "I'm here to help."

Christina instantly started crying, pulling her legs against her chest like a toddler. "Thank God," she choked.

Shay examined the handcuffs. "Does he have the key?" she asked.

The girl nodded. "He took me. I was so stupid. I thought it would be cool to see someone older. I was so stupid…"

"It's okay. The police are on the way."

"No!" Christina cried. "He's a policeman."

"I know." She patted the girl on the leg. "But they're looking for him, too. He has a history of hurting women. He's not going to get away with it this time."

"But why?" she asked. "All I did was tell him I didn't want to see him anymore. Why did he do this to me?"

"Because he could. It makes him feel powerful." Shay hesitated. "You left your ring behind?"

She nodded. "I was hoping someone would find it."

Shay smiled. "Someone did. Are you hurt?"

Christina shook her head. "I'm hungry. And I want to get out of here."

"Okay." Shay scanned the cabin. "Where is he?"

"I—" Christina shook her head. "I don't know."

A deep growl emanated from Buddy.

"Right behind you." Mac's voice rang out from the doorway.

Shay stood and whirled to face him, drawing the rifle against her shoulder.

Mac's face registered shock, and he lifted his hands slightly. "Whoa there." He began inching farther into the room. "No need for that."

Shay lifted the rifle and aimed. "Unlock her," she commanded.

"Sure, sure," Mac said, raising his hands a little higher. "It's good to see you again, Shay."

"Shut up and unlock her."

Mac drew a key from his pocket and approached Christina, who whimpered and scooted as far away as the handcuffs would allow. "Did you know," he asked the girl, "that Shay is my ex-wife?"

Christina's eyes flew to Shay, and she shook her head.

"And that's not all." Mac made a show of lifting the little key. "She's a witch," he said sarcastically.

Christina flinched. "Please. Please let me go with her. I promise not to tell."

"That's what they all say." He glared at Shay. "Isn't it. But you just couldn't keep your mouth shut, could you. You and your mumbo jumbo."

"I don't promise to keep quiet this time," Shay threatened, leveling the gun. "But I promise not to kill you if you do what I tell you to."

"Mmm." Mac shook his head and made an exaggerated display of fitting the key into the lock. "So, Christina," he said, almost casually, "you'd rather risk going with an honest-to-God witch than stay here with me?"

She nodded. "Please. I just want to go home."

"But there's more. Did you know that Shay here knows things, can see things in her head that no one else can? I'll bet that's how she found us."

The sound of a vehicle's engine echoed against the side of the mountain.

"Oh, I see you've invited others to the party."

"That's right." Shay smiled. "Now shut up and unlock her."

"Or what?"

"Or I'll put a bullet through your sorry head."

"No, you won't."

He grinned, and Shay saw the madness behind his eyes just before he drew a hunting knife from his belt. He grabbed Christina by the hair and tugged her against him, pressing the serrated blade to her throat.

Buddy began barking furiously, but didn't leave Shay's side.

"Shut that mutt up, or I'll cut her."

"Buddy, down." Shay motioned and the dog quieted.

"Christina!" It was Rand's voice.

"Daddy!" Christina cried, then whimpered as Mac's blade drew a drop of blood.

"Don't you dare," Shay warned.

And then Jack and Rand were beside her. Rand struggled against Jack, who was restraining him, preventing him from charging Mac.

"Oh, my God." Shay recognized Mattie's voice behind her, but never took her eyes off Mac.

"I'm sorry, Daddy," Christina cried. "I'm so sorry."

"Shut up, girlie!" Mac yelled.

Shut up, woman! Mac's voice echoed in Shay's head, followed by the memory of his fist against her jaw.

Shay cocked the rifle, aimed just over Mac's head and pulled the trigger.

Mac dropped the knife and threw his hands up to protect his head. When he pulled his hands away, they were covered with blood. Shay's pulse leaped with fear—and a little satisfaction—as she realized the bullet had grazed his scalp.

"You idiot!" he screamed, clutching his head as though he were dying. "You almost killed me."

She smiled, watching him scoot farther away from Christina and into a far corner of the room.

She followed him, cocking the rifle a second time.

She could hear the distant wail of sirens, and a peace flooded her. Behind her, she heard Rand rush to Christina's side, could hear the murmured soothings of father and daughter as they came together again.

"Shay." Jack's voice registered behind her. "Christina's safe now. You can put the gun down now."

"No." She shook her head. "Not yet."

She followed Mac as he flattened himself into the corner of the cinder-block wall, pressing his hand over his bleeding scalp and looking like a frightened animal. Is that how she'd looked when he'd cornered her?

"She's crazy!" Mac pointed to Shay.

Shay looked at Mac's raised hand, recalled the times that his fist had struck her. Only, then it had been her blood that had been shed, her blood on his hands. And then she saw Bruce's hand, gripping her arms and shaking her until she thought her neck would snap. And there had been others in between, boyfriends who shoved, forced and dominated.

No more.

Shay lifted the rifle and aimed.

Shay felt Jack's hand press lightly against her arm, but tugged away. "No, Jack. Leave me alone," she muttered. No more living with Mac's memories. No more returning to Bruce. No more victim.

"No." This time the word was small and laced with desperation. The voice was Christina's.

Shay hesitated.

"No more." Christina's voice was stronger this time. "Don't kill him."

Tears in her eyes, Shay turned to face the girl, who was wrapped in her father's arms on the cot. "You don't understand."

Christina straightened, wiping her cheek. "Yes, I do. I know that if you kill him, he'll be stuck in your head forever. You won't be able to get the memory out."

Shay looked at Mac, who cowered in the corner, his eyes wild with fear. She turned toward Mattie.

"She's right," Mattie whispered.

Shay looked back into Christina's eyes. There was an innocence she'd lost so long ago that it had become a distant memory, one that she could barely recall.

But it was there.

Shay nodded, then lowered the nose of the rifle.

The four women sat at the round bar table of the Stop-N-Bowl, sipping colas and eyeing the envelopes that lay piled, once again, in the center of the table.

"You first," Della urged, elbowing Mattie.

Mattie took a deep breath. Her letter lay on top of the pile. It was no longer pristine, but water damaged and held together with clear tape. And every single fantasy written inside had been fulfilled.

She shook her head. "Nope." She looked at Della. "You."

"Why me?" Della asked. "Shay."

All eyes fell on Shay. "No fair," she said, then turned to Erica.

Erica took a long sip of her drink, then lifted her accordion-folded envelope, turning it over and over in her good hand. But instead of ripping it open, she tossed it back into the pile. "Nah," she said, then took another sip.

"I've waited twenty years for this," Della protested.

"So you can wait another twenty," Erica responded with her usual bluntness.

Della brightened, grinning.

"Oh, good grief." Mattie sighed and slid a bar napkin in Della's direction.

Della scribbled furiously, then tore the paper into four squares and passed one to each friend.

They read "May 11, 2025."

Turn the page for another exciting NEXT read that will have all your friends talking.

*Here's an exciting sneak peek of
Jennifer Archer's newest book,
THE ME I USED TO BE,
available this month from Harlequin NEXT.*

After I pop the question to Warren, we decide to skip dinner and go straight to dessert.

He dips a strawberry into the whipped cream, slips it into my mouth, then unbuttons the top of my blouse. "Why do you want us to live together, Ally?" he asks, his eyes on mine.

Leaning back against the bed pillows, I swallow the strawberry and reach for his waistband. "Because of your great…" Grinning, I grab his belt buckle. "Big…" I begin to unfasten it. "Throbbing…" I slide the belt through the first loop. "Heart." Warren chuckles and I add, "Because we're good together."

He frees the second button of my blouse, his knuckles skimming across the sensitive space between my breasts. "Try again."

I close my eyes, feel the third button release. "Because I'm ready. Because we have fun." *And you make me feel beautiful...young...alive.* My breath catches as he opens the clasp between my bra cups. "Because I can't stand waking up in the morning without you beside me."

"Not good enough," he mutters just before his lips brush across the top of one breast. "Try again."

Seconds pass in a silence broken only by the sound of his breathing and mine. "Because I love you," I finally whisper.

He lifts his head. I open my eyes and Warren looks into them, grinning the dimpled grin I love so much. "Finally, it took you long enough."

It's true. I love Warren Noble. Funny, fabulous, fifty-six-year-old divorced father of two grown kids. Great conversationalist who challenges me. Skilled surgeon with a great bedside manner both in and out of the hospital. Marathon runner. Owner of magic hands. And my heart. I love him. I'm fifty-two years old and, until now, I've never said those words to any man. Only a boy of eighteen, and I was sixteen at the time. A girl, not a woman.

Now...after all these years.

It's as if a part of my soul that I've locked away too long has finally been freed. I'm laughing and crying and kissing him, and I can't stop; I don't want to stop.

Warren laughs, too. "Marry me, Ally," he says between kisses.

Oh, God. Bev's psychic. "Warren—"

"I've been waiting a long time."

"Not so long." Only nine months since the first time he asked. Then again three months later. After that, he quit trying.

"It feels like forever. We shouldn't just live together, we should make it official. I want the world to know you love me." He places his hands at either side of my face, slides his fingers into my hair, pushing it back. "This sexy, smart, fantastic woman loves me. And I love her." Our foreheads touch. "So much. I love you so much, Ally."

His lips taste salty from my tears. Salty and tender and oh, so sweet.

"Will you marry me?" he asks in a voice as quiet, deep and warm as the May night outside my bedroom window.

A "yes" wavers at the tip of my tongue. I'm still terrified, but I know it's the right answer. The only answer. I was crazy to believe we could ever do anything else. "Yes," I say quietly, then laugh and shout, *"Yes!"*

He pulls me into his arms.

"When?" I ask. "Where?"

"This weekend. I don't want to wait and give you a chance to change your mind. We'll fly to Vegas tomorrow afternoon. Hell, we'll fly to Hawaii, if you want, and say our vows barefoot in the sand."

Then I remember I'm catering a bridesmaid luncheon on

Sunday afternoon. Scooting off the bed, I start pacing. "Oh…no, honey, I'm sorry." I wince at him. "I can't leave this weekend. We have something going on at the restaurant on Sunday. It's for the mayor's daughter and I can't get out of it. Her bridesmaid luncheon. I've never left Teena and Joleen and Guy alone to do something so big. This probably wouldn't be the best event to start with." I bite my lip. "I don't know."

When I pass by him, Warren grabs my hand and tugs me back down onto the bed. I wrap my arms around him.

The doorbell rings. And again. Again.

"Damn," he mutters.

Letting go of him, I lean back. The doorbell rings a fourth time. "I'll get rid of them."

"Hurry."

I refasten my bra and start to work on the buttons of my blouse as I head through the bedroom and into my living room. The hardwood floors are cool beneath my bare feet. In the entry hall I flip on the porch light, then look through the front door peephole.

A boy wearing a sweat-stained backward ball cap stands on the other side of the door, staring down at his shoes. He looks to be fifteen years old, sixteen at the most. Here to sell me something for a school fund-raiser, most likely. I hope it's that, and not one of those poor dropouts who come around peddling magazine subscriptions. I hate seeing kids in that situation, hate turning them away when they look as if they're on their last dime. And so, inevitably, I end up with more subscriptions to add to my ever-growing pile of magazines I'll never have time to read.

I unlock the door and open it just wide enough to peer out. "Hello."

He has a tiny gold loop earring in his left ear. The shaggy tufts of hair curling out beneath the bottom of his cap are light brown.

"Miss Cole?"

Something about the shade and shape of his restless green eyes is familiar. Hauntingly so. "Yes?"

"Allyson Cole?"

I nod. "Can I help you?"

His eyes change, become as hard and cold as emeralds, sending a tiny shock of alarm straight through me. That's when I notice the large duffel bag at his feet. Lifting it, he steps closer to the door and gives me a cocky grin. "Hello, Grandma," he says. "I'm Nick. Nicholas Pearson."

Starting over is sweeter when shared.

What else could editor Elisha Reed do when she suddenly goes from single workaholic to mother of two teens?

Starting from Scratch
Marie Ferrarella

HARLEQUIN®

N**xt**™

HN17

Available November 2005
TheNextNovel.com

They were a father and daughter
who had never been close but
something about rebuilding the
lighthouse made sense.

Could a beacon of light that had
always brought people home be
able to bring understanding and
peace to two grieving hearts?

the LIGHTHOUSE
MARY SCHRAMSKI

REQUEST YOUR FREE BOOKS!

2 FREE NOVELS TO INTRODUCE YOU TO OUR BRAND-NEW LINE!

There's the life you planned. And there's what comes next.

A bear ate my ex, and that's okay.

Stacy Kavanaugh is convinced
that her ex's recent disappearance
in the mountains is the worst
thing that can happen to her.
In the next two weeks, she'll
discover how wrong she really is!

Grin and Bear It
Leslie LaFoy

The colder the winter, the sweeter the blackberries will be once spring arrives.

Will the Kimball women discover the promise of a beautiful spring?

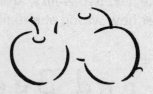

Blackberry
WINTER
Cheryl REAVIS